Not a Strong Enough Word

Not a Strong Enough Word

ALLIE SAMBERTS

PAGE & VINE

Page & Vine
An Imprint of Meredith Wild LLC

Cover Design by Okay Creations

Paperback ISBN: 978-1-964264-59-2

For Olivia. It has been so long and yet no time at all.
And for me. Because I'm strong enough.

Author's Note

It's interesting how stories come to life, isn't it? Some languish for years—decades, even. They sit in a writer's brain, slow cooking to perfection. Some seem ready, only for the writer to feel like each word is torturously being extracted, slowly and painfully. Some come on like lightning, flashing bright and falling onto the page like the subsequent rain.

Not a Strong Enough Word was a little bit of lightning, a little bit of torture, and a little bit of rain.

I'm not going to tell you this book was fun to write; writing about healing rarely is. But it was necessary. Scarlett's story, especially, was one I needed to tell. When her storyline came to me, I turned it around, looking at it from all angles, trying to find any other way besides the one that struck me like lightning to tell this the way I wanted to. Reader, when I say I sat on her story for weeks, I'm not kidding. I even quit writing it because I didn't think I could go through with describing her pain and heartbreak—it hits close to home, after all, and I didn't think I was ready.

But I was ready. I needed to write it. The only way out was through.

And in the process of giving Scarlett and Ryan their strength, I realized that I, too, am strong enough to tell Scarlett's story (which, in so many ways, is also my own), to give her the healing I needed, to see it through until the end, to bear witness to her messy life and the unbreakable love she and Ryan share, both because of and despite her trauma.

Dear reader, please stop here if you don't want spoilers, but it is my job to prepare those who might need a heads-up. First, my characters use profanity and there are two explicit scenes meant for mature audiences in chapters 16 and 24. I believe these are crucial to the development of my characters, but you can do whatever you see fit with that information.

Scarlett experiences intense burnout which results in depressive episodes, which are both described on page. She has a therapist, and she takes medication to help her manage this. There is also an early miscarriage described on page, and the loss of a parent off page.

I have tried to approach all of these subjects with authenticity and care. As someone who has experienced a late-term miscarriage, my story is different from what is discussed in this book, but a lot of the emotions are the same. There was a time when I wouldn't have been able to read a book like this, so if that is where you are in your journey, please put this aside for now. It'll be here for you when you're ready.

I've always been strong. I've had to be. But even over five years after my own loss, I'm starting to find a healing I didn't even know I needed. And that is because of you, dear reader. Every person who has read my words and given me the courage to continue to pursue this passion of mine has been a balm for my soul.

Thank you for being here. I hope Scarlett and Ryan offer you the same healing they've given me.

"It's the best thing you've ever written."

I'm a writer. It is my job to combine words into sentences. Or, at least, it was back when I was doing it regularly. But I still can't think of a better combination of words in the English language than the seven that come breathlessly from my agent's mouth the minute I answer the phone.

"Five years in the making," I grumble. I might be on cloud nine, but I can't resist a little self-deprecation. I'm fishing for another compliment. Sue me.

"Worth the wait," Trina rewards me again. She sniffles, and I hear the soft sound of tissues in the background.

"Are you crying?" I ask incredulously.

She's silent for a moment as the tissue makes noises against the phone. Then, without warning, she wails, "It's just so good."

I can't help it—I laugh. It's a harsh sound, raspy from disuse, and it almost hurts my chest. But this all feels so perfect. Even sad little me wants to jump for joy.

It's been five long years of beating myself up over blank pages. Five long years of depression, reclusion, lots of therapy, and some medication. Five long years of wishing I could call my former friends but being too afraid to be shunned again.

My agent, Trina, is the only one who has stuck with me through it all. I still can't believe she didn't want to drop me completely, but the way she put it, I was her first writer. I guess that means something. That and the royalties from my early books are still making her enough money to pay for groceries, so it's in her best interests to keep me around. I like to think it was more than that. A sense of loyalty, maybe. Or friendship. Genuine care and concern. But who knows.

Either way, she's still with me. She loves the new draft. This might be my way to get back in the game.

"Before I launch into anything else, I need to ask if you've eaten today," Trina says, dragging me back to reality.

"Uh..." I eye the dirty dishes that have piled up in my sink. It's unclear which is the most recent or what was on it. I've barely been able to clean my small condo since I started furiously writing about a month ago. Normally, this would be a concerning signal that I've relapsed into a depressive episode, but there's also an old adage that a writer can have a finished draft or a clean house. This is definitely a product of the latter.

I must hesitate too long because Trina sighs. "Please get some food. We can talk later."

"No," I say quickly. "I've been waiting for two days for your feedback. If I have to wait any longer, I'll burst."

"You need food."

I grab a piece of bread and hold the phone close to the toaster as I noisily press the lever down. "Hear that? Toast. I'll eat it while we talk. I promise." Even a year ago, I'd have lied and told her I had eaten recently so we could get on with the conversation, but she's known me for too long now. She can see right through my bullshit. And besides, she's right. I need to do a better job of taking care of myself, especially if I want to sell this book.

She hums, unconvinced. "Do you have anything to put on it, or are you just going to eat dry-ass bread? You need more than refined carbs, Scarlett."

Sighing, I look around my small kitchen for anything else that's edible. A bunch of bananas I did actually buy only a few days ago. Two empty takeout containers. An apple core...gross. I collect that and the takeout containers and throw them into the garbage.

Jackpot. "Cookie butter," I say triumphantly when I see the container that my little bit of tidying up revealed.

"You need protein," Trina protests.

"I'll go to the store after we talk. Promise. Now, please. I am begging you. Tell me you think you can sell this book."

"I think I can sell this book." I can picture her bright red painted lips breaking into a huge smile when she says it. "In fact, I know I can. JMP has acquired a new press and—"

"No," I cut her off. "Absolutely not. I'm not going back to JMP or any of their subsidiaries. Find somewhere else."

Now I can just about picture those red lips pressing into a thin, frustrated line. "Scarlett—"

"No," I repeat, more firmly this time. My toast pops up out of the toaster as if punctuating the sentence. I'm seriously lacking clean plates, so I toss it onto a paper towel and use the spoon that was resting in the jar to spread a generous helping of cookie butter on top.

"It's a totally separate imprint, despite the acquisition. New editors. Way better vibe. I've been working with one of the editors, Casey, on another project. He's great."

"Casey is not a new editor," I say around a mouthful. "I remember him from JMP."

"Well, yes," Trina says slowly. "He came over from JMP to help get the ball rolling. But as far as I know, he's the only one who made the move. And more importantly, his wish list has 'highly emotional literary fiction' right on there."

She's not going to let this go. Trina might be the only person in the industry who is more stubborn than me. It's one of the reasons we work so well together, but it sure is infuriating when I try to put my foot down and get blocked by her logic and reasoning.

"There are hundreds of imprints. Can't we go somewhere else? A small press, maybe?"

I don't want to say it out loud, but I'm not looking for another million-dollar deal. They don't just hand you a million dollars and say, *Go write a book!* No. They need to make their money back, and then some. Which means press tours and more books to generate more interest...It was too much pressure the last time, and it ended in me walking out of JMP's offices with the tatters of my torn-up pending contract for three new books in my hands and a broken heart in my chest. Not only did my career die that day, but I left the state and walked away from my ex-boyfriend, another one of JMP's editors. I spiraled into a deep depression, lost all my friends, my family—who had never been supportive of my career in the arts—more or less disowned me. And the rest is history.

My stomach sours at the memory, even five years later. I take a giant bite of toast to fill the emptiness.

"This is highly emotional lit fic, Scarlett. It's right up Casey's alley. Not to mention that I know for a fact that they're looking for a big name to put them on the map." She pauses for a moment as if considering whether or not to continue. But, of course, she does. "And you need the money. Or..." She draws out the word, and I already know I'm not going to like what she's going to say next. "We could shop it around. You'd probably get several offers. It'd go to auction..."

The very thought of this book going to the highest bidder sends a shiver down my spine. But I'm also probably about two months away from losing this apartment if something doesn't turn around. Not that I'd be sad to move out, but lacking any friends or family left in my life, I don't really know where I'd go.

"You can't live with me," Trina singsongs into the phone as if she read my mind. "I have boundaries."

"So do I," I fire back. "I'm not crawling back to JMP or this new imprint with my tail between my legs."

I had signed my first deal with JMP as a starry-eyed twenty-five-year-old fresh out of my MFA program with a novel on my hard drive and ten more in my heart. They made my debut a bestseller. And my sophomore novel hit just about every list, too. But when they started asking for more faster without any regard for the sleepless nights, weeks away from home doing interviews and signings, and constant stress they were putting me under, I broke. Two years after I signed my first deal, they tried to ploy me with a better one to soothe the hurt caused by the first. The thought of even less sleep and a worse work-life balance than I already had nearly pulled me all the way under.

And when all of your relationships are tied up in an industry where image is everything, the optics of being associated with the crazed, depressed, sleep-deprived writer who is tearing up six-figure contracts on her way out the door isn't great.

Trina knows all of this, of course. She was there. She's maybe the only one who supported my decision when I resurfaced two years later. Which is why it surprises me that she'd even suggest going back to the place that caused this whole mess to begin with.

"It's been five years," she says gently. Almost as if she doesn't want to poke the bear. "It's a new world. People are demanding work-life separation, and this new publisher respects that. This press is said to be better for authors. That's in their branding, which I'm assuming is why JMP acquired them. You weren't the only one with an issue, Scarlett."

"No, but I was the only one who burned a million-dollar deal to the ground."

"Right," she affirms. "But to be fair, they didn't hand out many million-dollar deals, so there weren't that many to burn."

"I don't think that makes me feel better," I mumble. I take another bite of toast to prevent myself from saying something I'll regret.

"Look, they want a fresh start. So do you. I get where you're coming from, but this could actually work in our favor."

The giant bite of toast scrapes against my dry throat as I try to swallow. I fill a relatively clean glass with water to wash it down. "What do you mean?"

"Everyone loves a comeback story. Especially readers."

"Are you talking about the same readers who took to the internet to talk shit about me in droves?" I remind her. "Their memories are long."

"Which is why I am going to suggest something a bit

unorthodox." She says it like a warning, and I brace myself for impact. "I want to submit this to Casey under a new pen name. When he tells me he's interested—which he will—we'll reveal who you really are before anything is signed. By then, they'll want the book enough to go along with this. We'll meet with their marketing team to come up with a timeline for releasing the information about who really wrote it. Everyone will have fallen as much in love with this book as I have, and the reveal will create another uptick in sales because you'll be forgiven."

"Or they'll buy copies to burn in effigy," I interject.

"Sales are sales!" she trills.

"We're going to have to agree to disagree on that one."

I poke a finger under the pile of dark hair that passes for a messy bun to scratch my head as I tip my eyes up to the ceiling in thought. It's a big risk, and it's a little bonkers, but it's also brilliant. I wouldn't be the first author to come back from disgrace. And I certainly wouldn't be the first well-known author to publish something under a different pen name. Worst-case scenario: If Casey rescinds a deal when he finds out who I am, I'm right back where I started. With the added bonus of shoving it in Trina's face with a nice *I told you so* dance to ensure she never submits anything of mine to JMP or its subsidiaries ever again.

This business won't break me again. I can't let it.

"Fine," I finally say. "This better not backfire."

"It won't." Trina can barely hide the glee in her voice. I hear a keyboard clicking in the background. My heart skips a beat at the thought that she might have had everything ready to send off and was just waiting for my approval. Is it out there already?

"Don't worry." She reads my mind again. "I wouldn't send it with you on the phone. No one needs that level of anxiety."

I breathe out a sigh of relief as my shoulders slump forward. "Thank you." I lean against the counter and idly tap the pointer finger of my free hand against it. "What's this new acquisition called anyway?"

"Anastasios Press," she says distractedly.

I snort. "Like the Greek name meaning *resurrection*?"

"Like the name of its publisher," Trina corrects. "But that definitely feels like a sign."

"I don't believe in signs," I say as a knock sounds at my door.

"I ordered you a burger," she explains. "It should be there now."

My cold, black heart swells just a little at her kindness. "You didn't have to do that."

"If you had said no, I might have sent fried Brussels sprouts."

"You ordered it before I said yes," I counter.

There's silence for a moment.

I open my door, and sure enough, a Styrofoam container is sitting on my doorstep. The smells coming from it make my mouth water despite the threat of Brussels sprouts. "Good thing I said yes, then."

"I knew you would. I ordered it before I even called you. How do you think it got there so fast? Now, go eat. I have work to do."

As we hang up, I'm filled with an excitement almost as pervasive as the rumbling in my empty stomach. If Trina thinks they'll offer me a deal, she's probably right. She's never been wrong before, and I doubt her skills have diminished in the past five years while my own have been languishing.

It feels good to have a plan again. I basically wrote that draft on a wing and a prayer, but knowing Trina believes in it gives me some hope that I might actually be able to get back to writing. And, more importantly, that I might be able to love it again.

There's nothing on my computer screen worth looking at. And yet, I've been staring at it for the past four hours, idly clicking on emails and opening documents only to close them and try something else.

Actually, that's probably not true. I'm sure some of these manuscripts could be really wonderful books. I'll probably even make offers to acquire some of them. I've edited some interesting books into shining stars over the past few years, but none of them have felt special.

"Anything?" I ask my intern, Margie, as she sinks into the armchair facing my desk. I know better than to get my hopes up, but I need to find something with a spark and fast. Slowly dying inside as the publishing industry passes me by was not on my bingo card for the latter part of my thirties, but here we are. More and more lately, I find myself longing for the days when I was fresh out of college, working my way up to senior editor at John Monroe Press where I got my pick of fantastic books and even more wonderful authors to work with. But somewhere along the line, either I got jaded or the manuscripts got worse. Or both.

Either way, now I'm relying on interns and slush piles. And that's after I made a desperate move to JMP's newly acquired imprint. I thought it would shake some things up for me. No such luck.

"There's a shorter book about..." She trails off and checks her notes, which isn't promising. We need books that stick with the reader long after the last page, not ones Margie needs to consult her notes about.

"You know what?" I hold up an impatient hand. "Never mind."

She slumps even further in her chair, pursing her lips to the side and regarding me with her wide, young eyes. A tiny little pang of regret hits me like it always does when I remember I'm supposed to be inspiring the interns, not dragging them down with me into the pit of despair I can't seem to dig myself out of.

I scrub a hand over my face, unintentionally upsetting the glasses on the bridge of my nose. There's a distinct possibility that I'm losing my ability as an editor if I even let a sentence that cliché pass through my brain.

"I'm really sorry, Mr. Whitlock. Maybe you can give me a few more specifics about what you're looking for, and I can try again?" She straightens in her seat and poises her pen over her notebook, ready to write.

Leaning my forearms on my desk and clasping my hands in front of me, I regard her for a moment. "Did any of those manuscripts make you feel anything, Margie?"

She tilts her head and pinches her brows slightly. "I'm not sure what you mean."

I shove off the desk to tip back in my chair. "Sometimes, identifying a winning manuscript is about a feeling. In your gut. Or in your heart. You read it, and you just know, even though you can't explain it." Sure, I'm trying to turn this into a teachable moment to assuage my earlier guilt over dragging down the intern. But maybe it'll help.

"Okay." She draws the word out and taps her pen against the edge of her notebook.

"What was the last book you read that moved you?" I ask her.

"Like, to tears?" She scrunches up her face. "I'm not much of a crier."

I huff a laugh. "Tears are a good signal, but it doesn't have to make you weep to make you feel."

One of the other senior editors, Casey, appears in my doorway. He leans against the door frame and crosses his arms. "Are you lecturing the interns again, Ryan?"

Margie pops up even straighter in her seat. "Oh, no. He was asking me about the last book that made me feel something."

Casey cocks an eyebrow and smirks at me. "Really? Well, I'm interested. What was it?"

"Um," Margie hedges. "Well, if you're asking me the first book that comes to mind...We read *In the Time Before* in our contemporary literature class last semester. By Scarlett Frye. Have you heard of it?"

My mouth goes suddenly dry, and I blink rapidly a few times. Casey pushes himself off the doorframe as his smirk turns to a look of concern. I try unsuccessfully to swallow, then clear my throat.

"Yes," I rasp. "I'm familiar."

Casey's eyebrows shoot up his forehead, but thankfully, he doesn't say anything.

Margie seems completely unaware as she continues on. "Well, I loved it. It was super emotional. Is that what you mean? You want me to find a book like that one?"

There is not, nor will there ever be, a book like that one. Scarlett Frye is a paragon in the literary community. Her ability to develop multifaceted characters and carve meaning from not only their misfortunes, but from the very words themselves is—as of yet—unparalleled.

In short, she is a literary genius. Or she was. And I remember her well.

Dark hair fanned out on the pillow around her pale face as she held pages up over her head to read them aloud to me. A smile, her dark eyes glittering. Somehow, that smile meant more from her, was more beautiful on her than on any other human alive.

"You like it?"

She didn't need my approval. She knew what she was capable of. But I gave it to her anyway. I always would.

"It's breathtaking."

Did I mean her or her writing? It didn't matter. She and her words were always one and the same. I hoped she'd never run out of them. Never stop sharing them with me. Never stop letting me see the inner workings of her big, beautiful brain.

"Ryan?" Casey's voice interrupts my sudden memory, and his short, black hair and dark skin replace the long, dark tresses and porcelain complexion from my vision.

I shake my head a little, if only that could dispel the thoughts. "Sorry." I give Margie an apologetic smile and idly scratch at the sleeve covering my right forearm. "That book holds a lot of memories for me. But yes, if you could find a manuscript that makes you feel something like *In the Time Before* did, that would be a good start."

Margie shifts uncomfortably in her seat. "Okay." Her gaze bounces back and forth between Casey and me. "If that's all...?"

I give her a curt nod. "Yes. Thank you, Margie."

She wastes no time unfolding herself from the chair and breezing out of my office. Casey's gaze tracks her hurried movement down the hall. Apparently satisfied, he plops into the now unoccupied seat.

As another transplant from JMP, Casey and I have been working near each other for a long time. His move over to Anastasios Press surprised me, but he assured me that the water over here was warm, and it was enough to get me to follow. That and I needed a change. I was drowning in memories over there, and I had to get away. Casey has done exceptionally well for himself here. I wish I could say the same. Though that might have something to do with the fact that his heart hasn't shriveled into some numb version of itself like mine has.

He crosses one long leg over another. "Are we going to talk about what just happened?"

I eye him over the black rim of my glasses. "I was reminded of a time long ago. Nothing to talk about."

"Wasn't *that* long ago." He looks at me pointedly. "And it looked like more than just a little reminder."

It was a straight-up fucking flashback, but I'm not about to unpack this with Casey. Even though he watched me obsess over that same manuscript and that same woman, and then her next one, too. Even though he suggested I fight for the offer we eventually made. Even though he watched the aftermath of that offer being thrown back in my face.

No. I've come a long way in the five years since. And even if I didn't come out of it with my heart intact, I still have my job.

I offer Casey a shrug and nothing more. He narrows his dark eyes at me, and I can feel the trepidation leeching into my skin.

"So, then maybe you'll tell me what that was all about with Margie?" He makes it sound like a question, but it isn't. Casey is nothing if not persistent, and I'm not getting out of this without answering him.

"Margie wanted to know what to look for in the slush pile," I say.

"And what did you tell her?"

"I was trying to get her to understand the feeling when you find something worthwhile. That punch-in-the-gut beauty of even a single line that makes the work promising, makes it something we want to spend a lot of time with before publication." I eye him over my glasses again. "You're not my boss, you know. What's with the third degree?"

"I'm not your boss," he agrees. "But I like to think I'm your friend." When I dip my chin in a nod, he continues. "What's going on with you? You haven't seemed excited about this job in a while. Time for a career move?"

"This was the career move," I mumble. When Casey doesn't say anything, I finally give in. I wave at my computer screen. "There are some really good submissions here. But none of them are...They don't strike me. There's no connection to them. I just want to find a manuscript that makes me feel something."

"Again," he finishes my already complete sentence.

"What do you mean?"

"You want to find a manuscript that makes you feel something *again*. Because I know for a fact there have been feelings about manuscripts you've worked on in the past. But I'm going to tell you that you're not likely to find that same feeling again, and you should probably stop chasing it."

He's right, of course. When words and books are tied up in bodies and souls to the point where you don't know where one ends and the other begins, there's not anything out there, no matter how good, that's likely to bring that level of emotion back to my life.

Maybe that's my problem. I got too high, and now nothing will compare. That's certainly what it felt like, working on that book. Being with her. Like a drug, injected directly into my veins. And silly me, I let myself get addicted to the feeling, thinking there was nothing that could ever come between us. Nothing that could ever stop her words.

I was so young. Now I know better. Not just because of her, but because this industry can, and does, tear writers down more often than it builds them up. I should have seen it coming. No one can fly that high forever.

When I don't respond, Casey inhales sharply, pushing forward in his chair so his elbows rest on his thighs and his hands meet between his knees. "I got a call from Trina McBryde today."

Back when Trina was representing Scarlett, she used to send all her new manuscripts to me. Since Scarlett disappeared five years ago, she started working more closely with Casey. It hurts, but I can't really blame her. In this business, loyalty is worth almost as much as a good book, and I know she will always be loyal to Scarlett, even if she's long gone.

"And?" I ask, trying not to show how affected I am by hearing Trina mentioned in quick succession with Scarlett.

"She's got a new book. Swears up and down that it's brilliant.

I read the first few chapters, and there's definitely something there. How did you put it—a punch in the gut?"

Casey waits for my reaction, but I don't give him one. I've become very practiced at shoving my emotions into the abyss where they belong, even if he constantly wants to try to get a rise out of me.

"Why are you telling me this?" I ask instead.

Regarding me carefully, he takes in a deep breath through his nose. "It'd be good for Anastasios if we took it on. *I can feel it.*" He emphasizes the last part as a nod to my sob story from a few moments ago.

I raise an eyebrow. "Good for the press or the man?"

"They are one and the same, in this instance. Regardless, I don't have time. I just signed three debuts that are going to need a lot of time and attention. And hand holding." He rolls his eyes at this.

I chuckle. "This one isn't a debut?"

"Oh, it is. The author's name is S.J. Falmouth. But it doesn't feel like a debut, if that makes sense. She's been around the block a few times. Maybe this isn't her first manuscript, just the first she's put on submission." He shrugs. "Who knows. But I think this might be just the one to get you out of your little slump."

I scoff. "Little" is the understatement of the century.

There I go with the clichés again.

"Look," Casey continues. "Let me send over the chapters. Read it with an open mind. See if you feel something. If you do, it's yours. If you don't...well, I'll leave that up to you. But if you could trust me and fake it, I'd owe you one."

"There's no reason why I can't at least take a look," I say.

"Great," Casey says as he stands. "I'll send it over. Trina mentioned this author is a little skittish, so if you think there's something there, let's have the initial contact go through me. We can do a virtual or in-person meeting, depending on the author's schedule, to introduce you before we really get started."

"Sounds great," I say to his back as he hustles out the door.

As I click through some more emails waiting for Casey to send the document over, I can't help but hope he's right about this one. I could really use the win.

Chapter 3

Scarlett

I KNOW IT's ten o'clock in the morning on a Wednesday in April. I don't care. My pajamas are comfortable, and there's a holiday baking competition on a streaming service and a spot on my couch that's calling my name. Curling up with my softest blanket and a mug of hot coffee, I start the first episode.

Baking competitions are a bit of a guilty pleasure of mine. Actually, I shouldn't say "guilty." I feel absolutely zero guilt about it. But I love them probably more than a reasonable, well-adjusted adult should. Though the jury's still out on whether or not I'm reasonable or well-adjusted.

All of this is to say that I could—and sometimes do—spend an entire day binging baking shows. This particular one has haunted me since I got serious about finishing the draft of my book in November. I told myself I wouldn't watch it until the draft was finished. By the time I've gotten to the fourth episode and downed another coffee, I'm settled in with my reward, and it feels so sweet. Pun intended.

That is, it's sweet until a banging sounds at my front door. It surprises me so much that I jump and hot coffee sloshes over the rim of my mug and onto my soft, white blanket.

"Son of a bitch," I curse, holding the mug up as if that's going to help anything and shaking my free hand to soothe the sting caused by the coffee.

The banging comes again, more urgent this time. My heart

starts racing; I don't think I've scheduled anything for today. In fact, I know I didn't because I was very serious about my date with the holiday baking competition. But I also notoriously need a calendar. Or an assistant. I used to have both, but since I haven't done anything of note in a while, I haven't seen the need for either.

"Open up, Scarlett. I know you're in there. I can hear the baking show," Trina shouts from the other side of the door.

I breathe out a sigh of relief at knowing who is out there before tensing up again because what the fuck is Trina doing at my apartment at two o'clock on a Wednesday afternoon without scheduling an appointment?

Gingerly, I remove the coffee-soaked blanket from my lap and set my mug down on the end table before marching the few steps to the door and throwing it open as violently as I dare. The poor thing isn't really meant for aggressive gestures, and I can't afford a new front door.

"There she is," Trina says with fake cheer, tilting her head to the side and smiling so wide, her signature bright red lips pull tight over her teeth. Platinum-blonde hair falls over her shoulder with the motion.

It only takes a second for her manufactured smile to turn into a very real frown as she takes in my pajamas soaked with coffee and my messy, dark hair that I'm sure looks like a rat's nest.

"In my defense," I jump in before she can criticize me, "I spilled the coffee when you scared the shit out of me by banging unexpectedly on my door."

Those red lips pull to the side as her hazel eyes narrow on me. "Why are you still in your pajamas?"

"Because I finished a draft of a book, which was a monumental thing. And then I cleaned my apartment, went grocery shopping, and showered every day this week, *Mom*." I don't mention that the last three things also felt monumental. Finishing my book and sending it to Trina gave me a lot of pride, but it has also left a void I'm not sure how to fill yet. Making myself do anything normal these past few days doesn't give me the same dopamine hit that writing has. And while that does feel depression-adjacent, I'm not in a full-on depressive episode. I'm even still remembering to take my meds, which admittedly doesn't always happen. I just wanted to take some time off. Hence the pajamas.

Trina peeks over my shoulder and into my apartment. "You cleaned?"

I roll my eyes like a petulant teenager and open the door wider so she can see. She doesn't waste a minute, brushing past me and waltzing right into the kitchen. I do say *waltzing* almost literally; she's wearing one of her brightly-colored, flowy skirts that kicks out around her ankles as she moves.

She inspects the kitchen for a few moments, even opening cabinets and my fridge. Apparently satisfied, she folds her arms over her ample chest and stares at me in silence.

"I wasn't lying," I grumble.

"Sometimes you lie," she retorts.

I open my mouth to reply but then close it. She's right. I know enough to know what looks bad, and I try to tell people what they want to hear to avoid their concern. It's been a while since I've done that with Trina, but I can't really blame her for not fully trusting me.

"Why are you here?" I ask instead. "Did we have something scheduled today?"

She eyes me up and down. I uselessly try to smooth my satin sleep shirt into something more presentable under her scrutiny.

"No," she says with disdain. "*I* scheduled you an appointment at the salon, so I'm here to take you there."

"What? Why?" My hand floats to my hair, which feels dry and brittle to my touch. Grimacing, I add, "Don't answer that."

That, at least, pulls a trill of laughter from her. She leans a hip against the counter, and her hands land on the curve of her hips. "Casey requested the full manuscript. He's going to love it, and we are going to meet with him to talk marketing before signing anything." She waves an imaginary circle in my direction. "So this depressed-writer chic isn't going to work in our favor."

"You seem awfully confident that they're going to make an offer." It's not even a protest, but I can't get my hopes up the way she can. It's never been real for me until the offer is signed.

"They will," she says simply. "Now, get dressed. On that note, do you have anything business-y you can wear to this meeting?"

My eyebrows inch up my forehead, and I feel something crusty stick in the creases. I might look worse than I thought. "The meeting we haven't been invited to yet?"

"The meeting we will be invited to within the next couple of days. So, do you?"

I squish one eye closed in thought. "Um..."

"Right. We'll hit up the store after the salon." She pulls her phone out of a pocket in her skirt and taps a few things into it as she chews on the side of her mouth. "Go get dressed. Our appointment is in twenty," she says distractedly.

I stand there, staring at her dumbly. "Why did you do this for me? If you had told me to go get a haircut and some clothes, I would have."

Without looking at me, she tips one of her shoulders up. "Would you have?"

"Yes," I insist. When she doesn't respond, I add, "I went grocery shopping when you told me to, didn't I?"

Her gaze pops up from her phone screen. "You did."

"I would have done this too. You're my agent, not my assistant. It's not your job to make sure I'm presentable."

"No, it's my job to sell your book. And that's going to go a lot better if you don't look like you've spent five years avoiding the world and holed up in your tiny apartment like a hermit." A tiny smile plays at those red lips, and her eyes sparkle. "I am your agent, but I also like to think I'm your friend, Scarlett. This is me being a friend."

"That's..." I trail off and swallow against the sudden lump of emotion that has lodged itself in my throat. "That's really nice of you, Trina. Thank you."

She breaks the emotional moment by waving her phone at

me. "I also booked an appointment with your therapist for you just in case this thing goes sideways, which is definitely more of an assistant move. So don't get used to it."

My heart starts pounding again of its own volition, and my mouth goes dry. Apparently, I had gotten accustomed to her bravado. "Do you think it will go sideways?"

"No," she says with what I think is real confidence. "But I also believe in being prepared. Which, frankly, you could learn from. Now, get dressed or we're going to be late. And you *know* I hate it when people are late."

I make my way to my bedroom to hastily dress and brush my teeth. I don't bother trying to do anything with my hair since a professional will be attacking it shortly anyway. When we leave the apartment, Trina links her arm with mine in a gesture of solidarity that fills me up to the brim. Knowing she's got my back goes a long way toward making me feel like this is all going to turn out the way she says it is. It feels almost as good as finishing that draft did.

Almost.

Chapter 4

Ryan

It has been days, and I can't get that book out of my head. The author, S.J., titled it *Becoming*, which is such a brilliant double entendre for the themes. It's a sprawling coming-of-age story about a young woman. Haunting in its simplicity, it's about a young girl literally becoming a woman. But at its core, it's also about how adulthood suits her. It is becoming on her, in an older sense of the word. The book is an achingly beautiful story of loss and hope. My heart still hurts thinking about the ending.

When Casey had sent over the initial chapters, I skimmed through them on my computer. Then, I read them again. And again, more slowly. It was a little rough around the edges, but it was clear this book had potential. I immediately asked Casey to get the full manuscript. Luckily, Trina acts fast. She sent the whole thing over, and I did something I haven't done in a long time—I printed the entire manuscript out on the industrial printer in the lounge area. It's something I only do for books that I have a desire to sit with for a long time. This was definitely one of those.

I took it home and read the whole thing in one sitting. I think it was three in the morning when I finished, but it was worth it. Casey was right—this one was special. I asked him to send an offer the next day.

But now, it has been three agonizing days of back-and-forth. Anastasios Press needs this book. *I* need this book. The need to get into those pages and muck around within those words to pull out the best version of them is almost an obsession.

From what I can gather, Trina is being a shark about this one. It's not so much about the money but that she wants an in-person meeting with us. Well, with Casey. She still doesn't know I'll be taking the lead on this. From what he tells me, the author is incredibly nervous—almost reclusive—and this request for a meeting seems strange enough that he doesn't want to drop that bomb yet. Trina has also insisted our publicist be present to talk marketing strategy before anyone signs anything. This isn't unheard of, of course, but in an industry that relies so much on gut feeling, the fact that Casey seems to think something is up is enough for me to wait patiently for any word from them.

But I also have a gut feeling that this book is going to be huge, even if it's off to a less-than-conventional start.

After an entire week of that back-and-forth, I find myself restlessly wandering around the office. Margie is still rifling through the slush pile, determined to find something usable, so I don't want to bother her. Most of the other senior editors are engrossed in something or working remotely while their kids are on spring break. While I don't want to bug Casey for the thousandth time, I catch his eye from across the room. He has his phone pressed to his ear, but he motions me over. He scribbles something on a pad of paper at his elbow and turns it toward me while he continues to listen into the receiver.

You free tomorrow at one? Trina and S.J. want to meet. Will loop in Meri for pub.

My heart leaps into my throat. I'm sure my schedule is clear, and if not, I'll clear it. My nod must be emphatic, because Casey huffs a laugh. He must be serious about this, too, if he's bringing in Meri for publicity. She's the best we've got.

"Yes," he says into the phone. "Mm-hmm. We will have everyone there." He pauses for a moment. "No, I don't think that's necessary, unless you do?" Another pause. "Okay, great. Thanks, Trina. See you tomorrow."

The phone is barely placed back into the cradle when I rub

my palms together in excitement. "She's going to take the offer?"

"I wouldn't go that far just yet." Casey indicates one of the seats facing his desk, and I sink into it.

"Trina wasn't happy enough with the outline for marketing you gave her?"

Casey shakes his head, his eyes wide. "I'm telling you, there's something different about this. Trina is being very cryptic. She says the author is insisting on a meeting before going any further."

"That's not unheard of. JMP always liked to pull their authors in for a face-to-face at least once in the process," I counter.

He purses his lips in thought. "You're not wrong. I don't know why I feel like Trina is being weird about this one. I thought it was because she doesn't fully trust us after what happened with Scarlett"—he eyes me warily at the mention of her name—"but that can't be it. We've worked together a few times since then with no issues."

I hum, not sure if I even want to voice what I've been thinking. When he raises his eyebrows at me in question, I go for it anyway. "This book...it *felt* like her. It wasn't." I hold a hand up to stop any of his protests. "I'm not saying that. The voice was entirely different. I'm just saying...the heart she had in her books. This one felt similar. Maybe Trina thinks she's got another star on her hands and wants to be sure we're going to handle this differently."

Casey scratches his jaw, his blunt nails scraping audibly against the well-manicured stubble. "That would make sense," he says slowly. "JMP really fucked that up, and we all paid the price for it." He regards me for a moment before adding, "Sorry, man."

I shake my head. "No need. That did get fucked up, and we lost her. The world lost her." *I lost her*, I don't say, but from the pinched sympathy on Casey's face, he knows how I'd finish that thought. What he doesn't know is the part I played in her departure. I'm not sure I fully understand it, but I know the blame is there. The guilt is, anyway. And the hole she left in my heart when she disappeared.

Coming out of his thoughts, Casey knocks definitively on the wood of his desk. "That must be it. I'll alert Meri so she can be prepared to handle this one with kid gloves."

"I'll do it." I stand quickly. "I don't have anything else to do, and I'm ultimately the one Meri and the author will be working with. Best I get involved now so the transition is smoother."

"Good thinking." He doesn't even wait for me to leave his office before turning back to his computer screen. "See you tomorrow."

"Yeah, see you." I try to keep my voice level, but my excitement seeps out anyway. I can't help it. There's no way I'm letting this book go without a fight. Anastasios Press is going to sign S.J. Falmouth, and I'm going to work on something important again. I can feel it.

Chapter 5

Scarlett

The Anastasios Press offices are located just outside of Chicago, about forty-five minutes away from JMP, which is right in the heart of downtown. The way Trina explained it, the suburbs have a bit of a slower-paced, family vibe that fits what Anastasios was going for when it was initially founded, and they negotiated with JMP to keep the building. Plus, more space with a cheaper overhead, which is probably the real reason.

Despite Trina's begging, I drive myself. She probably doesn't trust me not to bail. To her credit, I consider not going at least six times in the span of the hour it takes me to get ready. Thankfully, that trip to the salon actually did wonders for my self-confidence, so I'm able to wrangle myself into something I feel pretty good about. Before I can talk myself out of it again, I send Trina my location to keep me accountable, fold myself into my tiny car, and hit the road.

I arrive over an hour early, which is super great for the anxiety building in the pit of my stomach. But there's no way I'm going in there without Trina, so I try to read on my phone—*try* being the operative word. Once I've read the same page three times without processing any of the information, I switch to Solitaire.

Trina knocks on my passenger-side window about twenty minutes before the meeting is set to start, a small smile playing at her red lips. I vaguely wonder—not for the first time—how she keeps them so perfectly red all the time as she pulls open the door and sits next to me.

She wastes no time getting right to the point, which is one of the things I truly love about her. “Okay, game plan,” she says breathlessly as she folds the edges of her green floral skirt into the car and slams the passenger door. Then, she deflates. “Actually, I don’t have a game plan. I got the sense on the phone that Casey thinks this whole thing is super weird, even though I tried to play it cool. He’s already suspicious. So we’re just going to go in there, shake a few hands, and I’m going to launch into my pitch before they have a chance to say anything about you.”

“That...does not make me feel better.” I frown.

As she shrugs, her shoulders hit her giant earrings, making them jingle like little fairies. “It’s the best I’ve got.”

“You could have lied to me. Pretended like you have some kind of control over this.”

She shakes her head, and her earrings twinkle again. “Honesty is the best policy. Plus, I didn’t want to spook you in there. Now, get out of the car. Throw your shoulders back. Fake it till you make it. You’re Scarlett Frye, goddammit. You’ve already published two best-selling novels, and you’re about to publish a third. Act like it.” She nods curtly, punctuating her sentence.

I blink at her a few times, my brows furrowed. “That was quite the pep talk.”

“Thank you.” She smiles widely. “I was rehearsing it on the way over. Let’s go. Before you can second-guess yourself.”

“More like tenth-guess myself at this point,” I mumble as I get out of my car. Trina laughs, and I have to fight the urge to tell her I wasn’t trying to be funny.

Anastasios Press is a two-story building with windows everywhere, encasing almost every nook and cranny in bright, afternoon light. As Trina gives our names to the receptionist, I look out at the scenery. It’s idyllic. Peaceful. Two people are walking on a path amongst prairie grasses out back behind the building, and three more sit in light jackets at a table enjoying the spring sunshine. It’s a nice escape from the cold steel of the Loop, where I'm used to having meetings like this. I choose to take this as a good omen and use it to force my heart rate into something the receptionist can't hear. Trina was right; this is a different vibe. Different book. Different team. Different outcome, as my therapist would remind me.

Different Scarlett, I like to remind myself. I've come a long way since then.

Fortified against the nerves still threatening to take over my legs and make them run right out of here, Trina and I follow the receptionist up to the second floor and into a conference room. I don't see a soul in the office. Maybe they're all at lunch, which would be another one-eighty from the way JMP ran their editors into the ground. No one took breaks there. Even Ryan—

"They should be right with you," the receptionist says, thankfully stopping that train of thought in its tracks. "Have a seat. Help yourself to the waters on the table. Can I get you a coffee or something?"

Trina glances at me. I stiffly shake my head. The last thing my nerves need is caffeine.

"No, thank you. Water is great," she tells the receptionist, who closes the door softly behind us.

The sterile conference room, the paintings on the wall meant to be calming, the receptionist leading us in and telling us to wait. It feels so much like a doctor's office that I'm thrown for a second. Waiting for someone to come in and deliver bad news...

"Sit," Trina commands. When my gaze snaps to hers, her expression is neutral, but there's a concern flickering behind her hazel eyes.

I clear my throat, trying to keep myself from spiraling even further. "I'm not a dog," I say, but I drop into the nearest chair anyway.

No sooner does Trina sit in the chair next to me and grab a bottle of water for both of us than the door opens.

"Trina McBryde, it is so good to see you," comes Casey's booming voice. I haven't heard it in years, but it's the kind of voice you don't forget. Deep and rich, like a warm blanket. It'd be comforting if I weren't so jittery.

Trina jumps to her feet, and they embrace with him angled just enough so he doesn't see me. A woman enters the room after him. She has pin-straight black hair framing the bronze skin of her face, and she is wearing a bright yellow pantsuit that complements her features beautifully. I've never seen her before, but she smiles warmly at me.

"You must be S.J. Falmouth." She extends her hand, and it takes me a moment to remember that's my name here, at least until Casey gets a look at me. "I'm Esmerelda Chavez, one of the publicists here at Anastasios Press. But everyone calls me Meri."

I stand and shake her hand. "Pleasure to meet you, Meri."

"And this man who has apparently forgotten his manners is—"

"Oh, fuck," Casey curses. When my gaze snaps to him, he's staring at me slack-jawed with pinched eyes. He does not look at all happy to see me.

Stupidly, I give him a little wave. "Hi, Casey. How are you?"

"You two know each other?" Meri asks with a forced politeness, clearly trying to salvage the situation.

He drags a hand down his jaw and turns his head toward Trina, though his eyes linger on me. "I knew you were acting weird. I wish you had told me," he grinds out, ignoring Meri's question.

"Surprise!" Trina wiggles her hands in a sort of jazzy motion, the bangles at her wrists jingling with a cheeriness no one is feeling. "S.J. Falmouth is actually Scarlett Frye! Which is why we wanted to meet to discuss marketing."

"This is..." Casey trails off and finally drags his dark eyes away from me. They land on Trina, and not in a kind way. "This is not good."

She furrows her brow. "Why not? I mean, I know you weren't expecting this, but everyone loves a comeback, right? And I thought you said JMP doesn't really check up on you all over here, so..."

Trina goes on and on, talking a mile a minute. The door opens again, but my back is to it, and I'm too engrossed in this exchange to turn and look. Which is why I'm gobsmacked when the newcomer speaks.

"Sorry I'm late. There was some traffic coming back from lunch."

It's a familiar voice. One that used to be closer to my heart than my own. One that filled the gaps in my soul and whispered to me in the dark.

But surely he isn't here right now. I've just been stressed out about this whole thing, and I'm mistaking someone else's voice for his. That has to be it. There's no other explanation. Unless...

I freeze. Trina glances over my shoulder, and her eyes go wide. Her red lips form an O, and it would appear she's been rendered speechless. Casey watches me carefully, and poor Meri is just standing there in her bright yellow pantsuit with her hands clasped in front of her and a smile plastered on her face.

"What is going on?" comes that voice again, and I squeeze my eyes shut, trying to persuade myself that Ryan Whitlock isn't standing right behind me.

It's Casey who jumps in first. He clears his throat and puts a gentle hand on my shoulder, encouraging me to turn around.

"We were just getting started with introductions," he says as I turn as slowly as I possibly can to face my fate.

It is him standing there. The man I loved more than I loved my writing career, who pored over my words with me at such length, I wasn't sure which were his and which were mine. Bodies and souls and words entwined in a love deeper than any I've experienced before or since.

The man I walked away from when I rejected my offer from JMP.

People are saying things in a flurry behind me now, but I don't catch any of them. I have tunnel vision, laser-focused on Ryan standing in front of me, looking somehow better for the five years since I saw him last. He's wearing a thin, navy V-neck sweater and fitted gray slacks. His classic dark-rimmed glasses frame his brown eyes which also seem to be zeroing in on me. The brown hair I used to run my fingers through is longer now, and my hand twitches to find out if it's still as silky as it was then.

"Scarlett." His voice is several decibels lower than the frenzy behind me. And yet, it's all I can hear.

I can't move, can't speak. I can only nod slightly, and his hand flies to his mouth. He laughs, then—a harsh sound and not at all the joyous one he used to save for me. The room grows quiet at the noise.

"It was you," he says, and if I'm not mistaken, his words are laced with awe.

Chapter 6

Ryan

Scarlett Frye is standing in the conference room at Anastasios Press. At first, I'm almost sure I'm seeing a ghost, but no. She doesn't look like a ghost at all. Her skin is still smooth and milky white like it was before, but her cheeks are rosy, which they never were then. Not at the end anyway. She's curvier, too. Healthier. Like she's been taking time out of her day to eat—something I was never able to get her to do. Her dark brown hair is shorter now, falling just past her shoulders in soft waves. And her eyes...Those blue eyes are brighter. Sharper. Somehow lovelier than they were before. Or maybe they faded in my memory, though I don't think that could possibly be the case. My memories of her have consumed so much of my life since she left; every detail of her has been etched in stark relief in my mind's eye.

And yet, here she is. Even more beautiful than I remember.

Eventually, the commotion dies down. We sit with our team on one side of the large conference table and Scarlett and Trina on the other. Scarlett looks like she might bolt at any minute, with her back ramrod straight and her eyes fixed on the table in front of her. Trina lays a hand on her knee and glances at her questioningly. Scarlett merely nods but doesn't meet her gaze.

I see now why Trina was being cryptic with Casey on the phone. I also understand what it was about this book that had me in such a chokehold. It's Scarlett's. Her words have always had that kind of effect on me.

Casey's frustrated huff breaks the silence, but it does little to dispel the tension in the room. From the piercing gaze he has pinned on Trina and the drumming of his fingers against the top of the table, my best guess would be he's about ready to shut this down.

"Well," he starts, and the word sounds pinched. "This is less than ideal."

"Can someone explain to me what *he* is doing here? I pitched this project to you." If looks could kill, the one Trina gives Casey would have him on the floor.

"And I loved what I read." Casey's gaze slides to Scarlett, who still won't look up, and his expression softens slightly. "It's beautiful prose, and I guess now I know why. But I signed three high maintenance debuts this year. I'm booked. Ryan, here, has been in a rut, so I thought this would snap him out of it. I was right."

Trina's earrings jingle as she shakes her head. "That doesn't explain why you didn't tell me that from the start."

"I won't lie to you—we wanted this book," Casey says, and from the way Trina reels back, she didn't miss his use of the past tense. "You were the one who said the author is skittish, and you wanted this meeting anyway, so I figured this would be a good time to gently pass the project on to Ryan."

Trina folds her arms over her chest as she leans back in her chair. "You deceived us."

"So did you," Casey snaps.

"I like a little drama. So sue me." Trina throws her hands in the air and brings them down with a light smack on the table. "It's not every day a best-selling author stages a comeback."

"Let's everyone take a breath," Meri interjects, spreading her palms flat on the table. "All is not lost, surely. And while I don't know exactly why this is such an issue, from a PR standpoint, it's brilliant. Since we're talking about comeback stories, they're great for publicity, which is, in turn, great for sales. So, can someone please explain how everyone knows each other so we can come to some kind of solution?"

I glance at Scarlett, but her lips are pressed tightly together, and she's still staring at the table like it's the most fascinating thing she's ever seen. Dragging in a deep breath through my nose, I let it fill my lungs before saying, "We dated. Back when Casey and I were both with JMP. Scarlett was one of our authors." It's not enough to encompass all that we were to each other, but it's the best I can do without coming across as the sad sack I've been for the last five years.

Meri snorts, and everyone but Scarlett's gaze flies to her. "I'm sorry." Her voice is edged with laughter. "That's it? You dated years ago, and now you're both, what? In your thirties? And you can't work professionally together?"

"That's not it," Scarlett says almost inaudibly. Fuck, even her *voice* is more beautiful than I remember. Hearing it fills me with an ache so deep, I'm afraid I might never recover.

But I must have been the only one who heard it, because Trina barrels through. "Surely there's another editor who could take this on, then."

"I don't think that's a good idea. JMP will not like it," Casey responds immediately, without thinking. His hot-headedness is getting the best of him, and I know I'm going to need to speak up soon if we're going to save this deal.

"Why? You yourself have told me that Anastasios has full autonomy to buy whatever books you think will sell. And this book will sell." She stabs the table with each word.

"We have autonomy, yes," Casey admits. "But Scarlett is...not well liked over there." He avoids looking at her as he mumbles, "No offense."

Scarlett doesn't move.

That doesn't stop Trina. "You and your *other editor*"—she injects as much disdain as she can into the words—"think this book is great, which it is. Your publicity expert agrees that it could be brilliantly marketed, and I know Anastasios Press could use the buzz from what will not only be a bestseller but a comeback for the literary community. Right, Meri?"

Meri glances at Casey and winces apologetically. "We both know that's true, Casey."

"Book deals are about timing and gut feelings as much as the book itself," he counters.

"You can't honestly tell me your gut isn't doing a goddamn happy dance about this one," Trina shoots back. "You passed it off to him because you knew it was something special." It doesn't escape me that she has not once looked at me, nor has she used my name. I groan internally. This is going to be an uphill battle.

"Even so, it's soured a bit now," he replies.

"You really want us to take this book to another press, then?" Leave it to Trina to cut right to the chase and call his bluff.

Casey takes a breath to respond, but I don't let him. "No," I say sharply, leaving no room for argument. He turns his ire to me in a glare, but that's okay. I can take it.

I pin my gaze to Scarlett, silently hoping she knows what I'm about to say is for her and her alone. "*Becoming* is already one of the most breathtaking books I've ever read. I would be honored to work on it, but I'm smart enough to offer to step aside and let someone else here have it. That's how important I think this book will be. But Trina is right. Anastasios needs it. The world needs it." *I need it*, I finish silently. But this isn't about me.

Scarlett still won't look at me, but her throat works against a swallow. She blinks a few times, and it's the most emotion I've seen from her since I walked into the room.

Trina waves a hand in my direction. "See?" she says to Casey. "So find someone else to edit it."

"We can," I assure her, even though the thought of letting this book into someone else's hands pains me. "I would still love the opportunity, but regardless, Casey and I were prepared to offer a lot of money to acquire this title. He can get over his hurt pride for the sake of the press."

Scarlett winces at the mention of money, and Trina glances at her, as if checking in.

I frown at that. She was never one to balk at talk of money before. In fact, she never seemed to care about it, even in the end when JMP offered her over a million dollars for more. It was about the writing for her, she said. The importance of the art. Getting paid to do it was a bonus.

Casey and Trina start to go at it again, which has Meri looking like she's trying very hard not to roll her eyes into the back of her head, but something about the way Scarlett has withered from the healthy version of herself I saw when I came in to whatever silent shell she's become now has me on high alert.

"Stop," I say. When they don't hear me, I say it louder. "Stop."

They do, then, and turn to look at me.

I clear my throat. "We're all sitting here talking about this deal and this book and the author herself as if she's not sitting right in front of us with opinions of her own. Yes, this deal would be important for Anastasios. Yes, we were all deceived. And yes, even before knowing who wrote it, this book has meant something to me that I can't quite put into words. But I, for one, want to know what Scarlett thinks about this whole thing before we go any further."

That gets her attention. Her brilliant blue eyes fly to me, and some of the tension releases from her shoulders and face.

There she is, I think as my heart skips a beat. I give her a small smile, and she returns the ghost of one across the table.

I expect her to reject this whole thing out of pocket and prepare for how much it's going to sting when she does. But she keeps regarding me with those blue eyes, and I find myself mesmerized by them like I always was.

"You loved it?" she finally asks.

It takes me a second to realize she hasn't just shot me down. It takes another to register the hope in the lift of her chin and the angle of her brows. One more and it dawns on me that she's asking what I think, not because of any deal but because my opinion of her work still matters.

"Scarlett," I say, and her name sounds pained on my lips,

even to me. "*Loved* isn't a strong enough word."

Her eyes glisten as that hits home, like I knew it would. Everything goes still as I hold my breath, waiting for her to collect herself enough to respond.

"I want you to do it," she says.

And that's about when everything erupts again. Meri brings out her tablet to start drafting a marketing plan. Casey, begrudgingly on board, opens up his laptop to start taking notes on negotiations for the contract department to draw up paperwork.

Trina, to her credit, turns in her chair to fully face Scarlett and says, loud enough for everyone to hear, "Are you sure?"

Scarlett tears her eyes away from me to turn her attention to her agent. "No," she says, and I have to chuckle at her honesty. "But he loved the book without knowing I wrote it, without any preconceived notions. And if I know Ryan..." She trails off and looks at me again. "There's no one who will take care of my story the way he will."

As if that weren't enough to make my entire year, Scarlett smiles at me. It's a soft smile, one that only teases at the corners of her lips, but it's reflected in her eyes. It warms me from head to toe.

"I promise your book is in good hands," I say, because I have to say something before this feeling completely consumes me.

"I know," she replies with all the confidence in the world.

Chapter 7

Scarlett

Two days later, I'm sitting cross-legged on the couch in my therapist's office, the decorative throw pillow in my lap the only barrier against whatever awful, emotional work she's going to make me do after telling her exactly what happened in that meeting.

Dianne—as she's insisted I call her for the past several years, ever since Trina dragged me in here to see her—stopped writing on her notepad about halfway into my story. If I didn't know any better, I'd think she was engrossed in it.

"So you're going to be working with Ryan on a book that they believe will be another bestseller after walking away from both him and a deal that could have resulted in multiple other bestsellers and completely cutting him *and* writing out of your life?"

Huh. Maybe she *was* engrossed in my story.

"That's about the gist of it," I say drily. "When you say it like that, it sounds like I'm making a huge mistake."

"Do you feel like you're making a mistake?"

A grumble starts low in my throat. "I don't feel like being therapist-ized today."

She laughs. "I'm not, I swear. I'm trying to point out that mistakes are often a matter of perception. If you perceive this as a mistake, then it likely is, and vice versa. If you think you're not doing the right thing for your book—and, more importantly, for you—then you'll never be able to get past that to a place where you are happy with your decision."

I wrinkle my nose and pull at a loose thread on the pillow in my lap. "That actually makes sense."

"Don't act so surprised," she responds quickly. One of the things I love about Dianne is that she's not all gentle and kind with me. She'll put me in my place when I need it. And I often need it.

"It feels like it should feel like a mistake," I say eventually. It's the only way I can describe what's going through my head. "Working with Ryan is the right thing for this book. I feel it in my bones. But my brain disagrees. It's still connecting him with everything that happened outside of the last book."

"He is connected to more than work for you," Dianne says gently. I don't miss how she says "work" and not "books." This has always been her subtle reminder to me that writing is a job, and it doesn't have to infiltrate my entire life. Clearly, she's not a writer. "Have you had a chance to talk to him personally? Have you opened up about your—"

"No," I interrupt her before she can go any further. "There wasn't time. We negotiated, set up a few initial deadlines, and they were off to another meeting." I don't mention that I flew out of there before Ryan could even say goodbye. "Besides, this is about the book. Not me. It's not personal this time."

Dianne tilts her head to the side. "Isn't it?"

"What do you mean?"

"Art is intensely personal. Your art, especially. Are you really going to tell me that you have grown a sudden ability to completely divorce the past from the present? The personal from the art? Because if so, that's wonderful news." She doesn't sound like she believes me.

I truly consider her question for a moment. She's gotten to the heart of what has been bothering me about this for the past two days. Can I separate and compartmentalize enough to make this book into the best version of itself? In the end, that's what really matters.

"I don't think it's about completely divorcing myself from

anything," I finally say. "It's about moving on. Accepting what happened and coming to a place where I can work again. Working with him...I don't know. It feels like it might be healing in a way." I'm tempted to tip my voice upward at the end like a question, but I force myself not to. It's not a question. This is going to be good, for the book and for me.

It has to be.

Dianne's answering smile is wide and genuine. "Oh, Scarlett. I'm so proud of how far you've come. I hope you're proud of it, too."

"I am." I smile back.

After a moment, she gets serious again. "Lucky for you, we're out of time, so I can't bug you about talking to him about what happened five years ago, but I think you should. Soon."

I stand quickly, not wanting to go any further with that for now. I came a long way today. Let's not ruin it.

"Maybe next time." Even I can hear how uncommitted I am to that.

She laughs again. "Definitely next time."

THERE'S ONLY ONE thing that I can ever do after therapy, and that is watch baking competitions. Since my holiday baking marathon was so rudely interrupted last time, I'm itching to get back to it. I change into my pajamas, toss my hair up into a bun, make myself some tea because coffee this late in the day would be bad for my circadian rhythms, and snuggle in.

No sooner do I start the first episode of a new season than there is a knock at the door.

"Dammit, Trina," I curse loudly as I stand to answer it. Probably loud enough for her to hear me through the thin door. "You scheduled that appointment and texted me no less than eight times to make sure I went. You should know—"

I'm cut short when I pull the door open, because it's not Trina standing there. It's Ryan.

He's more casual today in dark jeans and a forest-green hoodie, but his hair is still done. There's a portfolio tucked under one arm, a laptop bag slung over his shoulder, and a question in his gaze that I can't quite decipher.

"I'm not Trina." His voice is laced with humor, though he doesn't let his face show it.

"I can see that."

His eyes flick over my shoulder, and then he gives a little half smile when he sees what's on the television. "You still love baking shows."

"Some things never change," I singsong in a desperate attempt to break some of the tension Ryan his decidedly brought with him.

That backfires, because his gaze slides over me as if he remembers every curve and dip and surface of my body. "Some things never do," he says softly as his eyes meet mine again.

It doesn't take much to remind me what I loved about Ryan all those years ago. In fact, I was reminded of it throughout my entire time at the Anastasios offices while he sat across from me, larger than life and overtaking my senses. He's still so confident. So unabashedly emotional. If I had to venture a guess, he's probably still so damn good at what he does, turning raw words into sentences that leap off the page.

Some things never change, indeed.

"Why are you here?" I ask. "And how did you get my address?"

Five years ago, in a fit of rage or depression or whatever you want to call it, I packed up a duffel bag and ran. After wandering for about a year, I had a service pack up everything that was important to me—which wasn't much—from my condo in Roger's Park and put it up for sale. That was when I came back to Chicago to move into this tiny apartment in the South Loop. It took me six months before I could call Trina again to tell her I was alive. I made her promise never to tell Ryan, swore her to secrecy. It took another two months of her building up my trust before I even gave her my new address. I never gave it to Ryan. Never called him. Never texted. I still go out of my way to avoid driving near his old place.

It's not that I didn't want to see him again. I did...and looking at him now, I remember even more clearly the way his body felt against mine, the way his lips brushed against my skin, the way his words sounded as he whispered them into my ear. But I was too afraid. If he had been angry with me or if I had ruined his career, I never would have forgiven myself. And so it just became easier to stay away for good. I convinced myself it was for the best.

But as his dark eyes search mine with a mixture of sadness and concern, I can see that he might have missed me almost as much as I missed him. And I don't know what to do with that information.

He clears his throat, breaking us out of whatever tense moment we were sharing. He lifts the portfolio from under his arm. "I have notes for you. And your address is on the contract."

Of course it is. I don't know why I didn't think of that. But I certainly never thought Ryan would just show up at my apartment.

"That doesn't exactly explain why you're here," I say over the noise from my television. "You could have sent the initial notes through Trina."

"Do you want me to send my notes through Trina? That's not typically how I work, but—"

"No," I cut him off. "I don't know why I said that. It's not how I work, either."

He idly fidgets with the gold ring he wears on his right middle finger. It was a gift from his late father, who passed away when Ryan was in high school. I hadn't noticed it the other day, but he never took that ring off when we were together. He left it on while cooking, jogging, in the shower, while he slept. While *we* slept. While he made love to me, the edge of it scraping against the skin of my hip as he pressed his long fingers into it...

"Can I come in?" From the timbre of his voice, it sounds like his thoughts went somewhere similar.

"Um..." I look down at my purple satin pajamas, the one luxury I cannot live without. "Do you think that's a good idea?"

"It's a better idea than me standing in the hallway."

He has a point. I open the door wider, and he walks inside. "Let me go put on something more appropriate."

"I've seen you in less." He smirks again as the door snicks shut behind him.

I gape at him. "Ryan," I whisper.

He shakes his head quickly. "I'm sorry. I was trying to be funny."

Blinking, I huff lightly. "It was. But maybe...too soon?"

"Fair."

We stand awkwardly just inside my door, unable to move or talk or look anywhere but at each other. All the while, I'm acutely aware of my rumpled pajamas, my unshaven legs, my messy hair, the face I scrubbed clean after therapy. Not that it matters what I look like to him. Not anymore.

Ryan is the first to break the silence. "It's good to see you." From the way he says it, I can tell he means it. It actually eases some of my self-consciousness.

"I'm sorry how all that went down the other day." I smile a little. "I'd say it wasn't my idea, but I went along with it. I should have told Trina—"

"No," he cuts me off. "It was a brilliant move on her part."

"Because you never would have read it if you knew it was me who wrote it?" I guess.

"Casey likely wouldn't have," he admits. His brown eyes pin me to the spot. "But I would. I'll read anything you write from now until the end of time."

"Even if I have another mental breakdown?" It's my turn to try to be funny, but it falls flat.

"Even then," he says with a marked intensity. "I never meant to be your enemy, Scarlett."

A lump rises in my throat. I try to swallow it away, but it's too thick. "I know. I'm sorry. I can't...I don't want to talk about this." I shake my head to clear it, trying desperately to find safer ground. "You said you had notes?"

Ryan regards me for a moment longer, then takes a few steps further inside to lay the portfolio on my kitchen table. Doing so brings him close enough to me that I can smell the almond and vanilla notes of his cologne. It threatens to pull me back under memories of him, but he speaks before I can go too far down.

"Just a few developmental notes at this point. Some suggestions about moving some scenes and a few to add for clarity. Nothing huge, but I thought you might want to get started."

"You printed it out?" I ask.

"I always work in print for the first round," he responds.

"Only for the books you really like," I counter.

He pins me with those eyes again, and I can hardly breathe. "Yes," he says simply. Then he adds, "I told you I loved it."

That's not what he said, and he knows it, but I'm not going to bring it up if he isn't.

"I'll leave you to it, then." He takes a few steps toward the door. "Wouldn't want to get between you and your baking show."

"Hey, Ryan?" I say to his back. "Thanks."

He stops, then turns slowly around. "For what?"

"For asking what I wanted. No one..." I hug my arms around my torso and pinch the satin fabric between my fingers. "No one did that all those years ago, and I wish someone had. I don't know if things would have turned out differently, but...maybe."

The hurt that flashes over his expression is unmistakable. I didn't mean to hurt him or imply that he should have been the one to ask, though he certainly could have. It would have meant a lot if he had asked before steamrolling ahead with a million-dollar deal that was going to demand more from me than I was already giving when I had nothing left to give. But he wasn't alone in that, and in his defense, who doesn't want a million dollars to write books?

"You're absolutely right," he says. "I'm sorry for the part I played in what happened."

The truth is that wasn't all of it. Maybe it's Dianne's suggestion I talk to him about it or the way his kind eyes have been drinking me in like I'm an oasis in the middle of the desert, but the rest is on the tip of my tongue. I almost unload all of it right then and there.

But he says, "I hope you can eventually accept my apology and that we can put the past behind us, where it belongs."

Of course. Moving on. That's the ultimate goal, right? To let bygones be bygones. What good would dredging it up do? It would only hurt him, and my goal isn't to break him like I was broken. I wouldn't even wish that on the villains of my stories.

"Yes," I say with forced cheerfulness. "Apology accepted. We're good, Ryan."

He looks at me for a little longer, some emotion in his eyes I can't quite name. Then, with a curt nod, he turns and leaves.

Almost immediately after the door shuts behind him, I look at the portfolio he left on the table. I glance between that and the elimination round of my holiday baking show. Ultimately, I turn the television off and dive into Ryan's notes.

I give myself over to the words. I always do.

Seven Years Ago

"ALL HAIL QUEEN Scarlett!" my three best friends exclaim in unison before we all toss back a shot of some kind of cheap liquor. I hiss through my teeth as it burns all the way down and then lingers.

"Pretty sure that took a layer off my esophagus." I grimace.

Ava slams her shot glass down on the bar and pats me on the back. "We need to toughen you up." She catches the bartender's eye. "Another round!"

"No!" I hold my hands out in protest. I'm still barely able to talk over the burning. "I can't be hungover tomorrow. I have to write."

"You don't have to do anything tomorrow, Miss I-Signed-a-Two-Book-Deal," Katherine says.

"They're eventually going to need that second book," I remind them.

"Yeah, *eventually*. You signed the deal. The check cleared. And only a week after graduation too. You don't even have to try to find some shitty coffee-shop job like the rest of us," Mandy adds. "Take one night to have fun with your friends. We're celebrating you!"

Mandy, Ava, Katherine, and I graduated from our various graduate programs a few weeks ago and decided to make the move to Chicago to pursue our careers. New York would've been closer to the heart of the publishing industry for me, but the great thing about writing is you can really do it from anywhere. Not to mention that Chicago has three things New York doesn't, and I'm currently watching them all do another round of shots.

I don't touch mine, but they don't seem to notice or care. They were so excited for my deal with John Monroe Press—a local publisher, no less—that they insisted we go out to celebrate. They did this when I landed my agent, too, who is also with a local agency. It's weird how everything fell into place for me, and they're so happy. Even though Mandy graduated from the same program I did and is currently querying agents for her first romance novel, none of them seem jealous. We're all filled with a youthful exuberance that even I—a youthful exuberant myself—can see. So, I didn't have the heart to tell them no either time, though this is so not my scene. I love them, and they're proud of me. I'm happy to be out with them, even if the music is loud and I have to get some coherent words on the page tomorrow if I'm going to make my deadline.

"Oh, I love this song." Katherine closes her eyes and sways to the beat of the music. "Let's dance, bitches!"

Mandy and Ava whoop loudly, drawing the attention of a few other people sitting at the bar. They head out to the dance floor while Katherine tugs at my arms to get me to follow.

"I'm going to get a beer," I tell her. "Go ahead. I'll be right there."

"Okay!" she shouts over the music.

Once she's out of sight, I lean my forearms against the bar with no intention of leaving this spot. Bars are not my favorite places, but I will tolerate them on occasion. I absolutely *will not* dance.

This bar isn't particularly busy for a Friday night, at least not yet. There's some kind of sports game happening on all three of the flat-screen televisions hanging around the place. By the way some of the people sitting here are cheering and groaning at regular intervals, it seems important.

The DJ is stationed around the corner from the bar and out of my line of sight, giving some separation from the sports while still being heard over the noises of the crowd. He plays another song that makes the crowd gathered in front of him squeal. If I had to guess, I won't see my friends again for a while. I groan internally. Leaving would mean going into the crowd of dancing twentysomethings to find them, which would lead to them dragging me onto the dance floor. Better to stay here and wait it out, I suppose.

I wave down the bartender and order that beer, if only to have something to do with my hands. When a seat opens up on the other side of the bar, I grab the just-delivered glass and make a break for it. But when I try to slide triumphantly into the chair, I'm met with something solid. This obstacle knocks the hand carrying my beer, and almost the entire contents slosh out over the side. I jump back enough that most of it lands on my shoes, but some of it splashes onto my blue shirt.

"Son of a bitch," I curse, loud enough to be heard over the music.

"She's not," the obstacle responds. When I look up from studying the wet stain welling up over my torso, I'm met with a man who would probably be tall if he weren't currently occupying my seat. Everything about him is practically monochromatic. Dark. I think he's trying to look brooding, but it's kind of missed the mark. He's dressed in a black Henley with the sleeves pushed up almost to his elbows and dark jeans. His brown hair is longish on the top, and I can tell it would be shaggy if not gelled into submission. Brown eyes peer out behind his dark-rimmed glasses. And an infuriating smirk plays on his full lips. He's the kind of academic-looking guy I would have swooned over in undergrad until I realized he was only interested in literature and himself, meaning I was only as good to him as how well I supported his pursuits.

In short, he looks like every other self-absorbed asshole I spent two years avoiding in my creative writing graduate program.

"What?" I switch my glass to my dry hand and shake the wet one to rid it of some of the beer. The man in my seat flinches as a few droplets hit his face. I don't feel bad about that in the least.

"You said, 'Son of a bitch.' The implication there is that my mother is a bitch. I said she's not," he explains.

"Oh, good," I mutter to myself and wipe my hand on my jeans. "He's probably self-absorbed, definitely an asshole, and he's pedantic too."

He smiles widely. "If you really want to hear something pedantic, I'd say you don't need the words *and* and *too* in that sentence. It's redundant. Good word, though—*pedantic*."

I pinch my brows together as my jaw drops. Is this guy serious? "Don't patronize me," I tell him.

Tilting his head to the side, he returns my confused look. "I'm not. It's a good word. Not one you expect to hear"—he looks around—"here."

A harsh laugh escapes me, which causes him to wince again. I shake my head incredulously. "An elitist, too!" I exclaim. Never mind the fact that I was internally bemoaning having to be here not two minutes ago. "What does *here* have to do with someone's vocabulary? And speaking of vocabulary, is *sorry* in yours? Because I haven't heard that *here*, either."

He regards me for a moment as the beat of the music intensifies, mimicking the angry pulse I can feel throbbing at my temple. His whole face infuriates me as it alternates between a frown and another smirk.

"You're right," he finally says, but it does nothing to ease my anger. "I shouldn't assume someone with a decent vocabulary doesn't enjoy a drink and some sports on a Friday night. I'd point out that I'm here, after all, and my vocabulary is at least good enough to recognize yours, but that would probably just be more evidence for you that I'm— How did you put it? Self-absorbed?" There's that maddening smirk again. "As for *sorry*..." He trails off and rakes his gaze over me as if seeing me for the first time. I try to ignore the way my skin reacts to his obvious appreciation of my body. When he's had his fill, his eyes meet mine again. "What exactly is it that I'd be sorry for?"

I wave a hand at his ass in the chair. "You took my seat."

His eyebrows shoot up, and he blinks a few times in surprise. "I truly didn't realize you had been sitting here." He immediately stands and turns the chair so the seat faces me. "My friends are dancing, I guess? I saw an open seat and thought it best to wait them out." Those brown eyes flick in the direction of the dance floor, then back to meet mine again. This man makes excellent eye contact, I'll give him that.

He's smiling genuinely now, and it changes his whole face. The skin at the corners of his mouth crinkle into almost dimples, and his eyes practically glitter in the dim light of the bar. I realize suddenly that he hasn't taken those eyes off me for more than a second since he bumped into me, and I'm not exactly sure how I feel about it.

"I wasn't," I admit. "Sitting here, I mean. You and I had the same idea, it seems."

His shoulders shake on a small laugh, which makes me smile too. "Ah," he says. His mouth twists to the side as if he's considering his next words carefully. "Well, I'll say I'm sorry your beer spilled, but I can't say I'm sorry I bumped into you."

I cock an eyebrow, the anger returning in a wave. "Why not?"

"Selfishly, I'm having fun talking to you." He dips his chin in the direction of my half-full glass. "Have a seat. Can I buy you another to make up for it?"

It's my turn to move my gaze over him. Now that he's standing—and now that my anger has simmered a bit, I can see that he is, indeed, tall. Almost a head taller than me. He's thin but not lanky, and he fills out the Henley nicely. The glasses suit his face, but I find myself wondering what he might look like without them. If he always wears them, or if he wears contacts sometimes. As he waits for my response, he tilts his torso forward slightly, but his grin doesn't falter.

He knows I'm ogling. That much is sure from the look on his

face.

"Sure," I say as I slide into the seat. "It's only fair, I suppose."

"What are you drinking?" he asks as he leans closer to the bar. The movement causes his chest to brush against my shoulder, and the scent of him overpowers the smell of wheaty beer wafting up from my shirt. It's sweet—vanilla and almond. Like paper.

I idly twist my glass on top of the bar. "312."

"A Chicago staple," he responds approvingly. "You're from here?"

"Midwestern." I shrug.

He rolls his lips between his teeth and narrows his eyes at me. The proximity of his body is making my own tingle. If I had to guess based on the fact that he hasn't moved away, he's feeling the same.

"You're going to make me work for information about you, aren't you?" he asks after the bartender takes our orders. "That's fine. I like a challenge."

The way he leans in and his voice drops an octave has my toes curling. I hadn't intended to make him work for anything, but now I can't think of a single thing I want more than to drag this out as long as possible.

"Take a guess," I tease as the bartender deposits our drinks. "I'll tell you if you're right."

"Hmm," he hums as he sips his beer. He makes a big show of studying me again, as if he hasn't been doing so this whole time. "Okay. You like words. You're out with friends, but if we're both avoiding the dance floor, this probably isn't your first choice for a Friday-night activity. Being Midwestern is interesting but probably not relevant. You're drinking beer and not something fruity, and your apparel would suggest you don't put much stock into your appearance—"

"Hey!" I interject.

He holds his hands, palms out, in a placating gesture. "I didn't mean it like that," he says through a deep chuckle, the sound of it warming me straight through to my core. "I meant you're not all dolled up. It's not a value statement. There's nothing wrong with that." His gaze dips, then he drags it back up to meet mine. "Some people might prefer it."

That shot earlier must be making me bold, because I respond, "Some people? Or one in particular?"

He tips his head back and lets out a loud, joyful laugh. It exposes his throat to me, and I take the opportunity to watch as it moves, the strong column of it long and rough with a five o'clock shadow.

"Quick witted, too." He wraps his long fingers around his glass where it sits on the bar top. A gold ring on his middle finger glints in the light and clinks against the glass as he taps it in thought. "Are you in journalism? Publishing?"

"Close." I dip my chin and take another sip of my beer. "I'm a writer. Based on your guess, though, I'm going to assume *you're* in journalism or publishing?"

"Editor," he says. "Would I have read anything of yours?"

"Probably not. I just signed my first deal. That's why my friends dragged me out tonight. We're celebrating." Another squeal comes from the area of the dance floor. "Well, they are."

"Congratulations on the deal," he says. "What house are you with?"

I can't help the way my back straightens with pride. Getting a deal with a major publisher is significant, especially as a debut. "JMP," I tell him.

He huffs a laugh as he shakes his head. Having expected him to recognize how awesome that announcement was, I frown and my shoulders deflate a little.

"What?" I ask.

"That's where I work."

"Oh!" I perk up again. "Really? What are the odds?"

"One in a million, probably. What's your name?"

"Scarlett Frye. What's yours?"

He coughs on his beer, pounding his chest to dislodge the liquid. "Are you fucking serious?"

"Yes," I say slowly.

"Holy shit. You're..." He trails off and stares at me with a slack jaw. "Everyone at JMP is talking about you. They've got all hands on deck for your book. You had senior editors fighting over who was going to get to work with you."

This isn't exactly news to me, of course. Trina had kept me updated about the whole process before I signed. I had multiple offers, and part of the reason I went with JMP was because of how badly they wanted my book. It felt like the right choice to go with a house that acted as excited about it as I am.

But watching this man regard me with obvious awe in the middle of a loud, crowded bar really drives the point home. If JMP has anything to do with it, this book is going to be huge.

It also probably means that my book is now more interesting to him than I am.

"Yeah." I avert my eyes, suddenly self-conscious and more than a little disappointed.

"Whoa." He moves sideways so he's in my line of sight, drawing my gaze back to him. "That was a shift. Are you not thrilled?"

"I am," I reply cautiously. "This is just going to change a lot of things for me is all."

He nods as if he understands, then offers his hand to me. "I'm Ryan Whitlock. Pleasure to meet you, Scarlett."

The edge of his ring scrapes against my palm as I shake his hand. He brings his other up to clasp mine between his, and he holds on slightly longer than is appropriate for a simple handshake. I don't dare move as the warmth of his hands seep into my own.

The intensity in his eyes coupled with his hands on mine as he leans further into my space dispels any concerns I just had about how interesting I may or may not be to him.

But, of course, my friends choose this moment to come back from the dance floor. Loudly. They surround me, seemingly oblivious to Ryan standing there as they sidle up to the bar.

"Scarlett!" Katherine draws out my name almost comically

as she throws an arm around my shoulders. "Time to move on to our next stop!"

I laugh as she shakes me back and forth. "What are you talking about?"

"We planned a whole bar crawl," Mandy says. "The next place is the one we did body shots at the last time we were out, remember?"

"*You* did body shots," I correct her. Knowing Ryan can hear me, it seems an important distinction to make. "I did no such thing."

"Because you're boring." Ava tilts her whole body back dramatically as she drags the word from her throat.

I can't really argue with that, so I catch Ryan's eye and shrug. He chuckles.

Mandy finally notices him, then winks knowingly at me. "Okay, ladies. After all that dancing, I could use some air. Let's wait for Scarlett outside." She rounds up the other two, and they make their way to the door.

I give Ryan an apologetic look.

"It's okay," he says, sliding a folded napkin across the bar top. "I need to find my friends anyway. But I really would like to see you again."

I unfold the napkin to see his name and number scrawled on it in ink. I laugh loudly. "This is so old school."

He clicks a pen and puts it in his back pocket. "A good editor always has a pen," he says, then indicates the napkin. "I hope you call me."

Pursing my lips against the smile forming is futile, but I try anyway. "I will," I promise. Then, I make my way outside to rejoin my friends.

AFTER LEAVING SCARLETT'S apartment, I go straight home with every intention of working remotely for the rest of the day. I wasn't getting anything done at the office; I couldn't stop thinking about her. And while I knew randomly showing up at her apartment could majorly backfire, I was willing to take the risk.

But when I get back to my Hyde Park condo and open my laptop on top of my desk, it doesn't take very long for my thoughts to drift. I have other projects besides Scarlett's that I'm working on, but after finding out who S.J. Falmouth really is, the directive from the higher-ups has been clear: All my other projects are secondary to this one. They know what a find they have on their hands, and they're going to put a lot of resources behind it.

I'm glad everyone at Anastasios seems to be on board. I would never tell Scarlett this, but after her dramatic exit five years ago, I was worried she'd be blacklisted in the industry if she ever tried to come back. But it seems, with enough time and turnover and a good enough book, they've been willing to overlook it.

Her book is good enough, that's for sure. It has stuck with me since that first reading when it latched onto something in my soul. I haven't been able to get it to let go.

That's not what's overtaking my thoughts now, though. Every time my mind drifts, whatever I had tried to focus on is replaced with the image of her in those purple satin pajamas, the fabric pooling at her bare feet, the chipped navy polish on her toenails peeking out under the hem. The way her blue eyes looked at me almost as eagerly as I left my handwritten notes on her table haunts me, and I'm not ashamed to admit that I wish she was more excited to see me than my editorial commentary.

I'm still thinking about it the next day as I wander into the office, hoping at least being there will keep me from looking at my bed, my couch, my kitchen counter, the makeshift desk she used to work at in my bedroom...everywhere she lingers even after all these years.

No such luck, though I am able to finalize a manuscript that's been sitting, almost finished, on my desk for a week. But the whole time I'm reading through the last chapter to make sure my notes are cohesive, I have to force myself to not compare this author's writing to Scarlett's. Not that it's a fair comparison; no one can out-write her.

The ding of an incoming email snaps me back to reality. Assuming it's the author whose work I just sent over with a quick thank-you, I hover my cursor idly over the alert, but Scarlett's name on the notification has me scrambling to click open the full email.

From: Scarlett Frye <scarlett@scarlettfrye.com>
To: Ryan Whitlock <rwhitlock@anastasiospress.com>

Subject: MS Notes

Ryan,

Respectfully, have you lost your mind? The bicycle is integral to the story and cannot possibly be omitted.

I will, however, begrudgingly admit that the rest of your notes are spot on, as usual.

—Scarlett

The bark of laughter I let out is so loud, Margie pokes her head in from the hallway.

"Everything okay?"

I clear my throat and brush a piece of lint off my sleeve. "Yes. I got a funny email is all."

"Oh, okay," she says. "You don't laugh very often, so I had to make sure." Then, she pops out of my field of vision.

I frown at the space her head just occupied, thinking about that for a moment. She's right, though I've never noticed that I don't laugh often when I'm here. It has me thinking about how often I laugh when I'm not here. I'm sad to admit it's not as often as I'd like. Thankfully, before I can go too far down that rabbit hole, another incoming email dings.

From: Scarlett Frye <scarlett@scarlettfrye.com>
To: Ryan Whitlock <rwhitlock@anastasiospress.com>

Subject: Re: MS Notes

Ryan,

Sorry about my brash question. I will be more professional in the future. But the bike stays.

—S

I don't waste any time typing up a reply.

From: Ryan Whitlock <rwhitlock@anastasiospress.com>
To: Scarlett Frye <scarlett@scarlettfrye.com>

Subject: Re: MS Notes

Scarlett,

No apology necessary. Your candor has brought some

levity to an otherwise dreary day.

I may have lost my mind, but it would be unrelated to this. I don't have a problem with the bike specifically. Surely you can see that you have multiple objects that are accomplishing the same thing; they all symbolize growing up, coming of age. By getting rid of one, you would strengthen the others. Do you have a suggestion for a different one that could go?

—Ryan

It's not strictly necessary for me to ask her opinion. A seasoned writer like Scarlett who has been through this process before might even read it as rhetorical—something to think about and nothing more—and not respond. She knows she can reject changes I suggest if she has good reasons. But I tell myself that I want to keep this line of communication open in case she needs more direction, even though I know, deep down, I want her to respond for entirely different reasons. So I am delighted a few moments later when she does.

From: Scarlett Frye <scarlett@scarlettfrye.com>
To: Ryan Whitlock <rwhitlock@anastasiospress.com>

Subject: Re: MS Notes

Ryan,

The bike is so much more than a symbol of Madeline growing up. It's transportation, freedom from the confines of her situation, but there are also limitations to that freedom because it can only take her so far. It's about fitting in with her friends who also have bikes but not quite being able to because her bike is secondhand and looks like a boy's.

I'm, frankly, amazed you didn't see this while you were reading. Is it possible you're losing your touch and not your mind?

As far as what else could go, I'll have to revisit the text and get back to you.

—S

Maybe I'm reading too much into it, but my chest swells with hope that she's asking a question for the same reason I did: She wants me to respond. That has to be it, otherwise why would she ask something that anyone else would find cutting? It's so similar to the way we used to tease each other—poking at each other's insecurities, popping them open until they deflated like balloons and took up less space—that I'm sure this is her intent. She wants to goad me into a reply.

From: Ryan Whitlock <rwhitlock@anastasiospress.com>
To: Scarlett Frye <scarlett@scarlettfrye.com>

Subject: Re: MS Notes

You probably won't believe this, but of course I noticed all of that. I do think several of your other symbols accomplish the same thing, and better. The birds, for example, do this and more while simultaneously creating beautiful imagery. The clouds, too. And don't forget the songs they sing together at the end. The bike is a wonderful symbol, but the others are gorgeous, rich, and help to create the visuals that really draw the reader in. The bike is...a bike. It's only in one scene, whereas the others are prevalent throughout, so they've been woven into the text more. But I am open to other ideas.

—Ryan

A giddiness rises up within me, like the bubbles in champagne zigzagging to the top of a glass. Effervescent. Shimmery. Natural, in a way. It has only been five emails, but this back-and-forth is familiar. It's like slipping on an old, favorite sweater. Scarlett and I started sparring the night we met and would continue to do so over the course of our relationship. It became almost a form of verbal foreplay and often ended with us in bed, exploring more ways to elicit different kinds of responses from each other. This feels so similar to that, and even though I know I shouldn't, I'm holding out hope that it's having the same effect on her.

Another email from her pops up in my inbox, and my excitement intensifies.

From: Scarlett Frye <scarlett@scarlettfrye.com>
To: Ryan Whitlock <rwhitlock@anastasiospress.com>

Subject: Re: MS Notes

The bike is gritty. Dirty. On the ground. Everything you mentioned is ethereal and sky-bound. The bike is not meant to be pretty or create imagery. It's meant to be tangible and real. And (again, I'm surprised I need to point this out to you), it exists in direct contrast to the birds and the clouds. A foil, if you will.

So, what I'm hearing is that I actually need to weave the bike into the book more, to make it inextricable from Madeline's story. Would that appease you?

The contrasting symbols did not, in fact, escape me, but the bicycle felt extra. The scene in which it appeared was stilted, almost as if Scarlett had been trying too hard to include it. But if she could work it in even more, make pieces of the book grittier and, by comparison, make the other scenes even more ethereal...

My elation at communicating with Scarlett morphs into the exhilaration of solving a puzzle. Something clicks into place. It's so satisfying—so obvious—that I can't believe it escaped me before.

From: Ryan Whitlock <rwhitlock@anastasiospress.com>
To: Scarlett Frye <scarlett@scarlettfrye.com>

Subject: Re: MS Notes

That's brilliant. Yes. More of the bike would solve the problem. But keep the bike gritty and real; keep the birds and clouds airy and light.

Her response is almost immediate. Yet again, I dare to hope everything I'm reading between the lines of these emails has been reciprocal.

From: Scarlett Frye <scarlett@scarlettfrye.com>
To: Ryan Whitlock <rwhitlock@anastasiospress.com>

Subject: Re: MS Notes

I might be rusty, but I'm not an amateur. Trust the process.

I'd better get to work on this. My editor is known to show up at my house unexpectedly with more notes.

Thanks, Ryan.

And even though I know that message is a clear indication that she's signing off, I risk another question anyway.

From: Ryan Whitlock <rwhitlock@anastasiospress.com>
To: Scarlett Frye <scarlett@scarlettfrye.com>

Subject: Re: MS Notes

Are you open to your editor stopping by with more notes in the future? I can warn him to stay away if you prefer.

I don't expect an immediate response. Her last email was final, and my question is loaded. There are a hundred reasons why she might not write back, and only half of them have to do with me making a move she's not ready for. But I still check my email frequently throughout the rest of the day. I'm disappointed every time there's nothing from her.

Later that night, after a lonely dinner of microwave lasagna and a cold shower that does nothing to calm my thoughts of her, I lie awake in bed, staring at the dark ceiling and kicking myself. First I show up unexpectedly at her apartment, then I ask if I can do it again? What was I thinking? I probably scared her away by being too forward. I should be handling her with kid gloves, like Casey suggested the other day.

Around midnight, as I'm just starting to drift off to sleep, my phone lights up with a text message. Groggily, I open the app without thinking, but I'm jolted awake when Scarlett's name appears at the top of my screen. She blocked my number when she disappeared all those years ago. It's been so long since she's texted me that our past messages have disappeared into the ether, so just one message sits in a little gray bubble at the top. Just the sight of it has my heart swelling up with longing.

Scarlett

If you need to hand-deliver notes, I wouldn't mind.

Chapter 10

Scarlett

For the next week, my days and nights are consumed by two things: bicycles and Ryan Whitlock. Thoughts of the two of them circle around and around, as if each occupies alternating spokes on the wheels of the very bicycle that is the object of my obsession. As they turn faster and faster, they blur into something one and the same—each inextricable from the other.

By the end of that first week, I've done more research on bicycles than any normal human would ever need. Everything I've found, no matter how seemingly unimportant, is printed and strewn about my desk and floor. Some papers have made it to my bed where they mingle with various red-inked pages of my manuscript. I make a habit of curling up there in the evenings with my research and Ryan's notes, adding my own responses to the margins and edits between the lines before going back to my laptop and typing up a more refined version. I work well into each night, falling asleep on top of the words and awakening with the sun to start the process all over again.

More of my time than I'd like to admit is spent staring into space and flipping through the pages in my mind until I land on a place to add a scene, but when it clicks, I jump out of bed and type furiously, unaware of the time or my body, completely lost in my work.

The words fly from my brain to the keyboard almost faster than my fingers can keep up. It's a high unlike any other, and

I'm addicted to the feeling. This is exactly as it used to be, when I would write and write and never need to come up for air. No, writing *was* the air, and I needed it like I needed to breathe.

I don't know how I lived without it for five years.

The truth is, I didn't really live for those years. Not well anyway. Giving it up was akin to cutting off oxygen. I had thought writing was like a drug and giving it up cold turkey was best for me in the long run. And who knows. Maybe it was for a while. If the way I've fallen right back into old habits is any indication, there might not be a way for me to do this job with any kind of balance.

But it's different this time in one very important way—Ryan is only involved at the surface level. The emails we shared at the start of the week were exhilarating. Bouncing ideas back and forth with him again was as easy as...well...riding a bike. But that's all this is. Even though I unblocked his number and texted him that it would be okay to come by again, he doesn't. He wouldn't have any notes yet anyway, since I'm still working through the first round, but that never stopped him before. His absence is all the reminder I need to keep my head down and the words flowing.

Different book. Different Scarlett. Different outcome.

Even if they are the same late nights and early mornings. The same dwindling groceries and forgotten meals. The same lost count of how long it's been since I've showered.

The same man. The same emails. The same quips and repartee.

I loved him once. But I loved writing once, too. Love for the latter has crept back slowly, in the lines and the margins, but love for him was never meant to be. The loss of my love for him is so completely intertwined with the loss of my love for writing then. Despite all the work I've done to separate the two, there's still a thread that holds them tightly together.

Yet as I sit cross-legged on my bed with my phone face down and buried in the comforter and pages strewn about, I chew on the end of my pen and wait for the dread that had been the third spoke of the wheel all those years ago. The knowledge that I couldn't sustain this if I wanted room in my life for anything but words. That there were things I wanted that I could never have with the schedule I was put on. That even Ryan was secondary to my work.

But the dread doesn't come. Instead, it's more like a piece of me that had been missing has found its way back and snapped into place. Like a lost earring found under a cushion. And instead of being painful to look at, Ryan's familiar, red-penned handwriting is comforting in the dead of night, like an old friend. The lack of sleep propels me forward rather than drags me down. Newton was right—a body in motion stays in motion. When a writer starts, she can't stop until the job is done. I'll sleep and eat when it's over. It'll be worth it again, just like it was before.

It has to. Because I'm starting to realize I don't fully know who I am without this.

As Friday night bleeds into Saturday morning, I finally send off the updated manuscript to Ryan and Trina and expect not to hear anything until Monday when they are both back in the office. I flop over onto my bed without bothering to remove the laptop from it and relish in the accomplishment.

My elation is rudely interrupted simultaneously by my growling stomach and several dings from my phone. Bleary eyed, I look around the bed, figuring it'll be easier to stop the noise from the phone than that from my stomach if my last raid of a mostly empty pantry is any indication. I pat the comforter and shift papers around, eventually shoving them off the bed since I don't need them anymore anyway. The phone dings again, which is when I realize the sound is coming directly from underneath me. Sure enough, when I scoot my ass over, I've been sitting on it. Thank god no one was here to see that. Ryan used to give me shit about that kind of thing all the time. For some reason, that reminder is painful, and an otherwise-forgotten memory comes clearly into focus.

"How is it you knew exactly where page sixty-nine was when

I asked you about the concert scene half an hour ago, but you can't remember where you put your phone?" Ryan poked my ribs teasingly.

I rolled over to my stomach and leaned my chin against his bare chest, waggling my eyebrows suggestively. "Probably had something to do with the page number and the promise of one such action if I finished early tonight. Which I did."

He cupped the back of my head and kissed my forehead. "Your big, beautiful brain remains a mystery to me."

My phone rang again from wherever it was hiding. "Well, it's a mystery to me, too, apparently," I said before we both jumped up to turn the comforter out. The phone hit the ground on Ryan's side with a thud. He picked it up and handed it to me with a cocked eyebrow.

I shrugged and laughed. "Hey, you found it."

His answering smile was warm and indulgent, as if he loved even this messy part of me. As if he could spend the rest of his life with me, between sheets and pages and words, discussing symbols and looking for my phone.

And maybe I could let him.

An unexpected pang of sadness at the memory catches me completely off guard. I rub at my chest as if that could ease the pain there, but my lungs squeeze all the air out of them when I click the screen on and Ryan's name appears with three messages.

Ryan

Scarlett, it's 2am.

Ryan

Please tell me you haven't been working this whole time.

Ryan

This book isn't that important.

He's clearly worried, and I should ease his fear about me falling back into my old ways, but the truth of the matter is, minus his physical presence here, this is exactly how it used to be, no matter how hard I've tried to tell myself it's different this time. He knows that because he was here with me then, even if he's not now.

What bothers me more is how easy it is for him to dismiss the importance of this book. It's not a comeback for him. It's not really anything for him except another part of the job he already has—the one he's had this whole time while I've been trying to find any kind of purchase on a cliff that seemed determined to move all the footholds just out of reach. For me, this book is everything. My work, my art, my identity. Who am I if I'm not Scarlett Frye, bestselling author? I've spent five years trying to figure that out, only to come to the conclusion that I'm no one and nothing without my words.

And so, here I am again. Back where I started and having to come to terms with the fact that this might be how it always is.

It's important to me.

The message is too simple, even as it holds volumes of words unsaid.

Ryan

I didn't mean that. I meant that it's not more important *than* you.

I should be touched by the sentiment. It should be a revelation and a warning to me, that I've gone too hard again and am going to pay the price. But what he doesn't understand, what he could never understand, is that my work *is* me. We are one and the same. It might have *felt* different this time, but that's a tenuous foothold on the same cliff I've been hanging from for five years.

I think of over a million different things I could type back, but ultimately, my growling stomach and good sense win out. I power down the phone and toss it somewhere to be found in the morning. I smear the last of the peanut butter on the last tortilla in my fridge and shove it into my mouth before finally collapsing face down on my bed.

Chapter 11

Ryan

"ALL I'M SAYING is that she sent it at two in the morning." I lean forward in my seat facing Casey's desk, as if that could make him finally understand the gravity of the statement I've repeated twice now. The timing of her email bothered me all weekend, so when Monday rolls around, I didn't waste any time searching out my friend for advice.

Casey twirls a pen between his pointer and middle finger. "And all I'm saying is that you got it at two in the morning. Just because someone is awake before the crack of dawn does not mean that person has made a habit of being awake at that time." He drops the pen, and it twirls in a circle on the smooth desktop. Disregarding it, he presses his forearms into the desk and clasps his hands. "I know you're worried about her, Ry, but..." He trails off and presses his lips together, shaking his head slightly.

"What?"

He lets out a slow breath through his nose. "It's not really your place anymore, is it?"

I open my mouth to respond, but nothing comes out. That old ache returns to my chest, and the best I can manage is a shaky inhale before snapping my jaw shut.

His expression softens, but it's too late. Like toothpaste out of the tube, he can't take it back. The damage is done.

"Look," he says, but I stop him with a shake of my head.

"No. You're right. My job is to edit this book. Nothing more.

She made that clear, too, and I should keep my nose out of it."

"What do you mean she made that clear? What did you do?"

"I...might have stopped by her apartment with my initial notes." I lean back in my chair and take my glasses off to rub the bridge of my nose. "In my defense, I didn't really want to take the time to type them up." Hopefully my hand hides the grimace I make, because even I can hear that's a feeble excuse.

"Ryan—"

"I know." I replace my glasses and drop my hands helplessly to my knees. "I know, okay? I had to see her again. I wanted to know she was okay."

"And was she?"

It's not the response I expected. Casey has every right to chew me out, and he probably should. Showing up at her apartment unannounced when she hadn't given me her address herself was a violation of her privacy, and Anastasios Press could easily terminate me based on that alone. But when I risk a glance at him, his eyebrows are drawn together, and his head is tilted in genuine concern.

Before I respond, I think back to that day, as if it hasn't been playing on repeat since I left her. But Casey's question adds a new lens to it. Was she okay? Her toenails were painted, which is something she only ever did when she had surfaced from her work long enough to give herself a little extra attention. The baking show has always been a comfort thing for her, but she had just had a meeting with us where she had seen me again unexpectedly. I suppose it's not out of the question for her to curl up with her emotional-support baking competition. Her apartment was clean. Her hair has clearly been cut recently. She wasn't wearing makeup, but she was never one for that kind of thing anyway. Makeup or no, her skin was glowing. She looked healthy. And she filled out her pajamas—also clean—in a way that has lived rent-free in my head since I saw her. But what it tells me now is that, as I had suspected at that first meeting, she's probably been eating.

I nod slowly. "Yes. I think she was."

"And was she pissed you stopped by?" He makes a show of looking me up and down. "You have all your limbs, and I don't see any obvious bruises. Since you walked in here just fine, I'll assume she didn't cut off your balls."

"Okay, asshole." I narrow my eyes at him. "She was surprised, obviously, but she seemed okay with it."

If you need to hand-deliver notes, I wouldn't mind.

She definitely wouldn't have said that if she didn't want me to stop by again. She must have been okay with it.

"Then no harm, no foul." He levels me with a glare. "But I wouldn't do it again. Boundaries are your friend in this situation. I know you still want to protect her, but the best way to do that is by staying away. She left you—I get that—but my guess is she was just as broken up about it as you were." He pauses again as if he's holding back, but this time it doesn't take any prodding for him to continue. "No one walks away from a million-dollar deal and someone they're in love with all in the same day without some serious shit going on under the surface. Don't stir the pot, Ryan. Leave well enough alone."

Casey's words roll around in my head for another full week. A week in which I'm so engrossed in Scarlett's manuscript that I almost feel like she's with me. Her voice is so clear, so brilliant, so haunting. And reading this time knowing it was her who wrote the words makes it all the more exciting. The changes she's made to the story based on our emails are even better than what I had originally suggested. The grittiness of the bike elevates everything else in the story and adds realism to her otherwise fragile and airy prose. It incongruously fills the book with even more hope than was there before.

It fills *me* with hope that Scarlett has found a way to ground herself like she's grounded the story. That she won't somehow float away. That she's filled with optimism, too.

I had planned to do several passes through the manuscript this time, but after I finish my first read-through, I'm itching to discuss it with her about it like we used to—papers strewn about, a light in her eyes as she talked through a particular scene. The way those eyes would go a little wider and she'd gasp just before scrambling off the bed to grab a notebook or her laptop or her phone, whatever was closest to frantically tap out whatever idea had occurred to her.

The way our bodies would tangle with the pages and the sheets, our tongues rolling around words, then around each other. Exploring both until we were spent. Waking up to do it all over again.

I shake my head rapidly. Casey was right. The best way to protect her is to stay away. No matter how much I want to pick up right where we left off, it might bring up too many old wounds. It could stop Scarlett from writing again. And the world needs her words. That, I know for sure.

But when Trina's name lights up my phone somewhere in the middle of my second pass of page fifteen, I scramble to answer it faster than I probably should.

"Hello?" I press the phone hard into my ear, suddenly and inexplicably breathless.

"Ryan? Are you on a run or something? I can call back—"

"No, no." I take a deep breath, praying I can get my shit together. "I was focused. You surprised me is all." The little lie slips easily off my tongue as I remind myself for the hundredth time in the past hour that boundaries are my friend.

"Sure. Anyway, I'm calling about Scarlett."

"Is she okay?" I ask a little too quickly.

"Yes," Trina says slowly. Suspiciously. "She mentioned you've had her revisions for a week or so now, and she hasn't heard from you. She didn't say so directly, but I think she's a little nervous. She's not used to not having...immediate feedback." There's definitely laughter in her voice there, and I imagine her bright red lips twisting into an indecent grin.

"Does she want immediate feedback?" The words tumble out of me before I can think better of it. And to make matters worse, I match Trina's innuendo. I cringe and toss my glasses onto my desk so I can rub at my temples as if that would take all the double meaning out of the conversation.

She snorts. "No. Like I said, she's nervous. I told her I'd check in."

"Right. Of course." I blink my eyes open, the words on my screen blurry without my glasses. "Tell her she has nothing to worry about. I finished my first pass, and her revisions are spot on. My second has been slower because of some other projects I needed to finish up"—another lie—"but I should have it finished soon. Maybe another couple of weeks."

"Great." There's a scraping sound as if Trina is shifting her phone to her other ear, then a car door opening and closing in the background. "She's started drafting her next book, so this will give her time to make some headway on that."

At that, another image overtakes the one I had of Scarlett and me tangled in sheets and pages and each other. This one is of her at her desk, sitting cross-legged on her computer chair, her face too close to her monitor and dark circles under her eyes.

"I needed seven thousand words today to stay on track, and I only got thirty-five hundred." Her voice was weak and small. She didn't bother looking up from her monitor as she clacked away at her keyboard, then cursed silently and deleted whatever she had just written.

I wiped the bleariness out of my eyes with the back of my hand. "Beautiful, it's four in the morning. Have you slept at all?"

"I'll sleep when I finish."

"When you finish it'll be tomorrow, with a new word-count goal. Come to bed, just for a few hours."

She waved me off without sparing me a glance. "It won't take much longer. Once I got going, the first half went really fast. One more hour, I promise."

But I had heard that before. "Another hour" would turn into "Why not get ahead?" and "If I write double, maybe I can turn this in early," which was almost always followed by a frantic "Nothing will ever be as good as In the Time Before*" and ten pages gone with the click of a button.*

I scrubbed a hand down my face and padded groggily to the kitchen to put on another pot of coffee. If she was going to pull an all-nighter, the least I could do was make sure she didn't delete it all when she reread it in the light of day.

"Hello? Ryan? Did I lose you?" Trina's voice cuts through the memory, scattering it like leaves in a windstorm.

I clear my throat and glance out the floor-to-ceiling window in my office, almost surprised to find the spring sunshine streaming in, casting the room in a bright, happy light. Those darker memories haven't been as prevalent as the other, softer ones, but this one felt real enough to be an omen. It dissipated, but it's lingering.

"No, I'm here. I'm sorry," I say, still blinking in the light from the window.

"I asked what you thought of the premise. Did you hear me?"

"Sorry," I apologize again. "I didn't. You were cutting out."

It's yet another lie, but this time Trina is onto me. "Mm-hmm," she hums, unconvinced. Then, after a pregnant pause, she says, "Scarlett is okay. This isn't like last time." Her voice is gentle, reassuring, but there's something underneath it. Agitation? Disquiet?

I run a finger over the edge of my desk to ground myself and take a guess at what she's upset about. "If it bothered her that much, I won't see her again unless I have to."

"Hmm?" she hums again, distracted this time. "Oh, no. She... well, she's an idiot mostly, as you know, and she actually seemed touched that you went out of your way to drop off those notes."

A soft smile curls half of my mouth upward, but the relief is short lived. "What aren't you saying, Trina?"

"I don't think it's a great idea for you to see her again. She's got systems in place now. Lots of therapy, medication...you know?"

There's an unspoken *but* at the end of her statement, so I wait her out.

Trina's sigh turns into a little mewling whine, and I know she's about to say something she wishes she could hold back. "The late nights aren't great for her. But I'm on it, okay? There's nothing to worry about yet."

I don't like that "yet" one bit, but Casey and Trina have both told me essentially the same thing, and I know the smart move is to listen to them. "Will you let me know if there is something to worry about?"

"Ryan." Her tone is a warning one. "I'm telling you, don't get involved, okay? This is hard enough without revisiting all the heartbreak on top of it. I've got her. I promise."

For a second, I think about protesting. Trina wasn't there during all those late nights. She wasn't the one to watch her try to push forward almost immediately after she got off yet another plane ride from yet another city on her press tour. She didn't see Scarlett start to second-guess every sentence, every word. She didn't hold Scarlett and listen to her talk about how numb it all felt.

But then the realization that I haven't been there for the past five years hits me like a ton of bricks. Trina has, and she's probably right—Scarlett has systems in place now that I know nothing about, and Trina is keeping an eye on her. They don't need me muddying the waters and causing unnecessary trouble.

My shoulders slump forward as I close my eyes against the sting of this new awareness. "Of course," I say. "Just...keep me posted, okay? And I'll have this round back to her as soon as I can."

When we hang up, I tell myself that the little pocket of dread that opened up when she sent her second draft at two in the morning is just bad memories coming back and nothing more.

I almost believe it.

Chapter 12

Scarlett

DEEP IN MY creative writing master's program, one of the members of my cohort mentioned once that he never deleted anything. He said he had a whole file titled *graveyard.docx* where he put everything he cut from any manuscript, no matter how large or small. He swore up and down that he would use it later, and that it saved him a lot of time when drafting similar scenes because he'd pull something from his graveyard to use in new works.

That guy was a moron. If it's garbage in one manuscript, inserting it into another isn't going to make it magically worth something. It's like putting makeup on a rotting corpse and pretending it's alive.

I much prefer to just let it die.

But I've done a lot of work with my therapist, and it's her voice in my head telling me that callously deleting the two thousand eighty-nine words that are currently highlighted on my screen would be two giant steps backward, both for my manuscript and my mental health.

I tuck my hands into the sleeves of my hoodie and sit on them as I narrow my eyes at the hot garbage in front of me. It would feel so good to just hit that Delete button. So easy...

"Bad Scarlett," I mumble as I move my hand from under my ass long enough to toss my laptop onto the couch cushion next to me. Step one: Remove the temptation. Step two...What is step two? Walk away? Have a snack? Call a friend?

The problem is I don't want to do any of these things. I want to delete the fucking words and start over because I know they're terrible, and it would be a waste of my time to try to fix them. Not even Ryan can fix this nonsense. He might still think he's some wise and witty syntax sorcerer, but he can't really do magic. Not this kind anyway.

The back of my head meets the back of my couch as I stare up at the ceiling and snort at the memory of the nickname he gave himself. That one popped up frequently over the years we were together, mostly when I wanted to give him shit for how good he thought he was at his job.

Never mind that he's the best editor I've ever worked with. Even before he was my actual editor, his feedback was always more useful than what I got from the people on my team.

I ball my hands into fists inside my sweatshirt sleeves, holding them tight against the desire to save him the trouble of trying to find something salvageable in this wasteland of prose. A growl of frustration starts deep in my chest and builds to a crescendo as I jump up off the couch and bury my fingers in my already-tangled hair.

This shouldn't be this hard. It shouldn't be this emotional. Leave it and move on.

Why is this so hard? Why is my kitchen a mess again? Why has it been so difficult to get out of bed? Even brushing my teeth has started to feel like a huge accomplishment. Anything that stands between me and working on the manuscript is something I can do later...and then something I don't do later. And right now, the manuscript itself is somehow standing in its own way.

I grab my phone from the kitchen counter and hover my finger over Ryan's name. He always knew what to say when I started feeling like I was buried alive under pages and words and books and contracts.

This is ridiculous. I'm not working with JMP anymore; I'm not beholden to their insane deadlines and strict timeline. I'm no longer required to pump out two bestsellers in less than a year or answer to editors who believe that tearing me down is the best way to build me back up again. So why can't I just enjoy it this time? *Becoming* flew out of me. There was none of this second-guessing myself. The last time I felt that good about a book was when I wrote my debut. When I was writing for the love of it, before the publishing industry decided my only worth was the money I made for them and disguised it as a boon for me in the form of a giant contract that essentially asked me to sign my life away on the dotted line. And smile while I did it.

The contract that had been Ryan's idea. Because he thought more money would soothe these wounds, not cause a million more problems.

I can't call him. I don't want him to know I'm barely better off than when we were together. The last time we talked, when he was standing here with my handwritten notes, I was well adjusted and able to handle this job. I don't want him to think otherwise. And I certainly don't want him to think that offering me more money would fix anything. I can't do that again.

My thumb drops a half inch to Trina's name. I push hers instead and put her on speaker so I can stand over my counter with my back to my laptop and lodge my fingers in my hair.

"How's my favorite writer doing today?" she answers cheerily.

"Tell me not to delete everything I've written." My voice is weaker than I thought it would be. When was the last time I ate anything?

"Scarlett..." Trina's tone immediately drops into worried territory. "What's going on?"

"I don't know," I moan. "I was *fine*, Trina. I was doing *fine*." With each sentence, I clutch at my hair a little more, letting the pain in my scalp bring me back to Earth. "What the fuck happened?"

"Is this about Ryan? Because I told him to keep it professional with you, but if he so much as said one word out of line—"

"No. God, Trina, what did you say to him?"

She groans, and I wince at how loud it is coming through my phone speaker. "He was all mopey. Totally distracted. I was trying to tell him about your idea for the new book, and he was barely even listening to me."

That doesn't sound like Ryan. There never used to be anything that could get in the way of him and his love of editing. Except me. My stomach clenches as a million reasons for that kind of distraction race through my mind. One, in particular, stands out, and I smack my forehead hard with my open palm. I can't believe I haven't thought about this before.

"Is he seeing someone?" I mutter. Then my eyes widen, and I clamp my hand over my mouth. "Shit, I didn't mean to say that out loud."

Trina's cackle is distorted by the speaker. Her mouth must be right on top of her microphone. "For a brilliant person, you are really dumb, you know that?"

"You've told me this before," I intone drily.

"Someday you might even listen to me."

Sighing heavily, I push off the counter and open my pantry. If Trina is going to razz me, I might as well put something in my stomach while she does it. There's an open box of cereal at the back. I remember buying it, though I couldn't tell anyone when that was, so it can't be *that* old. I shove a handful of it into my mouth dry because I know without looking that there's no milk in my fridge. It only tastes a little stale, so I grab another handful.

"He's not the type to get distracted," I say around my mouthful.

"I'm so glad you're eating that I'm not even going to tell you not to talk with your mouth full." Even though I know she's giving me a hard time, I allow myself a pat on the back for at least having the presence of mind during my earlier spiral to call her. Her sarcasm has knocked enough sense into me to push me to put some food in my mouth.

Let it go, I tell myself. *Don't ask. The conversation has moved on. It's only going to make you look desperate.* "What's going on with him, then?" I flatten my lips together as soon as I say it. Why do I never listen to my own advice?

Maybe Trina is right. Maybe I am really dumb.

"He's worried about you," she says as if telling me is against her better judgment. "In his defense, you should not have emailed him your second draft at two in the morning."

"But that's when I finished it."

The silence on her end of the line stretches for so long that I think she might have actually hung up on me. "Trina?"

"Dumb, I tell you. Like...you can't even see it?"

"See what?"

"*That you should not be up working at two in the morning.* It is not good for you to pull those late nights, Scarlett. Not sleeping is part of what got you into this mess in the first place. What would Dianne say?"

She must be serious if she's referencing my therapist by her first name.

"She'd probably tell me to set better work-life boundaries," I begrudgingly admit. "But I don't have a life anymore, so I don't think those boundaries apply."

I mean that to be cute and self-deprecating and not as sad and lonely as I fear it came across. Luckily, Trina laughs. "They do if it means the difference between you being able to continue this work sustainably or having another breakdown." Leave it to her not to mince words. But it's good. I need to hear this.

"I'm not going to have another breakdown."

"Oh yeah?" She clearly doesn't believe me. "Then why did you call me and ask me to tell you not to delete everything you wrote today?"

Touché.

"It was a moment of weakness."

"And how many moments of weakness have you had since you started writing this one?" she asks pointedly, but she doesn't wait for me to respond. "Listen, we negotiated better deadlines for you this time around. There is no reason why you need to be doing edits and drafting simultaneously anymore."

"I'm not. My edits still haven't come back."

"They will," she presses. "Take a break, Scarlett. Your problem right now is that you're not thinking past this next book. You're thirty-two years old, for fuck's sake. You need to figure out how you're going to do this for thirty-some more years until you can retire, because whatever is happening over there is not it."

"Boundaries," I mumble.

"Boundaries," she repeats triumphantly, as if she's so excited I'm finally catching on.

Maybe I do need to sleep more. I'm not really going to argue that, even with myself. Better sleep leads to better mental health. I found that out the hard way. But there are other boundaries that could protect me too. Here I am, thinking I need to do everything all the time. Thinking I need to work with Ryan again just because he said a few nice things. As if five years apart was long enough to forget enough of what we had together to make a work relationship plausible. As if the memory of his touch, his smile, his words didn't come crashing right back into me the moment I laid eyes on him in that conference room.

As if I haven't been burying myself in a new manuscript at least partially to avoid thinking about him. When he'll send edits back, what he thinks of my revisions, whether or not he'll stop by again. Why he hasn't stopped by again.

Why hasn't he stopped by again?

No. I'm not going there. And honestly, I need to eliminate all the reasons I've found for my mind to keep coming back to him.

I swallow hard. The last of the dry cereal scrapes against my throat. "Can you see if there's maybe someone else who could take over edits?"

Trina pauses for a moment. "Is that really what you want?"

"It's what I need."

"Those are not the same thing, I take it."

No, they are not the same at all. But boundaries are about what you need, right? And I need to separate myself from Ryan, no matter how hard it's going to be now that I've seen him again.

I drag my hand through my hair. My fingers get stuck on a

knot. “Everything is starting to feel really fucked up again,” I say honestly. “I’m not sure how much his involvement is tangled up in my mind, but I think removing him from the equation might be the best way to find out.”

She pauses again, then sighs. “I’ll see what I can do. But...take a break, too, okay? If he’s not working with you, I can’t guarantee the next editor will care as much about your well-being.”

When we hang up, I expect a load to be lifted off my shoulders. At the very least, I expect to feel moderately better. I’ve eaten something, resolved to step away without deleting thousands of words, and made a decision about my editorial team that I know is in my best interests.

So why do I end up curling myself in a sad little ball and falling asleep feeling worse than I did before?

Chapter 13

Ryan

"WHAT DO YOU mean she doesn't want to work with me anymore?"

Trina is standing on the other side of my desk, apparently having felt it better to let me down easy in person. She didn't bother to sit, but as a result, she's fidgety. Her arms are folded over her chest, but she keeps twisting and untwisting one of her bracelets around her finger, and the fabric of her skirt twitches in such a way that I can tell she's shifting her weight.

There's something she's not telling me, but at this point, I don't know if it's about me or Scarlett.

"Did I...Did I do something wrong?"

Her expression softens, and she drops her hands to her sides with a slap. "You didn't do anything but exist in her space when she wasn't ready for you to do so. Which was partially my fault. I will own that."

"I know this round of edits has taken a while, but I'm almost done," I assure her. "Scarlett's revisions were spot on, and I want to do the work this story deserves and—"

Trina interrupts me with a shake of her head. "You're not listening. It's not about the story. It's about you. It's not personal."

"What the fuck is it if it's about me, then, Trina? That's the literal definition of *personal*."

She throws up her hands in exasperation. "I'm not the wordsmith here. Don't shoot the messenger. I'm trying to say it's not about *you* you. It's about the idea of you. I thought after five years and a lot of work on her mental health, she'd be fine with this, but she's fragile, Ryan. We both thought this book would be good for her to get her feet wet. Dip a toe in, so to speak. But then you showed up and acted all swoony and shit—"

"How did I act swoony?"

Trina levels me with a glare that would have a lesser man quaking in his boots. "'Love isn't a strong enough word for how I feel about this book,'" she says in a deep voice that I assume is her mimicking my own.

It's not a direct quote, but point taken. I'm not sure how much Scarlett has told her about our time together, but either way, I know I delivered that line with some weight. Casey brought it up, too, in our debrief after they left the office.

"And now, instead of getting her feet wet and acclimating to the publishing world again, she jumped in headfirst. She's got the book you're working on, the book she's writing...and you."

The overwhelming desire to talk to Scarlett crashes into me out of nowhere. It's different from the everyday fight I've been having with myself about whether or not to call her or stop by just to see how she's doing. This desire is borne of desperation. If I could just have a conversation with her, we could sort this out. I'm not delusional enough to think she'd give me another chance. It's a pipe dream to think that she could possibly still be in love with me, and I'm going to have to live with that. But this book has awakened something in me I feared I'd never get back again, and at the very least, I want to see it through.

I clear my throat and run a hand through my hair. "I love h—" I stop myself before I can say *her*. "This book. You might think I was being swoony, but I don't know if I can quite describe what it has done for me. Reading it...I feel alive again." And knowing Scarlett wrote it has energized me. She's there in those pages; her voice is crystal clear now that I know for sure the words are hers. It has pulled a curtain back on the inner workings of her mind. She's alive and well, even if only in the book.

A stillness comes over the room. Trina tilts her head and

regards me with a heaviness that is entirely unlike her. "Is your excitement about a book really more important than her entire well-being?"

Trina's worried about her. It's right there, in the way her throat works against a hard swallow and the slight flare of her nostrils. She doesn't want to say it, but it's written on her face, clear as day.

My stomach bottoms out with the realization. Here is her agent, trying to help Scarlett save face and push forward with a publishing house that is already admittedly cautious about working with her again.

This could have been prevented. Maybe. But there's no telling how another editor would work with her. I know her, at least. And I can fix this.

As if she can see my thoughts playing out on my face, Trina's eyes go wide. "No. Do not get involved, Ryan. I'm telling you this for both your sakes. Find another editor to finish out this project, and I'll deal with the rest of it. Stay out of it."

"I didn't say anything." I feign innocence.

She circles a finger in the direction of my face. "You didn't have to. Those glasses hide nothing. And now I'm going to leave."

"Why?"

"Plausible deniability," she says as she backs slowly out the door. "I said what I came here to say, and if you fuck this up, you're on your own. Don't say I didn't warn you."

The door shuts behind her, and I'm left alone with my thoughts. Trina was clearly concerned. I know Scarlett. I can help. If Scarlett truly does want to cut ties with me, I'll honor her wishes, but even Trina suggested this was about the writing and not about our personal relationship. Maybe if we could separate the two...

My phone interrupts my thoughts when it buzzes where it sits on my desk.

Trina

Bring food, if you must.

Well, that is as close to permission as I'm going to get. It's practically the end of the day anyway. I grab my keys and am out the door before I can think better of it.

ULTIMATELY, I SETTLE on tacos. I would have gone for her favorite—deep-dish pizza—but I didn't want to wait for it when my drive from the suburbs to her apartment was already going to be at least forty-five minutes, and there are too many bad jokes to be made about being the pizza-delivery guy.

One of the best dates we ever had was at a hole-in-the-wall taco joint where we ordered one of everything. The entire menu. So I find a similar spot on the way and order one of every kind of taco they have available, and that is how I find myself thanking someone in Scarlett's building for holding the door for me—conveniently allowing me to bypass the buzzer—and making my way up to her fifth-floor apartment.

My heart is in my throat as I grip a full bag of tacos in each hand and wait for the elevator to take me up to her floor. Either her elevator is ridiculously slow or my nerves are altering my sense of time. Hard to say, because I felt the same way when I was here the other day too.

Finally, the elevator spits me out on the fifth floor, and I walk the few feet to Scarlett's door. I knock, then wait. Nothing. There's no light filtering out from beneath the door, no sound of anyone moving around inside. It's almost as if she's not home. For a moment, I'm equal parts disappointed I won't see her and overjoyed she's venturing out of her apartment. If she's going out, she's okay. But I knock one more time anyway, just to be sure.

"It's open," comes Scarlett's muffled voice. It's hard to tell through the door, but she sounds hoarse.

The first thing that hits me when I open the door is a faint musky smell, like someone has left garbage sitting for too long without taking it out. Sure enough, when I glance toward her kitchen, dishes are piled high in the sink, and several take-out containers litter the countertops.

When I step further into the apartment, I can see the television is replaying a silent teaser for a baking competition. Scarlett is sprawled out on her couch, her satin pajamas rumpled up over her calves. She has one sock on, and one foot bare, and her hair covers most of her face.

Papers are strewn about the kitchen table. I push enough of them aside to clear a space for the bags of tacos. She still hasn't looked my way by the time I've deposited them onto the table, and I wonder if she's been making a habit of letting anyone into her apartment who comes knocking. And then I wonder if anyone has come knocking, and the realization that no one has causes an ache in my chest.

"Not interested in watching actual baking?" I'm trying for lighthearted teasing, but the question sounds strained, even to my ears.

Scarlett's body goes stiff at the sound of my voice. She clearly wasn't expecting me, but she doesn't make a move to lift herself from the couch or even turn in my direction. "I finished it. The bald guy won."

"When did you finish?"

"What time is it?"

I check my watch. "Five thirty."

She groans and turns her face so it's buried in a throw pillow. "Three and a half hours ago."

I don't have a lot of experience dealing with people who are in a depressive episode, but my best guess is that if I act alarmed or shame her in any way, she'll only sink deeper into whatever mood she's in. So I simply walk around the couch and tap her feet in a signal for her to move them over. She does, and I sit far enough away so I'm not touching her.

"What's going on, beautiful?" The nickname slips out, but she doesn't seem to notice. She just curls her legs into her chest and stares at the television screen.

"Trina told me to take a break, so I did. But..." She trails off and swallows audibly. Her lips are cracked, and her eyes are half-closed. I consider sitting on my hands so as not to touch her, but I clasp them in my lap instead while I wait for her to continue.

"I don't know what to do with myself when I'm not writing," she finally says. Her voice cracks, and my heart cracks wide open with it. She draws in a shaky breath but doesn't cry.

"What did you do after you quit?" If I can find out what has been working for her, I can help her replicate it, surely.

She huffs a laugh. "Traveled. And...this, mostly. For about a year until Trina dragged me to see a therapist. And a psychiatrist. Then..." She trails off again, then shakes her head slightly as if she's shaking off a memory. "Well, I never stopped writing. Not really. It was never writing that was the problem."

Before she disappeared, Scarlett had been frustrated with me for being unable to understand how publishing had ruined writing for her. Truth be told, I could never grasp how that could be the case. For me, the magic was in the revisions that came along with publishing. The way I saw it, she would write something for herself, and the editors would help turn it into something for an audience. It was a symbiotic relationship for everyone involved—Scarlett got to write, we got to revise and reshape, and the readers got to enjoy her work. But the further into the process she got, the more she hated it. I tried to tell her to hold out for the next deal. I even worked behind the scenes to push for a much better offer than they were going to give her. The hard work was going to pay off for her in a way she deserved. But it wasn't enough.

"I'm glad you kept writing," I say simply.

"Yeah, you've got another bestseller on your hands if you play your cards right."

Even in all of our conversations before her breakdown, I don't think I've ever heard her sound so bitter. It hurts to hear her sound so jaded. I frown down at her, but she doesn't look at me. She just stares vacantly ahead.

Something about the raw vulnerability she's showing me

makes it all the more important for me to make her understand that it was never about editing a bestseller for me. "After you left, I didn't know what to do with myself." I don't know why I decide to go down this road, but there's no turning back now. "I kept going to work, but not because I wanted to. At first, I think the only thing that kept me going was sheer hope that maybe one day, you'd show up again. And then I needed to pay my bills, I guess. I signed authors, got promoted, did decently well. But none of those books were memorable in any way. Not like yours. And then *Becoming* landed on my desk. It woke me up, Scarlett. It meant something. I haven't felt like that since the last page I read of yours."

She rolls her head slightly so she can look at me. The bags under her eyes are intensely purple. She looks five years older than the last time I saw her. I want to pull her close to me and soothe away every negative emotion clouding her head.

"You're so dramatic," she teases, though the words come out flat, as if she doesn't have enough energy to put any bite into them.

"Like you said, some things never change."

A corner of her mouth tips up slightly, then falls. Her eyes drop with it, staring into space again. "Do you think I can change? Do you think I can ever publish books and be happy at the same time?"

I don't hesitate. "Yes."

"I wish I had your confidence."

"You just need a little help. You're overwhelmed. Take it one thing at a time."

She seems to think for a moment, then nods as her blue eyes meet mine again. "What's first?"

"Tacos," I say. "Then a bath."

"I am hungry. And dirty." There's that little smile again. A squeezing sensation in my chest accompanies it.

I stand and offer her my hand to help her up. She takes it, and though she's a little shaky on her feet, she interlaces our fingers and squeezes, looking up at me with those devastating eyes.

"Thank you," she whispers.

Without thinking, I lean in to kiss her forehead. When I realize what I've done, I pull back, afraid she's going to get skittish and order me to leave. But the smile she flashes up at me is wide and genuine and heartbreakingly gorgeous.

I never thought I'd see that smile again, but now that I have, there's no way I can let her walk out of my life a second time.

Seven Years Ago

"TACOS?" SCARLETT ARCHES a dark eyebrow in my direction. She glances warily at the hole-in-the-wall restaurant in front of us. "I know we've been seeing each other for a few months now, but I was hoping you'd try to impress me for a little while longer."

I put a hand over my heart in mock offense. "How dare you. Tacos are the perfect food."

She purses her lips skeptically. "*Perfect* is a pretty strong word for what is essentially a sandwich."

"Take it back this instant," I tease. "A measly sandwich has nothing on a taco. There are so many options! Crispy or soft, any meat or vegetarian filling you want, beans, cheese, salsas, guacamole, sour cream. Should I go on?"

"Sour cream is disgusting," she counters.

I tip my head back and forth, thinking. "I'll give you that one."

"If I didn't know any better, I'd think I should be jealous of your relationship with this particular food item," she says sardonically.

"You joke, but I take my tacos very seriously."

"I can see that."

Stepping forward, I hold the door open for her and motion for her to go inside. "Reserve your judgment until you try them, okay? At the very least, they'll be easy to take where we're going."

As she passes me inside, her shoulder brushes mine. I have to fight against the urge to grab her and pin her against the wall with a searing kiss. She's so strikingly beautiful, with her dark hair hanging long down her back, the silky strands tempting me to run my fingers through them. Of course, she's wearing my favorite color on her, too—a royal-purple tank top that brightens the hue of her eyes and dark wash jeans. As her hips sway on her way into the restaurant, I know she's intentionally made herself hard to resist.

Three months with this woman, and every day I feel like I've hit the jackpot.

"We're not staying here?" she asks over her shoulder. "Where are we going?"

"I thought we could take our food to a park nearby. Set up a picnic. Maybe read a little." I shrug like it's no big deal, but I surreptitiously rub my sweaty palms against my jeans.

Scarlett joked about me trying to impress her, but every date I've planned so far has been carefully crafted around something I think she might like. She's not the type to enjoy large crowds or loud spaces—I gathered that from the night we met. Most of the time she spends on her own has something to do with her writing, whether she's drafting or editing or working with her critique partners. JMP has her slated for a small press tour with the possibility of expanding it when her book releases, so some of her time has been spent shopping for outfits with her roommates. I know she's nervous about all of that, but she doesn't have anything to be worried about. Her book is fantastic, and even though she describes herself as painfully introverted, she lights up a room when she's talking about her work.

So far, when I've planned dates for us, I've been careful to avoid things she doesn't enjoy but even more attentive about what she likes. Just the other day, she was bemoaning the fact that since she signed her deal, she doesn't have any time to read. I grabbed the book that has been sitting on her nightstand for weeks, hoping she wouldn't miss it if it was gone for a few days, and planned this afternoon for her to unwind.

Scarlett turns to face me, pouting. "You should have told me. I don't have my book."

I wink at her and look up at the menu hanging above the cashier. "Let's order."

"What are you up to?" She sounds skeptical, but I don't look at her. If I do, I'm likely to spill all my deepest, darkest secrets, and not just the fact that I have her book in my backpack.

"Trying to impress you," I say simply. "Now, what kind of tacos do you like?"

She sighs and turns her attention to the menu board. "I'm assuming you've been here before, so you tell me what's good."

"It's all good. Like I said, tacos are the perfect food. You literally cannot go wrong." I think for a moment, then add, "Unless you top them with sour cream."

"We'd better get one of each, then."

She's joking, but I nod and step forward to order one of everything on the menu. It's a small restaurant, so the menu isn't extensive, but Scarlett can't stop laughing about how serious I am.

As we wait for our food, we chat about little things. Every once in a while, she'll catch one of the cooks eyeing us, then rolling their eyes, and she'll burst into a fit of giggles all over again.

I'd probably order one of every type of taco in existence just to hear her laugh like that again and again.

It doesn't take too long for them to get our order together, and the teenager behind the counter passes me four foam containers that squeak when they rub against each other. I thank the kid, leave a massive tip in the jar next to the register, and ask Scarlett if she can hold the door for me. She laughs as she pulls the door open.

We walk down the street to a small park. The summer sun is warm, and the heat of the tacos is seeping through the containers to warm me even further. It's a relief to finally set them down in the grass while I spread out a large blanket from my backpack.

Scarlett sits cross-legged on top of it and starts opening containers of food. "I'll admit, it does look good."

Joining her on the ground, I inspect the tacos. I grab a shrimp that has fallen loose and pop it into my mouth. "Mmm," I hum in satisfaction.

"You like the shrimp ones?" She clasps her hands in her lap and leans forward slightly, curious.

"They're tied with carne asada for my favorite."

She nods as if she's packing away this information for later. "Well, I'm starving." Her fingers wiggle over the tacos as she makes her decision. Carefully, she extracts a pork taco from one of the containers. When she takes a bite, her whole body relaxes on a moan. All the blood in my veins rushes south, and I have to shift to hide what that noise does to me.

"Okay, you were right. This is heavenly."

After she takes another bite, some juice from the taco runs down her chin. I use a finger to wipe it off, but before I can pull it away, Scarlett dips to draw it in her mouth. She swirls the digit with her tongue, and then there's no hiding what she's doing to me.

"Fuck, Scarlett," I groan.

She releases my finger and smiles. "Maybe later," she says coyly. "Right now, I want to enjoy the sunshine and these tacos." Her expression becomes shy, and her cheeks turn a gorgeous shade of pink. "And you."

I kiss her then, because how couldn't I? It occurs to me as my tongue dances with hers that I could kiss her every single day for the rest of my life, and it wouldn't be enough.

She pulls away, smiling, her joy spelled out across her face. I grin back as I grab my own taco and start eating.

We chat and watch people play catch while we eat. She doesn't make a big deal about it, but I notice she leaves the shrimp and carne asada ones for me. When we've both eaten our fill, I throw the empty containers into a nearby garbage can and pull her book out of my bag. She squeals in delight, and we both lie on the blanket. She curls up against my side, her head on my chest.

I've had several relationships, though none of them got very serious. I should be wary of such strong feelings for her so soon, but for some reason, I'm not. If someone were to tell me right now that I wouldn't be spending the rest of my life with this woman, I'd tell them to check again. It's simply unimaginable.

Once, before he died, I asked my dad how he knew my mom was the person he'd spend his life with.

"How do you know I love you?" he said.

I furrowed my brow in confusion. "What do you mean?"

"It's simple. How do you know I love you?"

"I just do," I said, feeling like I was missing the point.

He nodded sagely, as if I had gotten it right. "I just knew I loved her, too."

That was that. I thought I understood at the time, at least as well as a ten-year-old boy could. But now, as Scarlett turns a page and shimmies a bit to get more comfortable, I realize that I didn't understand at all. Because if anyone were to ask me how I feel about her, I'd probably tell them she's it for me. And if they asked me how I knew, I could point to the weightlessness of her head on my chest, the effervescence of her laughter, the brilliance of her mind. But all of those things pale in comparison to the truth.

How do I know? I just do.

Chapter 15

Scarlett

RYAN MUST BE applying for a promotion to sainthood. Not only has he brought me one of every kind of taco available to mankind, but he quietly cleans up my kitchen and draws a bath while I eat them. When I offer some to him, he shakes his head and tells me he ate already. I skip the shrimp taco and the carne asada one because I know those are his favorites. And when I offer them to him, he flashes me a wide grin and practically inhales them.

As he makes his way through my kitchen, tossing out containers and loading the dishwasher, I allow myself to watch shamelessly. The lean muscles of his shoulders stretch his pale blue, lightweight sweater. When he bends over to put a pod in the dishwasher, his glasses slip down his nose. He pushes them back up, then goes to check the bath, seemingly oblivious to my attention.

When he comes out of the bathroom, his glasses are fogged up. I laugh lightly, and his responding goofy grin would have my knees going weak if I weren't already sitting down. There's something about having him here again that has already lifted some of the crushing weight I had been feeling. And yeah, it could have been the tacos, but I'm pretty sure it's mostly him.

"Ready?" he asks as he leans against the doorway.

I don't trust myself to stand steadily when he's leaning and smirking and looking so adorably perfect. It's almost like we haven't missed a beat.

Some things never change.

"You make it sound like I'm in for an experience," I deflect as I try to buy myself some time to get my libido under control.

"The Ryan Whitlock Bathing Experience is one unlike any other." He tips his head back toward the bathroom. "Come on, beautiful. Let me take care of you."

My mouth goes dry, and a warm heat pools low in my belly. "Are you...You're not..."

His smile widens. "I won't look," he promises. "There's a lot of bubbles." A look of pure earnestness crosses his face. "I want to help, Scarlett. Please let me."

I try very hard to swallow and bring some moisture back to my mouth to no avail. This is bonkers. I should absolutely make him leave. He's done enough, and I feel better. I can probably take it from here. But what happens after this bath, when I get out and dry off and realize I still don't know what to do with myself? And worse, what happens when he's gone and I miss him again?

There's no use denying it. I want him here, even if it's a terrible idea.

There's a quip on the end of my tongue about him trying to assuage some guilt for taking so long with my edits, but it dies there. All I can muster as I stand on shaky legs is an equally shaky, "Okay."

He's at my side in a flash with an arm around me for support. I don't really need his help to walk the five steps to the bathroom, but I lean into him anyway. Even if it is a thinly veiled excuse to feel the hard planes of his body pressed into mine.

When we get inside the bathroom, he takes a step back into the hallway. "Kick your pajamas out when you're ready. I'm going to throw them in the laundry."

"You don't have to do that," I say.

"I want to," he replies quickly. "Besides, your kitchen towels stink."

"Is *that* where the smell is coming from? Glad it's not me," I joke. He laughs lightly, and for a moment we both stare at each other, not quite sure what to do and both afraid to make the first move.

He blinks rapidly as he snaps back to his senses and steps out of my view.

Okay, then.

Leaving the door open a sliver, I shed my satin pajamas. These things have seen better days, that's for sure. I'm not sure I could identify the stains on them anymore. I kick them out into the hallway, then lower myself into the tub.

Ryan wasn't kidding. There are a lot of bubbles, and the water is almost scalding, which is exactly how I like it. I'm touched he remembered such a simple detail.

The idea of a baptism pops into my head. It's a great symbol, though it does get used fairly often. But it's nice to think that your sins and worries can be washed away with some water. *Worth a shot*, I think as I plug my nose and dunk my head under. When I come up, I don't feel any better than I did before, though my face thanks me for this bare minimum of cleanliness. I can't remember the last time I washed my face, either. Dianne would shake her head in dismay if she knew. That's one of the things she urges me to do every day, even if I don't feel like it. Oops.

I hear the laundry machine start through the wall, and I relax against the edge of the tub, closing my eyes and letting the heat of the water and the rhythmic whirring of the machine lull me into something close to peace.

Vaguely, I'm aware of the door opening and closing, then the sound of a shampoo bottle snapping open. There's a presence next to me, warmth radiating off of him and his almond-and-vanilla scent mixing with the lavender of the bath. I'm suddenly too tired to open my eyes or protest. *Nothing he hasn't seen before anyway.* The thought has me smiling.

"Something funny?" Ryan asks, his voice low and soothing. I want to crawl into the sound of it and sleep.

"No," I lie. That warmth from earlier collects between my thighs. If I weren't already underwater, I'm sure there'd be an obvious wetness there, too.

He hums as if he doesn't believe me but doesn't say anything else. The next thing I know, his fingers work their way into my scalp, pressing and massaging with delicious pressure.

"Oh my god," I moan. "That feels amazing." Any remaining tension rushes out of my body, and it's replaced with an aching desire that cuts through my exhaustion and starts my heart racing in my chest.

His fingers leave my head for a moment as he shifts into a more comfortable position, then they return to their work. I crack an eye open to find him looking down at me with such tenderness that my pounding heart skips a beat.

I have to look away. If he continues to look at me like that, I might cry. Because he used to look at me like that. I long for him to keep looking at me like that. But when he's done here, he's going to leave. This isn't permanent. It can't be.

My gaze trails down his chest. The light blue of his sweater is speckled with dark spots where the water has splashed him. His sleeves are rolled up, and some black ink catches my eye.

"You got a tattoo?"

"Hmm?" he hums as if he had been distracted. "Oh, right. Yeah. Maybe four years ago now?"

"What is it?"

He turns his forearm over so I can see. It's designed to look like his skin is paper, ripped open to reveal the page of a book. I lean in to get a better look at the words, but he flips his arm and starts massaging my head again.

"It's pretty badass." My eyes drift closed as his ministrations have their desired effect. "Did it hurt?"

"Not as much as some things," he says.

My breath catches in my throat, but I keep my eyes carefully shut. His hands go still as if he's wishing he could take it back.

"Ryan, I'm sorry—" I peer up at him, then, wishing I could lay it all out for him right then and there, but a sharp shake of his head stops me. Dianne had urged me to tell him exactly what happened five years ago, to make him understand what pressure I was under, exactly what I had lost, and clear the air. Maybe she was right about that, and now feels like as good a time as any. Not that I want to hurt him even more, but if it could just tell him...

"Water under the bridge," he says before I can work up the courage to continue. He sounds choked up, so I stuff everything back into the box in my heart and close the lid. Lock it shut. Throw away the key. I certainly don't want to cause more damage than I already have by opening up old wounds. What does it matter now anyway?

This isn't permanent.

He continues lathering my hair in silence for a few minutes before telling me to rinse. I dunk my head again, and this time it does feel a bit more like a cleansing, if not a full baptism.

"Are you okay to get out by yourself?" he asks, sitting back on his heels and rolling the sleeves of his sweater down.

Unable to speak, I simply nod. He leaves the room. When the door snicks softly shut behind him, the sound reverberates through my brain. It feels final somehow, like he's shutting the door on us. Like this was some kind of goodbye.

Trina said I was dumb, but right now I don't know what's the worse decision: Asking him to stay like I so desperately want to or letting him think I don't want him to be my editor and watching him walk out of my life. Again. But I do know that having him here feels good, and I'm willing to follow that feeling, even if chasing any kind of true happiness is futile.

But the finality of that shutting door makes me afraid he's on his way out of my apartment. I scramble out of the tub and throw my robe around my shoulders. I tie it quickly but don't bother drying off. It sticks uncomfortably to me. Water pools at my feet and drips off the ends of my hair. I step carefully on the wet tile to pull the bathroom door open in a rush.

Ryan is sitting on my couch, one ankle crossed over his knee and his arm spread out over the back of it like he belongs there. And that's when I realize that I really do want him here. Maybe just tonight, maybe forever. I don't know. I can cross that bridge when I come to it.

I'm not sure what my face is doing, but it must be something weird because his brow furrows with concern. "You okay?" he asks.

I nod, trying to tamp down the sudden swell of emotion rising in my throat. "I wanted to catch you before you left."

He tilts his head to the side and smiles. "I'm not going anywhere."

And that's when I sit down right there, in the middle of my floor, and burst into tears.

Six Years Ago

"Why don't you ever wear red?" Ryan is standing in my new bedroom, adjusting his tie in front of the full-length mirror.

I eye him from where I'm sitting on the edge of the bed, trying and failing to secure the buckle on the one pair of strappy sandals I own. "What?"

"I've been watching your social media updates and television interviews for weeks, and I realized I've never seen you wear red. Not once. I took a peek in your closet just now to see, and I was right. Not a stitch of red."

"Do you want me to wear red?" I ask.

"I think you'd be stunning if you ever did, but you're always stunning. So no, not particularly. It just seems like a staple color in a woman's wardrobe."

"This is the strangest conversation I've ever had," I mumble.

Ryan chuckles warmly, running his hands through his hair. "It's just something I noticed, and I was curious."

"My name is Scarlett," I remind him, as if that's explanation enough.

"And?"

"It'd be a little on the nose, wouldn't it?"

He shrugs. "Maybe."

I watch him fiddle with his clothes in the mirror some more.

A few months ago, Ava met someone who she swears is the love of her life. I've heard that from her before, but this time she fell in love with another woman, which she swears has made all the difference. I suppose when you know, you know. And now that I've just arrived home from two weeks on the road, we finally have a moment to meet them out on a fancy double date.

Watching Ryan scrutinize himself in the mirror is maybe one of the most adorable things I've ever seen. Even after almost a year together, he still gets nervous and wants to impress my friends. I wish we didn't have to go, that we could have the night all to ourselves, but I miss my friends too.

When my lease with Ava, Mandy, and Katherine was up, we decided to go our separate ways. Or rather, I did. I had earned out my advance from JMP about a month after my debut released, and it didn't look like anything was going to slow down anytime soon. Besides, I had been splitting most of my time between writing and a lengthy press tour with interviews and signings and the whole shebang. When I'd get home, I'd go straight to Ryan's condo anyway, because he lives alone, and having an adult relationship with three roommates is awkward to say the least. It only made sense for me to buy a place of my own.

I bite my lip as what he said really sinks in. "You watched every interview?"

"Of course I did," he answers easily. He catches my eye in the mirror and smiles, then goes right back to fixing his hair.

I allow myself a minute to drink him in. His dark hair is longer now than it was when we met. He got new glasses, too, though they are a barely different version of the old ones. But that ass is the same, and it's exactly as delicious as it was a year ago.

I don't have much room to talk about Ava and how fast she fell for the love of her life. It didn't take me long at all to know Ryan was special, and it wasn't long after that when I realized spending the rest of my life with him seemed like a fun prospect rather than a daunting one. We slipped into each other's lives so easily, as if we were occupying spaces that had been left for us.

Soon, I was staying over at his place for several nights, then weeks at a time. We'd work well into the night—or at least as long as we could last as we tried to resist each other's small touches and suggestive glances—then wake in the mornings and share coffee and breakfast before he'd leave for work. It felt domestic, but not in an oppressive way. In an exciting way. A picture of the life we could lead together had emerged on the horizon, and I liked it. Loved it, if I'm being honest. And once I admitted that to myself, I started daydreaming about all of our options. A house in the suburbs. A little son or daughter running around in the backyard or shoving wrinkled pages of a story they wrote into our hands. A dog? No, probably a cat. Neither of us have the patience for a dog.

I mean, I certainly can't have any of that now, while my book is still climbing the charts and I'm being asked to do more and more signings and interviews. But someday.

Even now, as we both get all dolled up to meet another couple out for dinner, I relish in the domesticity of it. This is something real couples do. Normal couples. Ones without a half who has to travel for weeks on end. It feels right. We're just two people in our late twenties—him climbing rapidly toward a position as a senior editor, and me writing bestsellers—with a world of possibilities in front of us. I'm almost worried it's too good to be true, but then there are moments like this, when he casually drops into conversation that he has watched me while I was gone. That he noticed something like my preferred wardrobe colors. When he catches me watching him over his shoulder in the mirror and winks at me. Such a small thing, that noticing, that wink, but indicative of something so much bigger.

Love? Maybe. We haven't said it yet, but it sure feels like we could.

"Like what you see?" He tips up the corner of his mouth in a small smile, then does a three-sixty for me to see the whole picture.

"Always." My sandals finally buckled, I push myself off the bed. I make sure to give my hips an extra sway as I walk slowly toward him, and I'm rewarded for it with a darkening of his eyes as I loop my arms around his neck.

"You're remarkable," he breathes into the space between us. "I still can't believe you ever gave me the time of day."

"It was your giant...vocabulary," I tease. "They say size doesn't matter, but the bigger, the better, as far as I'm concerned."

He chuckles, then trails a hand down my spine to cup my ass. Warmth floods my core, and I lick my lips in anticipation of their meeting his. He indulges me by tipping his face downward, kissing me innocently at first, but it's not long before he's dragging my bottom lip through his teeth. As he soothes the little sting with his tongue, I moan. He swallows it greedily, his hands roaming and exploring.

"This dress is doing things to me, Scarlett." He kisses down my neck and bites gently where it meets my shoulder.

A delicious little shiver works its way down my body. "We're going to be late if we do this now," I caution.

He squeezes my ass, pressing me against the hardness between his legs. "I don't give a damn."

I groan. "I'm starting to care a lot less, but Ava will never forgive me if we ditch her."

Ryan grumbles something incoherent but releases me. When I step back, he adjusts himself before rolling his shoulders to stand taller. His eyes are hooded when they meet mine again. I step up to straighten the tie I rumpled, and he smiles down at me.

"What?" I ask when he doesn't speak.

"Nothing," he says quietly, shaking his head. "I like this."

I return his smile, a different kind of warmth blooming in my chest. "Me too."

Dinner goes off without a hitch. Ava's girlfriend, Marcie, is a delight. She has us in stitches most of the evening, telling stories about her time as a clown for hire and all the wild things she saw at kids' birthday parties. She does mostly data entry now, but when she tells stories, Ava watches her with hearts in her eyes. They ask about my book, but not too much, which is nice. I've been talking about my book for weeks; I want to talk about other things.

The whole time, Ryan finds excuses to touch me. His hand rests casually on the back of my chair so his thumb can brush against the nape of my neck. His thigh presses up against mine under the table. He brushes my hair off my shoulder and leans to whisper something into my ear. At one point during dessert, his hand lands on my knee.

By the time we leave, I'm desperate for him. The ride back to my condo is excruciating, especially because he strokes a light finger up and down my inner thigh under the cover of darkness as we sit in the back of the cab. When we get to my building, I run ahead of him up the steps and through my hallway—heels be damned—so I can unlock my door for us to tumble inside.

He slams the door shut behind him, then spins me so my back is pressed against it. Wasting no time at all, he presses a hot kiss against my fevered neck. "I missed you." Another on my collarbone. "I missed this." Another on top of the swell of my left breast above the scooped neck of my dress. "And this." Then, my right breast. "And this."

"Ryan." I exhale as he drags the hem of my dress upward.

"I missed those little noises you make." He pulls the fabric up so it pools over my hip, leaving my soaked panties on display for him. His finger meets the cotton material, and he groans, dropping his forehead to my shoulder. "Fuck, Scarlett. Have you been this wet all night?"

"For you," I say breathlessly. "Always for you."

He tucks my panties to the side and dips a finger into my waiting heat. I cry out in pleasure, digging my nails into his shoulders, trying to gain purchase through the fabric of his shirt so I can ride his hand. He pushes another finger inside, and the way he stretches me is exquisite, even if it's not quite enough. As if he can read my mind, his palm meets my clit. His dark eyes meet mine before he swallows my breathy moans with a kiss. Pressure builds in my core, and I claw at his shoulders, begging for more.

"I missed this, too," he says, pulling away just enough to watch. "I want to see you come, Scarlett. Can you come for me, beautiful?"

"Yes," I gasp. "Yes."

He circles his fingers inside me a few more times, and I shatter, clenching and unclenching around his fingers as he tastes my mouth with his tongue.

As soon as I can breathe again, he releases me. We waste no time shedding clothes on our way to the bedroom. I don't know where anything ends up, and I don't care. We're too frantic for each other, too eager. Clothes are tomorrow's problem. Right now, we're only skin and heat and need.

I lie on my bed. Ryan takes off his glasses and lays them carefully on the nightstand before crawling over me, dark eyes glinting in the moonlight that filters in from the window. He kisses my hip, then the valley of my waist, my stomach, the underside of my breast. Swiftly, he draws a nipple into his mouth, sucking hard, nipping at it with his teeth. I gasp and rub my legs together, trying to relieve some of the pressure already building again between my thighs. My palm meets his hard length, and he lets out a gruff moan into my chest as I pump my hand a few times.

Quickly, without warning, he circles his broad hands around my waist and flips me onto my stomach. I arch my back, which pushes my ass up into the air. He rubs a hand over it and squeezes.

"I'll never get tired of this view." His voice is gravelly. He uses both hands to spread me open for him, then notches himself against my entrance.

"I missed you," I say as I rock backward, taking him inside me. We both let out a noise of relief, and I gasp as he presses even further, filling me. Another thrust, and his hips meet my ass. I sigh, content.

There are no more words as he sets an unhurried pace. All the frenzied need from earlier is gone now, replaced with a tenderness punctuated by our soft sighs and the sound of our skin meeting in the darkness. At one point, he reaches around to place a warm palm on my stomach, then drags it downward to stroke my already-sensitive clit.

"Can you come for me again, beautiful?" he asks, his voice reverent and full of emotion.

"Yes," I breathe, arching my back even more so he can reach the spot I need. "Can you use a little more pressure?"

He obliges, and I cry out, burying my face in the blanket in front of me. His thrusts start coming harder and more erratic. I feel him stiffen inside me, and with another swirl of his finger, I come again. While waves of pleasure are still crashing into me, he shudders his own release.

After we come down from our high, Ryan goes to the bathroom. He returns with a warm washcloth and starts to clean me up. I can't explain why, but from the way he concentrates on the task, it feels like this is important to him. When he's done, he tosses the cloth into my hamper, then lies down and pulls me against him. We slip into a deep sleep together, holding each other close the whole night.

When Scarlett and I met, she was a spitfire. On our first two dates—which were a month apart because she wasn't sure she wanted to see me again—we spent half the time trying to one-up each other with literary knowledge and the other half making out like teenagers. Over the course of the two years of the rest of our relationship, I think I saw her cry twice, and neither of those times were the waterworks that explode from her when she crumples onto the floor in a literal puddle of bath water and tears in the hallway outside her bathroom.

By the time I walked out of that bathroom, I knew I had crossed a line. The flush of my overheated skin and the hardness between my legs were clear signals, and even though I knew leaving right then and there was probably the best thing for everyone involved, I sat down on the couch to wait for her, as if touching her hair and imagining her curves below those bubbles had caused my body to act on its own.

But the look on Scarlett's face when she flew out of the bathroom, her threadbare robe clinging to those curves that had only existed in my memory, was thankfully enough to spur me into action.

"Oh, shit." I jump to my feet as her ass hits the ground. "Scarlett, what happened?"

Huge, aching sobs are wrenched from her throat. That's the only way to describe the sound—it's as if she's having an out-of-body experience, the entirety of her pain and emotion being sucked out of her with each cry.

I drop to the ground next to her and pull her close. She doesn't even resist; she just folds herself into me and presses her cheek to my chest. The warm water from her hair blooms over my sweater, soaking through to my skin. I wrap my arms around her and hold on tight as waves of sobs crash out of her.

I don't know how long we sit like this. All I know is that when I exited the bathroom, the sun was just starting to set, and by the time her sobs have calmed to more manageable sniffles and the occasional gasp, it's almost completely dark outside.

She shifts so the crown of her head rests just under my chin. I kiss it without even thinking. Even in her sadness, touching her like this is automatic. As easy as breathing. And now that I've done it again, maybe it's as necessary, too.

"What happened?" I risk asking quietly.

She sniffles and wipes her nose with the sleeve of her robe. I make a mental note to wash that later for her, too.

"I don't know." Her voice is hoarse. "I don't usually...That's not..." She lets out another gasping sob.

I squeeze her even tighter. "Hey. It's okay. I'm here."

She nods against my chest and wraps her arms around my torso. I rest my cheek against the still-wet crown of her head.

"The last time this happened," she starts haltingly, "was the day after I quit writing."

I hum, and she snuggles closer to me as if trying to chase the sound of it in my chest. "You had a good run, I guess."

She huffs a wet laugh, wipes her nose again, and goes back to squeezing my middle.

"It makes sense, though," I say. "You had a lot going on then. You're going through a lot of change now, again. Sometimes you have to let it all out."

Scarlett had held me like this once, on the anniversary of my father's death. He died when I was in high school, but there have been so many times in my life when I have wished I could ask him one more thing. One more piece of advice. Whether or not I'm on the right track. If I'm good man. If I could be a good husband, a good father one day...

She had found me drowning my worries in a bottle of whiskey. I hate whiskey, but he loved it. I thought maybe one drink would make me feel closer to him, but the situation quickly devolved. Scarlett let herself into my condo after I hadn't answered her calls, silently cleaned up my picked-over meal and the glass I had forgotten after I started drinking directly from the bottle. She pressed two ibuprofen into one palm and a glass of water into the other. When the glass clinked against my father's ring, I lost it again. When the wave of sadness passed, she urged me to take the medicine and finish the water, then she wrapped me up in herself and a blanket and held me until morning.

"Sometimes you have to let it all out," she said. "There's nothing wrong with missing your dad."

I hadn't even told her what was wrong. That's how well she knew me—how in sync we were.

A tear leaks out of the corner of my eye as the full weight of the loss of her hits me again, as it has so many times over the years. It mingles with the wetness on her hair.

"You sound like my therapist," she grumbles, tearing me away from the memory.

"I sound like you."

Her body stiffens ever so slightly under me. "Ryan—"

"I'm sorry," I say quickly, then shake my head as I backtrack. "No. I'm not, actually. I won't pretend that I haven't missed you, Scarlett. I can keep this professional, but I won't lie. I loved you, and I won't wish that time of my life away. Not for anything."

She's quiet for a moment, which is about as long as it takes me to replay everything that happened in the last ten minutes and decide that the best course of action is to curl up in a hole and never come back out.

"This is...keeping it professional?"

I can't see her face, but I can hear the smile in her voice. The relief that washes over me is intense. This is the Scarlett I know: teasing, irreverent, sarcastic. I can work with this.

"I go above and beyond for my writers, Scarlett. I am often their editor, confidant, and meal-delivery service."

"Do you bathe them, too?"

Chuckling deeply, I plant another kiss on her head, hoping it's an innocent enough gesture. "That one's special for you."

She pushes off of me and scoots about an inch away. Immediately, my body leans toward her until my brain rudely reminds it who we are now and what we're doing here. As she rolls her shoulders, her robe slips down to expose the smooth expanse of her skin, and I have to ball my hands into fists at my sides as a reminder that her skin is not mine to touch anymore.

"Well, I wouldn't want to keep you from taking meals to your other writers." The way she ends the sentence, it seems like she's going to continue, but she doesn't.

"I can stay," I whisper, afraid that if I speak any louder, it'll startle her into remembering she didn't want me around to begin with.

Her blue eyes are rimmed with red, and her nose looks like she could guide Santa's sleigh through the darkness, but her expression is something akin to hope.

"It's okay." She clears her throat. "I wouldn't want your other writers thinking you're giving me preferential treatment."

"My other writers haven't been around as long as you. It's a seniority thing."

Snorting, she turns her eyes to the ceiling and presses her left thumb into the palm of her right hand, making soothing circles as she thinks.

"Look," I say before she can talk herself out of it. "You need rest, and I want to help. I'll stay until you fall asleep. I have some work to do anyway."

A crisp nod is my only response, but I'll take it. The cold tile floor bites into my palms as I press against it to stand up. I reach out to help her up, but she stands by herself. I try to remind myself that's a good sign rather than feel the sting of her choosing not to allow me to touch her again. She retreats into the bathroom, and I hear the water running from the sink faucet. I busy myself with digging my laptop and some papers out of my bag, so when she emerges from the bathroom and closes herself in her bedroom, I'm not looking at her.

After a few minutes, I'm left wondering if I should set myself up on her couch or her table. As I'm weighing my options, her bedroom door opens. She's not standing there like I expect her to be, but it seems as clear an invitation as any. I gather up my things and peek inside the door. She's snuggled under the comforter, her face turned away from me and her brown hair falling in waves over her pillow. Her body is tucked all the way to the right side of the bed, and there's a space on the left. Every other light in the room is off except for the one on the left-hand nightstand.

She left a space for me.

Swallowing thickly, I walk around the bed and sit on top of the blankets, stretching my legs out and crossing them at the ankle. Scarlett's face is visible to me now, her eyes closed and her expression slowly relaxing. She must have been exhausted to slip into sleep this fast.

I tell myself I'll work for an hour until she's more deeply asleep, and then I'll leave. That was what I told her, and though I could stare at her all night, I don't want to freak her out. So I wiggle a bit to get more comfortable and drag my laptop to my lap.

It isn't long before I become focused on my work. The book I'm working on isn't the most interesting, but it's fine. Working on Scarlett's manuscript while I'm sitting next to her would feel too much like times long gone, so this one will have to do.

My fingers quietly glide over the keyboard, and I let the sound of the keys lull me into a rhythm. I always did my best work sitting next to Scarlett. It would seem that hasn't changed in all these years, either.

As I'm puzzling over a passage that isn't quite right, I feel something on my thigh. When I look down, Scarlett's hand has found me in her sleep. My heart cracks wide open, and my breath catches in my lungs.

A glance at the time tells me it's long past the hour I told myself I'd stay. But now her hand has found me, as if she needs me to stay as much as I want to be here.

I'll leave when her hand moves, I tell myself.

It's not long before I drift off to sleep too.

Chapter 18
Scarlett

I'M USED TO waking up in a fog, usually from working late the night before. Sometimes from waking up too early to do it again. Words blend into each other, jostling and fighting for space in my brain. They rarely leave room for anything else except, occasionally, a nagging feeling that I'll never do enough, be enough, write enough.

But there's only one word in my mind when I wake up the next morning.

Ryan.

The sun is streaming through my east-facing window when I crack my eyes open. Dust dances in the beams of light, and it feels like an accurate metaphor for what I'm feeling right now. Cobwebs and dirt are illuminated by the golden hour, all the more beautiful for how they move and shine. My brain isn't clear, but I can see the grime. Maybe that's the thing that needs to happen before I can clean it out.

And Ryan was the one who shone a light on it all. I had been deep in my own world, convinced this is just how it is for me: I can write and live a life of isolation and exhaustion with Trina as my only connection to the outside world, or I can never write again and cobble together some semblance of a normal life. But with only one evening having him near me, I can already see that a happy medium might be possible, because the way I feel now, I could conquer not only this manuscript but maybe even another.

Smiling to myself, I reach out to where I had felt the mattress sag next to me last night as I was finally, blissfully drifting off to sleep. Only now, it's empty.

Of course it is. He said he was going to stay until I fell asleep and then leave. A quick glance at my phone reveals no messages from him, and the fact that it's already eight in the morning. I can't remember the last time I slept this late. And as late as it is, Ryan is probably long gone by now.

The sting of disappointment is enough to keep me in bed all day, but Dianne's voice nags me at the back of my mind. *Get out of bed, even if that's the only thing you do. Then when you feel able, do the next thing.*

Groaning audibly as if there's anyone here to hear it, I violently roll myself over and land with a thud on the ground. Actually, it's a good thing no one was here to see that bullshit. Whatever. She said I had to get out of bed, not *how* I had to get out of bed. I'm putting that one in the *win* column.

That done, I untangle myself from the comforter that came with me and toss it in a heap onto the floor. I'm pretty sure the next thing should be to make the bed, but I don't care enough about the aesthetics of my home to bother. Instead, I rub the dried tears from the night before out of my eyes and pull on a pair of joggers that looks clean enough. I make my way to the kitchen, pleading with the universe that I still have enough coffee grounds left to brew myself a cup.

"Good morning," a deep voice greets me.

My hand flies to my chest as I stumble back a step. "Fucking hell," I breathe, pressing myself against the wall and trying to catch my breath.

"Did I scare you?" Ryan smirks. He's leaning against my counter, and he takes a smug sip of what I really hope is coffee from a mug out of my eclectic collection. This one has a classic, intricate, blue-and-white design on it, but when you look closer, there are little dinosaurs chasing people among the detailed blue houses.

"Yes, you fucking scared me. I thought you had left." My heart is still racing, though I can't tell if it's from lingering adrenaline or from the fact that he's still here, looking fresh as a daisy even in yesterday's clothes.

Still smirking, he hands me a mug. This one says *I stayed up all night to see where the sun went. Then it dawned on me.* He had bought this for me years ago as a joke about how late I tend to work, but I can't help but wonder if he was in my head this morning.

"Sleep well?" he asks as if it's totally normal for him to be standing in my kitchen at eight in the morning wearing clothes he must have slept in and handing me a warm mug as the early-morning light casts the whole scene in a glow.

I eye him over my mug as I take a slow sip. It is, indeed, coffee. A little, appreciative moan escapes me, and I could swear Ryan's eyes flash. It's gone too fast to be sure.

"I did, actually. Why are you still here?" As if I hadn't been bemoaning the fact that he was gone not two minutes ago.

"You were out of coffee, so I went to get some." That's not really an answer to my question, and it occurs to me to wonder how he's been getting up to my apartment without being buzzed in. Because he did leave, apparently, and came back with this nectar of the gods that is currently warming my cold hands.

Narrowing my eyes at him, I try to put on an irritated expression, but if I didn't notice this until now, I don't know how concerned I really am about it. "How are you getting in and out of here?"

Ryan has the good sense to look sheepish. He sets his coffee mug down on the counter and clears his throat. "Well, I—"

"Are you stalking the door and waiting for people to open it? I swear to god, Ryan. That could get me in trouble with the super."

"It's not my fault Midwesterners are nice and hold the door open for people. They should know better in this day and age. That's a definite security risk." He levels me with a pointed look. "There are a lot of people in and out of this building, Scarlett."

"Don't deflect blame on me for choosing the most nondescript building I could. I wasn't in my right mind when I moved here. Last time I checked, you still have your sanity. You shouldn't be sneaking up here. Use the buzzer like a gentleman."

He tilts his head and is silent for a moment. His throat works against a hard swallow. "Would you have buzzed me up?"

My gaze falls to his hand resting on the side of his mug where it sits on the counter. The light clinking of his ring tapping against the side of the mug fills the silence between us like a metronome. No, like a clock, ticking the seconds away. Or like the timer on a bomb, counting down to my response.

But like a bomb, there's no avoiding the inevitable answer.

"I'd always buzz you up, Ryan," I say to his hand, barely audible.

That finger stops clinking against the mug. The resulting silence is deafening.

"Scarlett," he says, his voice strained.

"I was never mad at you," I choke out, still not looking at him. "It wasn't that I didn't want to see you specifically. I couldn't see anyone. It wasn't anger or shame or anything like that. It was a physical inability to have a conversation. A mental block. And by the time I sorted it out..." I shrug. "I guess I figured you all were better off without me after I ruined everything."

The vague awareness of his body leaning closer to mine pokes through the watery haze that's developing at the corners of my eyes. I don't know if I realized how bad off I was five years ago until I said it aloud just now. But I know it's true in the way I know it when my words are hitting right on the page—it's a gut feeling, and I'm not deleting any of it.

"I wasn't," Ryan whispers. He clears his throat, then speaks louder. "I wasn't better off without you."

The blue fabric of his sweater blocks my view of the counter as he steps in front of me. His hand comes up to cup the side of my face, the warmth of his palm incongruous with the cold metal of his ring lightly scraping against my skin.

"Look at me, Scarlett."

I take in a deep breath before I do, the aroma of vanilla and almond and coffee working its way into my senses. Slowly, I drag my eyes up his chest, letting my gaze linger on the brown stubble that speckles his usually clean-shaven skin before I meet those dark eyes, framed by even darker glasses.

He's everywhere. He takes up so much space that it's hard to breathe.

"You are more important than the sum of all your words." There's an intense seriousness in his voice that's matched in his eyes. The press of his palm won't let me look away.

"I'm not suicidal, Ryan. I've been depressed. There's a difference." I don't know why, but it's important to me that he knows that.

Those brown eyes assess me for a moment before he nods once. "Right. But you're not really living like this, either, are you?"

My gaze falls again, even as he holds my face in his hand. I had thought I was doing okay. And maybe I was, though I can see how he, as an outsider, doesn't think so. But is okay really something to strive for? Is that the kind of existence I want?

No. I want words and pages and the high of holding my book in my hands, of trailing my fingers over the beautiful cover, letting them linger over my name on the spine. The way it used to be, before everything went to shit.

"We did it," I said, my grin stretching so wide it hurt as I drank in the cover art, the way the letters of the title curled into the drawings below and gave way to my name at the bottom.

"You *did it," Ryan corrected, but his smile rivaled mine.*

I shrugged. "You helped. I mean, you're in the acknowledgments."

He flipped straight to the end, his eyes tracking quickly across the page, then slowing when he found it. His smile softened as he dragged his bottom lip through his teeth. "Thank you, most of all, to Ryan Whitlock. Weak words have no place here. Only the strong will survive," *he reads. In one motion, he clapped the book shut, it landed on the love seat, and he pulled me into a kiss.*

I want him.

It should be a harsh realization that crashes into me. That's how it happens in all the books anyway. But it's not. It's warm and soft as it slides into my mind and over my heart. It feels like coming home.

His hand falls away from my cheek and he takes a step back. "I'm sorry. That was out of line."

I huff a laugh. Out of line. Sure. If he only knew that I can't stop thinking about kissing him, holding him, having him in my life again.

"It wasn't." My voice is raspy and raw. "You're right. I need...I don't know. Something else. Something I can do besides write and get in my own head."

Ryan runs a hand through his hair. It stands out at odd angles, and a lock of it falls over his forehead. "You mean besides watching holiday baking shows?"

"Make fun all you want, but you have to admit that there's something really soothing about watching cake batter pour into a pan."

His chuckle is quite possibly the best thing I've ever heard, and the sound of it draws my own rusty laugh out of me. We linger in the light humor, mirroring each other's smiles, our eyes locked as if neither of us wants to look away. The earlier tension between us isn't broken, but it's subdued—a candle flame rather than a roaring bonfire.

We both open our mouths to speak at the same time, then laugh again at the awkwardness of it. But before we can do the *You first, No you* thing, a loud ringing sounds from Ryan's pocket. His shoulders tense, and he looks around as if he doesn't realize it's his phone making the sound. When he figures it out, he pulls the phone from his back pocket. A glance at the screen has him tensing even further.

"I have to take this," he says apologetically. "Can I..." He motions to the bedroom.

"Sure. Yeah. Of course." I nod emphatically like a fool who

doesn't know how to work her own body. *Get a grip*, I tell myself as Ryan slips into the bedroom and shuts the door behind him.

When he's out of my line of sight, I deflate. I slump against the counter, and my hand knocks against my coffee mug, almost tipping it over. I right it quickly, but my Ryan-induced lack of control over basic movements is starting to get annoying.

I sip my coffee and try to calm my racing thoughts while I listen to Ryan's muffled voice through the door. I can't make out any of the words, but the deep tones resonate through the wood. It soothes me.

He stayed. He brought me coffee. He's here.

Even though I majorly fucked him up five years ago. Even though I can barely keep it together now.

I'm falling for him again. As much as I would like to shove that inconvenient fact into a box and pretend it doesn't exist, I can't. The little touches, the warmth of his presence, the thoughtfulness. His ability to see me at my worst and still only think the best.

I don't want him to leave.

And if we're going to try to keep this professional, I am royally screwed.

Chapter 19

Ryan

THE MINUTE I see Anastasios Martis's name light up my phone before I've even left for work, I know this is not going to be good. I'm glad I excused myself from Scarlett's kitchen, and not only because looking at her standing there—vulnerability written in the curve of her shoulders and the blue of her eyes—was going to break me into a million pieces in about two-point-five seconds. There's only one reason why the publisher and namesake of the press would be calling me.

Sure enough, the first thing he says when I answer the phone is, "I have been thinking about this, and I'd really like to meet Scarlett Frye."

I move my glasses out of the way so I can massage the bridge of my nose. It doesn't ease any of the tension, but it was worth a shot.

"Well, sir, I'm sure she'd love to meet you too," I start as diplomatically as I can, "but she's under some pressure with her next deadline. I think it might be best to let her work uninterrupted—"

"That's actually why I want to meet with her," he interrupts. "I trust you can be discreet about what I'm going to tell you?"

"Of course, sir," I say because I know what's good for me.

"I'll be honest, I was hesitant to sign her on given her history with JMP. But with you vouching for her current manuscript, I felt like it was less of a risk. Your word goes a long way, Whitlock. I hope you know that."

"Thank you, sir." I rub my hand over the itchy stubble on my jaw that has grown since last night.

"It's still a risk, though. JMP sank a lot of money into that third book of hers, only to end up having to pull every resource they had slated when she backed out."

"All due respect, sir, but they did that before their offer was even on the table. There was always a chance she would walk." I keep my voice as measured as I possibly can. Anastasios Press was acquired two years after Scarlett left, and though I'm sure Anastasios heard rumors about it all, she had become both a pariah and a thing of the past by that time. Her status was almost mythological among the ranks at the press, and the speculation about her breakdown ranged from courteous sympathy to downright anger. Her disappearance only fueled the flames of conjecture for a while, though I'm not sure how much of that speculation made it up the ranks to the top.

It was always their intent to have Anastasios remain at the head the acquired imprint—even allowing him to keep the name under the guise of his name meaning *resurrection* and it being a symbol of rebirth for the company. They desperately needed a new image after Scarlett's disappearance gave a number of authors courage to come forward about the stresses they themselves were under. But by the time the imprint was up and running, Scarlett's situation was so far in the rearview mirror that I doubt he learned about any of the finer details. Like our relationship, for example.

"Trust me, there were conversations about their strategy behind closed doors. JMP's relationship with risk has permanently changed because of that very debacle. But it got me thinking. She could walk again, you know."

I'm immediately defensive. "She won't," I say. It comes out harsher than I meant, so I take a deep breath and try again. "She signed the contract this time, and she's been in direct contact with me as we work on revisions. Everyone involved agreed that it's been long enough for her to have changed and that her manuscript was good enough for a second chance."

"For now, yes. But if this goes where I hope it's going, she'll be important again down the line with more books and bigger deals. I need to protect my investments at this imprint." His voice trails off as if he's musing on something else, and I hear the clicking of his keyboard over the phone. I wait for him to finish whatever it is he's doing.

"Listen," he says when he comes back to the conversation. "I promise this isn't sinister. I know editors can get protective over their authors, especially the more delicate ones." The editor in me wants to ask if it's the authors or the editors who are delicate in this situation, but I bite my tongue. "We've all been there. I just want to meet her. This isn't anything against you or your work. Call it idle curiosity, if you will."

I bristle at the suggestion that Scarlett is something to be gawked at, like a caged animal. Or worse, that she's a commodity. But I don't see any way out of this. Anastasios Martis is my boss, and it's in everyone's best interests to keep him happy.

"I can see if she has any availability." I grimace to myself at how easily I give in, though I'm not sure what the point of resisting him would be other than to write my own professional epitaph. I'm just a company man, I guess.

"Excellent." His chair squeaks in the background as if he's standing to mark the end of a meeting. "Call my secretary when you have a date so she can get it on my calendar. I look forward to it." He hangs up before I can say anything else.

Groaning, I toss my phone on top of Scarlett's bed. It's when the phone lands with a dull thud and not a soft flop that I notice the comforter piled next to the bed, on the floor. I guess that explains the noise I heard just before she exited her room this morning.

I pick up the comforter and lay it out on top of the bed for her, smoothing it as I go. The memory of me nodding off on top of it last night—like a perfect gentleman—comes back as I run my hands over the damask pattern. I should have left. I know I should have left. But being with her again—watching as her body relaxed into sleep, her hand reaching out to me like a moth to a flame—I couldn't leave.

I like to consider myself a strong man. And where Scarlett is concerned, I've thought I was at least over her enough to move on with my life. I used to think that if she ever appeared in my life again, we'd exchange pleasantries, maybe catch up a little, and go our separate ways. But this whole situation has blown that out of the water.

Dragging my hand down my face, I groan again. I am well and truly fucked.

When I finally exit Scarlett's bedroom, I find her opening and closing cabinets in the kitchen with what seems like growing panic. She's muttering to herself, but when she hears the door open, she whips around. The cabinet door slams behind her, and she starts a bit.

"Everything okay?" I ask, stepping toward the counter and the coffee I left there.

"Well, yeah. Sort of." She shrugs, then winces at me. "You didn't put a little orange pill bottle somewhere when you were cleaning up, did you?"

My eyes tip upward as I search my memories. "You mean like a prescription bottle?"

"Mm-hmm." She nods as she lifts her eyebrows.

I shake my head slowly. "No, I don't remember anything like that. Why?"

She sighs, slumping against the counter. "I'm on some medication. Antidepressants?" Her voice tips up at the end like a question. She eyes me, waiting for a reaction. I keep my expression carefully neutral, unsure of which reaction would be the appropriate one for information I technically already knew. Apparently appeased, she continues, "Anyway, I can't find them, which makes me think I might be out."

"How long have you been without them?" I ask carefully.

She lets out a puff of air which buzzes her lips until she closes them and blows out her cheeks. Her eyes slide to me, and she sends a cautious eyebrow skyward. "I don't remember."

My feet, with minds of their own, shuffle toward her. "You can't just not take your meds, Scarlett." I try to sound stern, but my voice is laced with an unmistakable concern.

She drags her bottom lip through her teeth. "I know. I'm usually really good about remembering, I swear. But I was working on revisions for you, and then I started this next project, and when I get to working, the days all bleed together, and I can't remember if I took it or not and—"

"Scarlett." I tuck a wayward hair behind her ear, which effectively stops her guilty rambling. I allow myself to run a thumb over the softness of her cheek, but I drop my hand before I can give into the urge to drag that thumb over the place where she just bit her lip. "It's okay. We'll refill your prescription, and then I'm going to set an alarm in your phone as a reminder for when you need to take it each day."

Her dark eyebrows crumple together in confusion, and she blinks at me a few times. "We...You..." She shakes her head rapidly as if to clear it. "Why did I never think of that?"

A chuckle bubbles up out of me, riding up on the high of being able to help her do this simple thing. As if acting on muscle memory, I cup my hand behind her head, weaving my fingers through her hair, and kiss her forehead. It's such a natural action—one I made countless times, years ago—that I barely think anything of it until my lips touch her skin.

"Because your big, beautiful brain is full of other things." Suddenly very aware of our proximity, I take a step back quickly. "Besides, that's what you have me for." I try to put on a reassuring expression, but my lips are still practically vibrating from their contact with her.

Scarlett's gaze drops, and her features contort with concern. "I didn't have trouble remembering before this," she mutters, probably to herself.

I respond anyway. "Hey, it's okay. We'll get you set up and back on track. No problem."

Her eyes fly to mine, and the concern etched on her face

is replaced with skepticism. "Why are you doing all of this? It's Tuesday. Don't you have, like, a job to do or something?" Like a cloud passing over the sun, her expression clears. "I guess I am your job now, huh?"

There is no world in which I wouldn't help Scarlett get what she needs now that I know what that is. But I don't have to tell her that. "Your book is my job," I deflect.

"Well, I wrote the book, so it's definitely in your best interest to make sure I write the next one they signed me on for."

"I said it once and I'll say it a million times, Scarlett. You're more than your writing."

She shrugs with an air of forced nonchalance, like a maladjusted teenager pretending not to care. "Yeah." Then, she brightens a bit as her spine straightens. "Speaking of my writing, though, would you maybe want to read what I've got so far in this draft? I could use some feedback. It's hard writing in a vacuum."

"Shouldn't you ask your critique partners before you ask your editor?" I tease, but from the way she winces, I know exactly what she's going to say before she says it.

"I...uh...I don't have any critique partners." She shrugs in that jerky, uncomfortable way again. "I haven't since, well, you know. It's like they think mental breakdowns are contagious or something. Or they don't want to be associated with someone on publishing's blacklist."

That's when I realize she's not just trying to rebuild a career. She's trying to rebuild an entire life. One that collapsed in the wake of her decisions. She didn't just walk away from her career and from me that day. She walked away from *everything.*

"You're not on the blacklist," I tell her, because starting there seems easier than trying to dissect the more complicated emotions rising in my chest. "In fact, Anastasios Martis wants to meet with you later this week."

"That sounds ominous."

"It's not." I try to reassure her, even though I'm not entirely certain about this myself. "That was him on the phone just now.

He was asking me to set up a meeting with you."

"Hmm." She narrows her eyes skeptically. "When?"

"Whenever you're available."

Her arms lift from the sides of her body, as if they're encompassing the entirety of her life. "As you can see, I'm completely booked, but I suppose I can squeeze something in," she says with a healthy dose of skepticism. Then, she grows serious. "Maybe the end of the week? Or early next week? I'd like to get some shit together first, if you think that'd be okay."

"I think that'd be fine," I say gently. "And I'll be there. I'm not sure if that's reassuring or not, but—"

"It is," she cuts me off before flashing me a half smile. "I'm glad you'll be there for me."

I'll always be there for you, I want to say, but I don't. I've crossed enough lines today. Instead, I grab her jacket from the hook next to the door and help her into it. "Let's get your prescription, and then I want to read this next draft of yours."

She shrugs into her jacket and pulls her hair loose from the collar. The dark strands fall over the green vinyl of her windbreaker. "You do?"

I jam my hands into my pockets in a feeble attempt to resist running my fingers over the loose ends of her hair. "Of course I do. I already told you I'll read anything you write. Always."

It feels like an admission, and the words hang between us. But when Scarlett smiles, it's like a rainbow after the rain. And as we ride the elevator down from her apartment and step out into the spring sunshine, everything feels better. Lighter.

It doesn't even matter that we aren't together anymore. I'll do anything to make her smile like that again. For as long as she'll let me.

"Do you want me to come with you?" Trina sounds distracted, even though she was the one who called me this morning before my scheduled meeting with Anastasios Martis at his office. It's still unclear if she called to make sure I get my ass out the door or to ask—yet again—what this meeting is even about.

I switch over to speakerphone and rest my phone on the edge of my bathroom counter so I can try to do something with my hair. "It's not like I need union representation, Trina." My brush gets tangled up, and I curse as it pulls at my scalp. "Dammit, that fucking hurts," I mutter.

"Are you tweezing those eyebrows finally?"

"What? No, I'm combing my hair." I squint at myself in the mirror. "Why? Do I need to tweeze my eyebrows?"

"I mean..." She trails off. I wait for her to finish her sentence, but there's only silence.

"I like my eyebrows," I grumble.

"Okay," she says simply.

I roll my eyes and sigh as I pass my brush through my hair again. It's much smoother this time. "Whatever. I'm fine. Besides, Ryan will be there."

Trina makes an indecipherable noise that sounds like a cross between a scoff and a hum of disapproval.

"What's your problem now?" I try to keep the defensiveness out of my tone, but I can't help it. It's been over a week since

Ryan spent the night here, and even though it was a completely innocent evening, I haven't mentioned anything to Trina about it. Somehow, it feels private. Like a secret. Something I want to keep close to my heart.

My hair is finally untangled enough to braid it, so I start crossing strands over each other while simultaneously scanning my messy counter for a hair tie.

"I don't know, Scarlett," she says on a sigh. "Things didn't exactly end well for you two. And now all of a sudden, he's in your life again, editing your book, no less. Dropping off notes at your apartment unannounced, bringing you food—"

"How did you know he brought me food?"

"Uh..." she hedges. "Well, I told him if he must see you, he should bring food with him." She has the good sense to sound sheepish, but her tone quickly turns agitated. "So of course now I know he saw you and he brought you food because you just admitted it. Come on, Scarlett. Only an idiot wouldn't be able to see what's going on here."

My fingers pause mid-braid. "What do you mean?"

"Literally the dumbest smart person I know," she mumbles. Before I can protest, she practically shouts, "That man never fell out of love with you."

I wince, rubbing my ear before turning down the speakerphone volume. My braid falls apart as soon as I let go of it. I run my hand through my hair to fluff it up a little and decide, fuck it, it looks good enough as it is.

"You're being ridiculous," I protest, making my way to the bedroom to get dressed. Even though I had wondered the same thing as his strong fingers were working their way into my scalp while I lie naked under the bubbles in the bathtub. "I left him high and dry, remember? *Ghosted* isn't even a strong enough word for what I did to that man. He'd be even dumber than you think I am to come back to me."

Damn, I hurt my own feelings with that one. I'm glad I'm not looking in the mirror anymore, because I'm sure it'd only reflect my pained expression, which would somehow make it worse.

"Oh, honey." Trina's voice is soft. "Do you want him to come back to you?"

"It wouldn't be a smart move," I say, but even I can hear how uncommitted I am to the words.

"That's not exactly an answer," she counters.

It may not have been a direct answer, but that's an answer in itself. Do I want him back? Of course I fucking do. I probably would have spent the rest of my life with him if things had turned out differently. "I think you know that it is, actually."

"This is going to sound crazy, but maybe this is a sign. Maybe it's time for you to start dating again. Get yourself out there."

"You're right." I pause as I pull my white T-shirt over my head and knot it at my hip. "That does sound crazy."

"Bitch, I thought you were going to agree with me to go on a date," Trina yells.

I wince. "Please stop shouting."

"I will stop shouting when you start listening to my advice."

My gaze bounces to the clock on my wall as I pull on a blue skirt with little white flowers. "Oh shit. I need to go. Listen, I will be fine. I'll call you when the meeting is over and fill you in on everything. Don't worry about me."

"I always worry about you," she grumbles.

"That's why I pay you the big bucks," I retort. "Love you, bye!" I quickly press the red button and grab my purse and keys on my way out the door.

By the time I park my car in the lot outside the Anastasios Press building, I've worked myself up into an anxious mess. Even my deep-breathing exercises aren't helping my heart calm down. Maybe I should have had Trina come with me.

I'm a writer, dammit. I'm supposed to be holed up in my house with a cup of tea, making up worlds and characters in my own little head, not having unexpected meetings with publishers who have no clear agenda.

Head down, I push my way out of my car and rush inside as fast as I can before I'm able to talk myself out of it. I'm not looking where I'm going, too distracted by my own racing thoughts, which is why I'm absolutely shocked when I run into a wall of solid muscle. I drop my purse and take a step back, my eyes wide as they trail up from a thin, navy sweater stretched over very well-defined pecs. Those biceps are testing the limits of the sleeves that barely contain them. Upward still, a strong neck and jaw covered in a dusting of golden-brown hair. Full, pink lips curved upward in an indulgent smile. Green eyes, sparkling with mischief.

"I'm so sorry," I say breathlessly but unable to move. Either I haven't gotten out in a while, or this man in front of me is one of the most beautiful men I've ever seen. Maybe both.

He bends down to pick up my purse from where it fell on the ground. By the way he chuckles when he hands it to me, I know my mouth is gaping.

"Not a problem." His voice is warm and smooth, like the feeling of really good whiskey sliding down your throat and settling into your belly. "You seemed distracted, Miss..."

It takes me a moment before I realize he's asking my name. And then it takes me another moment before I remember what name I'm supposed to give him. "Fr—Falmouth," I correct myself quickly. "S.J. Falmouth."

He extends his hand, and I shake it. The rough callouses of his palm scrape deliciously against mine. It sends a jolt of electricity up my arm, which serves to wake me all the way up. This man is hot, and he must be in publishing in some capacity if he's in the lobby of the press offices. How does someone who sits at a computer all day have such rough hands? It's patently unfair. But I'm distracted from that question by the gentle rubbing of his thumb against the inside of my wrist, which would seem to suggest he likes what he's looking at.

It's me. He's looking at me.

Trina's voice nags at the back of my consciousness: *Get yourself out there.*

If she were here, I'd kick her and tell her to shut up.

"I've heard of you," the man is saying. "You're debuting at the end of this year?"

"Uh..." God, I wish I had rehearsed some answers to these questions. "Yes. Right."

He chuckles good-naturedly and releases my hand. "Congratulations. I know. It's a weird feeling to talk about your work at first. You get used to it. I'm Charles Hall. It's nice to meet you."

That snaps my jaw shut. Charles Hall published his first book three years ago, just about when Anastasios Press was acquired, but as far as I know, he was with a competing house. His book was a bestseller. It sold almost as many copies as my debut. Almost.

"Wow, okay," I say, acting duly impressed. I am actually pretty excited to meet him, but I make the snap decision to lean into the persona of my pen name for a minute. S.J. Falmouth is debuting this year and would be starstruck at meeting this guy, but more importantly, she isn't depressed, doesn't have to worry about falling for her editor *again*, and didn't leave the publishing world to have a mental breakdown five years ago.

It won't last. Eventually, people will figure it out. But maybe, for a minute, I can pretend.

He leans forward conspiratorially and winks. "Anastasios is courting me for my next release. You never saw me here."

"I won't tell a soul." I make a zipping motion over my mouth and toss away an imaginary key.

He laughs again. "Were your ears burning?"

That, actually, does surprise me. "What do you mean?"

Tipping his chin upward, he indicates what I imagine is the direction of the publisher's office upstairs. "We were talking about you, just now. I was in a meeting with the man himself, and he mentioned your book. Must be something pretty special to have Martis talking about you in casual conversation."

My heart skips nervously, but I maintain an unaffected air. If this meeting is any indication, Anastasios Martis isn't nearly as interested in my book as he is in me, but I'm not about to disclose this information. That would make my game of pretend far too complicated. "Something like that."

Charles tilts his head and studies me for a minute. His gaze trails decadently down over my body and back up to meet my eyes. A little shiver follows in its wake. "What does S.J. stand for?"

I open my mouth to respond, but just then, a door opens to my right. "Scarlett," Ryan says as he enters the lobby. "There you are."

"Scarlett," Charles croons. "Beautiful name."

As if Ryan has just noticed him there, he stops almost mid-stride. His nostrils flare slightly as his gaze bounces back and forth between the two of us, and he crosses his arms over his body, pulling his gray dress shirt tight over his shoulders. His eyes land on my companion and narrow. "I see you've met Charles Hall."

As if Ryan's sudden presence snaps me back to reality, two things occur to me at once. The first: Charles has no idea who I am, which, from the clear tough-guy image he tries to uphold with his muscles and calloused hands, makes sense. He probably surrounds himself with a bunch of writer bros and doesn't bother keeping tabs on anyone writing books that might appeal to a different audience.

And the second: Ryan is jealous as fuck.

Looking at the two of them side by side, I can see why. Charles has *Golden Boy* written all over him, from the carefully trimmed blond hair and beard to his obviously curated muscular form. Even the navy sweater seems to have been selected to make his green eyes pop. He's an image. A mirage. Too good to be true. His picture on dust jackets is what sells his books. I'd be willing to bet Charles Hall isn't even his real name, though I don't have a lot of room to talk there.

Ryan, though, exists in stark opposition. His hair and eyes are dark, accentuated by the black frames of his glasses. He's tall but not as tall as Charles, and his lean frame makes him look more bookish than quarterback. The scowl on his face isn't winning any awards for America's Sweetheart, either.

"I was actually just going to ask S.J.—do you want me to call you S.J. or Scarlett?" Charles is saying. I've been too busy staring at Ryan, who is staring at Charles, to realize he's talking to me.

"Hmm?" I blink a few times and turn my attention to him. "Oh. S.J. works."

He studies me for a moment like he doesn't believe me but then carries on. "Anyway, I was going to ask if you want to join me for dinner tonight."

"Me?" I squeak just as Ryan huffs. He barely conceals an eye roll, but Charles isn't paying any attention to him.

Charles lets out a hearty laugh, one that says he's used to starstruck women falling all over themselves to go to dinner with him. "Yes. I thought it might be nice to chat about our books. You know, writer stuff." He winks at me again, and I can feel the waves of irritation coming off Ryan from where I stand. "Where do you live?"

"In the South Loop," I say before I can think better of it.

"Wonderful. I know a great tapas place there. Can I get your number so I can send you the details?"

"S.J." Ryan's voice oozes disdain over the letters. "We really need to head up."

I don't know where I get the audacity, but I check my watch. "We have ten minutes. I'm sure I can spare one to give Charles my number," I say sweetly.

It's not my intention to stoke whatever flame Ryan has burning right now. It's really not. But a dinner out sounds nice. I haven't been out to eat with someone in a really long time. The last time was probably with Ryan, actually. And while I don't think I'm in the right headspace to date someone else, there can't be any harm in meeting up with another writer to talk craft. When Ryan mentioned critique partners the other day, I was overwhelmingly sad about the loss of them all. It would be amazing to have another writer to talk to again.

Charles hands me his phone, and I type in my number. When I hand it back to him, he taps out a text and sends it. "I sent the information. Good luck with your meeting, S.J. I'll see you tonight." He flashes a pearly-white smile at me, then turns on his heel to leave.

Ryan stands perfectly still, his eyes tracking Charles's movement through the lobby. It isn't until the door has shut behind him that Ryan allows himself to relax a fraction. He closes his eyes, and his chest rises and falls with a deep breath.

"Tapas," he mutters under his breath. He opens his eyes and pins me with a look. "Really?"

"I was flustered," I say defensively. "Besides, you suggested yourself that I should have some critique partners again. How else am I supposed to meet other writers who are willing to be associated with me?"

Ryan flinches. He never did like my self-deprecating humor. "I don't think he's interested in critiquing your work."

I shrug, but the motion feels robotic and stiff, even to me. "So maybe he also thinks I'm okay to look at," I say. "There's no harm in that."

He stares at me for a moment, so still, I'd think he was made of wax if I hadn't been talking to him. Then, he shakes his head slowly and turns his back to me. "Come on," he says. "We're going to be late."

As much as I hate it, with that movement, I'm sure Ryan knows as well as I do that we can't be together anymore. Before he turned around, the defeat was written on his face, disappointment etched in the curve of his shoulders. It wouldn't be good for us or for the book. Even if the feel of his fingertips grazing my jaw in my kitchen days ago have lingered far longer than my fleeting handshake with Charles. It lingers, still.

But I have to put it out of my mind, at least for now. What's done is done, and it would be best for me to move on.

Chapter 21

Ryan

I SAW SCARLETT smile at Charles fucking Hall. I haven't seen that flattered, genuine smile in *years*. The first time I saw it was shortly after I ran into her in a bar, and I had to work for it. That asshole got one out of her in just a few minutes with hardly any effort at all.

In the elevator, I avoid looking at her, though I watch her wavy reflection in the metal doors. As the elevator ascends, she takes in a shaky breath and lets it out slowly, wiggling her hands at her sides.

My attitude softens slightly. "It'll be okay," I say with as much gentleness as I can. "Anastasios wants to meet you, that's all."

"I'm not worried about him," she mutters.

I bite the inside of my cheek so hard I almost draw blood. "Nervous for your date, then?" I spit out the word "date" so hard that I'm surprised she doesn't react to it.

Scarlett simply flicks her blue eyes to me as she sucks on her teeth. "It's not a date. He wants to talk about writing." She pauses, then adds, "I can't write in a vacuum, Ryan. Recent events have proven that."

If I could pull her into a hug right here in my workplace, I would, but the elevator pings, signaling we've arrived at our floor. This woman can shatter my heart into a million tiny shards that pierce me again and again with their sharp edges. I want this for her. Truly, I do. But she's kidding herself if she thinks Hall isn't after something else. He hasn't signed with us yet, but the publishing world is small, and I've heard enough about him to know what he's about.

We both stand there for a second too long, and the elevator doors close again. Scarlett sighs and turns to face me. "I get it. You want to shelter me from the worst parts of this job." She swallows audibly, then licks her lips. "You've always tried to do that for me."

I huff, almost defeated. "I failed."

"You absolutely did not." She says it with such conviction, with such a fire in her eyes, that I go completely still. "You did not fail me," she repeats, punctuating each word. "That was...it was out of our control in a lot of ways."

"I pushed for that deal," I practically whisper, my words fighting their way out around a swell of emotion. "I thought more money would make it easier on you. You could hire someone to help, or..." I trail off and shrug. It doesn't matter. "And now you're here, having this meeting you shouldn't need to have." And meeting hulky men in the lobby and going to dinner with them later when she should be *mine*. But I don't say that part aloud.

"More money always means more product," she says simply. "I'm an investment. And now, I'm a risk. The only surprise here is how long it took Anastasios to meet with me, not that it's happening at all."

I shove my hands into my pockets. If I don't, I won't be able to resist folding her into my arms, smelling her hair, kissing her. "You are surprisingly well adjusted about all of this."

She snickers and tosses her dark hair over her shoulder. "It helps that I've been taking my meds." Pursing her lips, she adds, "I know what I did, Ryan. Walking away from that deal was my decision. Even at the time, I had a good understanding of the consequences. Publishing again was my decision too. I knew what I'd have to overcome when I sent that manuscript to Trina, even if parts of it have been harder than I thought they would be. And even if I never expected you'd be part of it."

"I can still find someone else to edit the next one or take over this one if you want," I offer half-heartedly. We talked briefly about her directive to Trina to find a different editor, but she ultimately decided to stay with me. Though it was unclear if she actually wants me on the project or if she's afraid of looking like she's asking for too much on top of everything else.

She shakes her head but doesn't say anything else.

"I don't suppose I can talk you out of dinner with Charles tonight?"

She continues shaking her head, but her lips curl up into a wicked smile. I stifle my annoyance. I know her well enough to expect that the harder I push, the more she'll want to see him. Spite has always been a pretty powerful motivator for Scarlett, as has pushing my buttons just enough to make me want her more. Though I can't imagine wanting her more than I do right now as she challenges me with a light in her eyes I haven't seen in a long time. Since before she left, I realize with a start. I only wish I had noticed the absence of it sooner.

Tipping her chin toward the elevator doors, she presses the button to open them and says, "Let's get this over with."

As she exits the elevator, I trail behind her like a dejected puppy, back to imagining her and Charles Hall tucked into a corner at a small, romantic table, sharing tapas and wine with her smiling at him the way she was in the lobby.

I shuffle a little faster to open the door to the conference room for her. It's a smaller room than the one we were in the last time she was here. Anastasios is already there, waiting. He has a presence about him that makes it easy to see how he climbed the ranks in the publishing industry. At fifty-two years old, his dark hair is now more salt than pepper. He wears it long enough to dust over his ears, and there's a notable shock of gray running from his right temple over his forehead. His beard has even more gray in it, adding to his distinguished air. He is slightly shorter than me, but he doesn't exude any less power for it. He's always dressed in a three-piece suit—today's is a charcoal gray with a blue dress shirt that pokes out the top, unbuttoned at the neck. He never wears a tie. I think he wants to look more approachable, though that's hard to do when he turns heads every time he enters a room.

Usually, he's commanding but also comforting. He has solutions to problems and answers to questions, which is something everyone wants in a boss, especially in an industry that thrives on negotiations and deadlines. But the tense silence that reappeared between Scarlett and me when I asked her to cancel her date has put me so close to the edge that I know I'm not going to be in a good place during this meeting.

Luckily, I don't have to do much. Anastasios stands immediately when we enter the room, and Scarlett turns on her charm. I've seen her do this before; it's like a veil she puts on in meetings and interviews like this, all bright smiles and easy laughter.

"Scarlett," Anastasios says warmly, taking her right hand in both of his. "It is a pleasure to finally meet you."

"The pleasure is all mine," she replies.

He releases her and motions to the chairs placed around a round table. "Please, let's sit."

We do, and I catch Scarlett adjusting the fabric on her blue skirt in a motion that means she's nervous. Anyone who doesn't know her as well as I do would miss it, but I'm hyperaware of her every move. I have to actively resist covering her fidgeting hand with my own and telling her it's going to be okay.

"Thank you for meeting with me today," Anastasios says politely.

Scarlett clasps her hands together on top of the table, leaning forward on her elbows. "Of course. Let's cut right to the chase, shall we? I know you're worried about me and what happened last time, but I can assure you that will not happen again."

Anastasios's eyes widening slightly is his only tell that he's surprised. I, on the other hand, gape at Scarlett. What is she doing?

Silence stretches for so long that I wonder if someone is going to explode, and I worry very much that it will be my boss. Hopefully, I'm not watching an oncoming train wreck as I bounce my gaze back and forth between the two of them.

Suddenly, he bursts into loud, deep laughter that shakes his whole body. "You sure know how to cut through the bullshit."

Scarlett smiles wide, but the stiffness remains in her spine. "I won't lie, sir. I'm nervous about why you called me in here, so I figured we should address the elephant in the room before we go any further."

Anastasios dabs at the corners of his eyes, then leans back in his chair. There's a mirth about him—just a little air, like he's amused. "All right. I'll bite. What happened five years ago, and why are you so sure it won't happen again?"

"I can't tell you everything." Scarlett, however, is all seriousness. "Some of it was personal, and I owe a lot of people explanations that I haven't had the chance to share yet. But the gist of it was that I burned out and broke down. The pressure of a grueling press tour, deadlines for edits and drafts stacked on top of one another, and more of each on the horizon had me asking some very serious questions about whether or not that was what I wanted my life to look like in the long run. The answer was no."

"They offered you a seven-figure deal for three more books." Anastasios cocks a bushy eyebrow. "You didn't want a million dollars?"

"All due respect, that made it worse, sir."

I recoil slightly at that, knowing the hand I had in making that deal for her. Scarlett very carefully does not look at me, though. It seems like she wants to, but she keeps her eyes trained on Anastasios.

"How so?" He pushes forward in his chair again, his lips flattened together.

"With more money comes more expectations," she explains. "You and I both know they weren't going to give me a million-dollar advance and then let me take time off to enjoy it."

That was the piece I hadn't seen at the time. I had thought she loved the work but felt she wasn't being compensated appropriately for what was expected of her. But what she had wanted was fewer expectations and more reasonable deadlines.

In my twenties, everything had been about the money. My classmates who had gone on to get MBAs were making seven figures by the time I started at JMP. My only thought was that if I could get Scarlett that kind of money to write, surely she would have felt successful. And we had talked about it too—what we would do with a million dollars if we had that kind of money. I should have gotten the hint when her fantasies were always about moving to a cabin in some remote area, luxuriating in hot tubs with bottles of wine with nothing but time to read and write and be together.

"True." Anastasios snaps me out of my reverie. "But you could have negotiated that later, after you had been more established."

Scarlett nods slowly, as if that's a fair assessment. "Yes, but I needed it then. I don't know if you've experienced burnout, Mr. Martis, but it feels like..." She trails off, then sighs deeply. "Nothing has any joy anymore. There's no sparkle, no excitement. Colors aren't as bright. Songs you used to love grate on your nerves. Everything feels like too much and not enough, all at once. The people you love become a burden. It's hard to get out of bed. Puts a real damper on the creative process."

Anastasios tilts his head, regarding her. "Sounds an awful lot like depression."

"There's a lot of overlap, at least in my case. After all of that, I isolated myself, which did lead to depression. Eventually, I got help. I have a plan now, and a support system, even if it is small. And my agent negotiated a contract with longer periods of time between deadlines and a cap on the press I'll do when you decide to release my identity, as I'm sure you know."

He rubs a hand over his close-cropped beard and nods once in acknowledgment. "There are a lot of people at JMP who are still very angry with you. If it gets out prematurely that we signed you here, there could be consequences."

"I don't blame them, sir. But I was young and inexperienced, and I didn't have the vocabulary to clearly express what I needed at the time. The irony of me being a writer and not having the words does not escape me, but it doesn't make it less true. I could tell a story, but I couldn't figure out my life."

"There were many other authors who spoke up about their work-life balance after you left. JMP had a lot to consider." Anastasios dips his chin to look at her across the table.

"So I've heard," Scarlett responds without missing a beat.

I don't think Anastasios is trying to intimidate her or make her feel bad in any way, but she's not backing down. She's frank and unapologetic in her explanation of what happened, and even though I know it's not the full story, I'm so fucking proud of her. For everything. For working through all of that, for getting to the place she's in now. Even if there are slip-ups like she had a week ago, she's trying so hard to get her life back to where she wants it, and she's unashamed of the journey. Of course, hindsight is twenty-twenty, but I'm even proud of her for walking away back then. She did what she needed to do. Even if it broke my damn heart.

He nods slowly, narrowing his eyes and taking her in. "Thank you for your candor, Ms. Frye. It wasn't my intention to ask straight away, but I appreciate the information you've given me. And, more importantly, I am sorry. I can't speak on behalf of JMP because I wasn't there at the time, but you deserved better. My goal is that here, at Anastasios Press, we can provide that for you."

She smiles, and this time it's more relaxed. "I appreciate that."

"I'll say it again, though. We have to keep your identity under wraps until our team is ready to do a reveal. We are still owned by JMP, and there are a lot of people over there who wouldn't be too happy if they knew you signed with us. We'd like to be ready to provide sales data to show them, irrefutably, that signing you was a worth the risk." He shoots a warning glare at Scarlett, then turns the same look to me.

"I'm also hoping that there's a plan to mitigate some of the anger I incurred when I canceled my press tour," Scarlett says, drawing his attention back to her.

With that, Anastasios launches into an outline of the

marketing and publicity plans Meri has mocked up, complete with a tentative timeline for everything with *Becoming*. Scarlett listens attentively, asking questions where appropriate.

After that, the rest of the meeting goes off without a hitch. He asks her about the new book she's working on, and she lights up when she starts explaining the plot to him. Watching as she speaks—her hands waving wildly in the air and her expressions changing rapidly the way they always used to when she was talking about her books—I can't help but realize I'm falling a little more for her with each minute that passes. She's still the Scarlett I was in love with all those years ago, but better. She's more confident. Her eyes are clearer. Excitement radiates off her in waves.

She's magnetic, and I'm a piece of metal, powerless to resist her pull.

Eventually, the meeting comes to a close. Anastasios asks me to stay back to discuss a few other projects that are on the docket. On her way out, Scarlett grins at me, clearly relieved the meeting went so well. That glittery smile reminds me of the one she was flashing Charles when I came down to bring her up to the meeting. In my pride for her, I had almost forgotten about her date tonight, but now I can't get it out of my head.

All throughout my conversation with Anastasios after she leaves, I try to avoid seeing them together in my mind's eye. It distracts me, and Anastasios has to repeat his questions a couple of times before he ultimately dismisses me, telling me to get some more sleep so I can focus.

I have no right to be as obsessed with this dinner as I am. Scarlett deserves to have writer friends she can talk to. Just a few days ago, I was hoping she'd find new critique partners, which makes me a hypocrite. Admittedly, I had hoped she'd reconnect with her old roommate, Mandy, or something, but I guess beggars can't be choosers.

And yet, even though I know it's wrong, there's no way I'm getting any sleep tonight while Scarlett is out with that guy.

Six Years Ago

"I DON'T THINK *secluded* is a strong enough word."

Without looking, Scarlett waves a hand over her shoulder to swat at me. I take a step back, laughing as she narrowly misses knocking the glasses off my face.

"Will you please not read over my shoulder? You're interrupting greatness here." Her keyboard doesn't even stop clicking as she speaks. If I hadn't been witness to her process for over a year now, I would think she was just click-clacking at fake words to make a point, but she's not. She really can talk and type at the same time.

Sort of. Sometimes I find little snippets of our conversation buried in parts of her draft where they have no business being. I quietly delete those for her with a soft smile, unlike when I find familiar phrases very purposefully woven into the fabric of her writing. I bask in those and let them warm me to my core.

Scarlett is likely only vaguely aware of the way I'm watching her right now. She's sitting cross-legged on a chair we dragged in from the kitchen at a table turned desk in the corner of my bedroom. There's a perfectly good home office in the next room, but she insisted on this setup. I like to think she wants to be close to me as she works, especially as more and more of her time has been taken up by working. The requests from book clubs and podcasts and other interviewers have continued to roll in, especially now that her second book is getting closer to release. I picked up editing some of it in order to speed up everything and save her some time. Writing, editing, and doing press has proven difficult for her. On more than a few nights. I drift off to sleep and wake up before the sun rises to her clacking keyboard, sure she hasn't slept at all.

But right now, she seems relaxed. Calm. Happy. She's wearing black joggers and an oversized T-shirt that hangs off her bare shoulder. Her dark hair cascades down her back, and every once in a while, she pauses to twirl a strand of it around a finger before leaning forward and typing again. She's never been one for makeup, but she wears absolutely none when she's working. Once, she told me that she touches her face and bites her lip too much while she writes to bother, and either way, it doesn't matter because who is watching her anyway?

Me. I watch her. She's so fucking beautiful like this—at home in my space and hyper-focused on creating her beautiful art. I can't look away.

It's a moment before I realize the sound of the keyboard has stopped. She doesn't move, but she drags her bottom lip between her teeth, and I hurry out to the kitchen to busy myself with making some tea before she realizes I've been ogling her like a creep.

"What's a better word, then, Mr. Editor?" she calls from the bedroom. She leans back to look at me through the open doorway. The chair creaks as it accommodates her new position.

I drop two tea bags into their respective mugs and smile to myself at how perfect they look together on my counter. "Personally, I prefer Ryan Whitlock, the Wise and Witty Syntax Sorcerer, Wielder of the Red Pen, and Master of Manuscripts."

Scarlett throws her head back and cackles, exposing the long column of her throat. The chair almost tips from underneath her, but she catches herself at the last second without interrupting her laughter. "I meant instead of *secluded*," she says when she can finally talk again. "But if we're naming you instead, I have some ideas." One of her dark eyebrows ticks up, and those lips, swollen and pink from being dragged through her teeth, curl up into a smirk.

I take the steaming mugs back into the bedroom and set one on a coaster next to her laptop. Using my now-free hand, I tuck a wayward strand of her hair out of the way, letting myself linger in the softness of her skin. The mirth drains slowly out of her round, blue eyes as it shifts into something closer to desire.

"I'd very much like to hear what names you have for me in that big, beautiful brain of yours." I press a kiss to her forehead as if I could kiss her brain right through her skull.

"Hmm." Her eyelids flutter closed. "I don't think you want to know what I call you in my head." She lets out a breathy sound that's somewhere between a laugh and a sigh. "Most of the names I call you when going through your edits aren't very nice."

"No?" I tip her chin up so I can kiss her nose. "That doesn't seem fair. Every name I have for you is exceptionally kind." A chaste kiss to her lips. "*Brilliant.*" Another. "*Beautiful.*" Another. "*Amazing.*" I use my tongue to soothe the swelling where she's scraped with her teeth.

"You really missed an opportunity for alliteration here, oh Wise and Witty Syntax Sorcerer," she teases against my lips. Her hand snakes up to the back of my neck as she pulls me closer and opens for me.

"In my defense"—more kisses, as if even a moment separated is too long—"I'm distracted."

"Mmm." The sound of her hum vibrates through me and goes south, settling between my legs. "The Master of Manuscripts is slacking on the job."

I put my mug on the desk next to hers. "I'm not on the clock," I correct her, returning to kiss a line down her neck to that bare shoulder that has been plaguing me since she pulled her laptop out to start working. "You shouldn't be, either."

At that, she practically wilts. Where there was a tangible sexual energy between us not one second ago, now there's nothing.

I rest a hand on the edge of the desk and another on the back of her chair, caging her in before I pull back to see her wincing in apology.

"I'm almost done with this chapter. I need to get it out, or I'm going to be behind. Can we...put a bookmark in this, maybe?"

In the year since we started seeing each other, I've never once resented Scarlett's writing process. She has always been intensely focused, sometimes going silent for weeks on end if she's working out a difficult passage. It has been fairly recent that she's let me be in the room while she works at all, and being able to watch her create is a privilege. Having any part in her work is exhilarating. Her writing is full of emotion. It regularly moves me to tears, and I want to support her in any way I can.

"Of course." I plant one more kiss on her neck for good measure, then make my way to the bed. Leaning against the headboard, I stretch out my legs and grab the manuscript I had printed out at the office before coming home tonight.

We work in silence for who knows how long. Scarlett seems lost in her own world, and it doesn't take long for the rhythmic clicking of her keyboard to become background noise to my own reading. Soon, I'm so engrossed in the story in front of me that I don't notice when the sound stops, and the room falls into complete silence.

"What about *love*?"

She's so quiet, I almost don't hear it. Her back is to me, and she's staring at a dark laptop screen. It must have shut off while she was thinking.

I gently lay the manuscript on the nightstand and my red pen on top of it. "What about it?"

From this angle, I can make out the thumb of her left hand pressing circles into the palm of her right. I've seen her make this exact motion when she's on the phone with her editor and she isn't quite sure how to proceed.

"I...I was wondering if it's a strong enough word. *Love*."

Ever so slowly, I swing my legs over the side of the bed and stand. Scarlett doesn't move to look at me, but her shoulders tense and her thumb stops its movement.

"It doesn't seem strong enough." She laughs, but there's no humor in it. "Not by your standards anyway. But I can't think of another one that would be more appropriate—"

"Scarlett," I say, my voice low and soothing. "What are you trying to say?"

She does turn to look at me then, draping an arm over the back of the chair and pressing her chest into it as if she could hide her vulnerability. Her brows are pinched together, and her bottom lip looks like she's drawn blood by chewing on it so much.

Those blue eyes meet mine, and I could swear I see turmoil playing out in their depths. "I love you?" Her voice tips up on the end like a question, and her eyes fall to the ground. "See? It's not right," she mutters to herself as she shakes her head.

I take two steps and fall to my knees in front of her. She opens her legs to accommodate me as I push my torso between them and reach up to cup her beautiful face in my hands. "You love me?"

"I more than love you," she whispers shakily, as if she might cry. "I don't know how to say it."

"*Love* isn't a strong enough word," I whisper back. A tear trails along her cheek, and I swipe at it with the pad of my thumb. "Not for how I feel about you, either. I don't think the English language has a word that can describe it."

She barks out a wet laugh. Her trembling hands circle my wrists as she presses her eyes closed, tears leaking from them. "English sucks." She sniffles. "You'd think the Wizard of Words would be able to come up with something."

"Syntax Sorcerer," I correct her softly.

"I was referring to myself," she fires back. Those eyes open and land right on mine, and they almost glow in the soft light of the room.

Chuckling, I wipe her lingering tears away. I want to scream from the rooftops or do a dance. Maybe burst at the seams. I don't think I've ever been happier than I am in this moment. But instead of doing any of those things, I say as calmly as I can, "I suppose *love* will have to do."

And then, I decide that my mouth is better used to kiss her than to unsuccessfully try to find words to adequately tell her how I feel. Gently, I pull her closer, and she obliges. Her mouth opens immediately, and she lets my tongue dance with hers. When she scoots forward on the chair to press her chest into mine, I can feel her racing heart. My own is still soaring, beating in time with hers.

Scarlett loves me. She *more than loves me*. And I feel the same way about her.

She pulls back to look at me, studying my face like she's committing it to memory.

"*Love*," she whispers, as if trying on a new word to see how it feels.

"*Love*," I reply, turning the word this way and that.

We share a smile, letting the word settle between us. And even though I can tell she's just as happy as I am to have finally shared this with me, there's something else tugging at her attention. Instead of annoyance at having to share this moment, though, I am filled with a giddiness that I know her well enough to be able to tell when she's fully here with me and when she's not.

I know her. I love her. And she loves me. That's all that matters.

I smile indulgently at her. "Do you want me to read through your chapter?"

"Oh. It's late," she protests half-heartedly.

"I want to."

She leaps off the chair and grabs her laptop. I recline on the bed against the headboard in my original position with my legs spread out, and she crawls over the expanse of the bed to hand the laptop to me.

"I'm really excited about this one." She kicks her legs under the blankets and lies on her stomach with her hands making a pillow under her cheek as she looks up at me.

If history is any indication, she'll be asleep in minutes. I don't mind—the love of my life is deeply satisfied, both emotionally and artistically. There's no small amount of pride in knowing I've played a part in both, and with all the late nights she's been pulling recently, she needs the rest.

Sure enough, I haven't even gotten to the second new page before her breathing evens out. A quick glance in her direction tells me her eyes are closed, and her body is relaxed into the mattress.

I smile softly as I watch her and send up a quick thank-you to whatever higher power put this woman in my path. *She loves me*, I think, and my smile grows even wider.

Trying to focus, I turn back to Scarlett's laptop. But after another page, I feel her hand on my thigh, chilled even through the fabric of my sweatpants.

She sighs contentedly in her sleep, and her breathing slows even further. Her hand anchors herself to me like she'd been adrift in her dreams and needed something to hold on to.

No, like she needed to hold on to *me*. I'm what she's chosen to anchor herself to. Not her job or her words or any of the other options she has to ground herself. Me.

Love might not be a strong enough word to describe how I feel about her, but I resolve, right then and there, to be strong enough for her so she can anchor herself to me forever.

Chapter 23

Scarlett

WHAT DOES ONE wear to a not-date? Because, regardless of what Ryan had been clearly brooding over for the entirety of our meeting with Anastasios, this is absolutely not a date. And, I tell myself, even though Charles is objectively good looking, he's not my type.

It's just a casual dinner between two writers, talking about writerly things.

But I still don't know what to wear.

There's no way I can call Trina and ask her, either, because I won't get past the first sentence without her needling me about dating, and this is *not a date*. I'll leave the conversation late to dinner without any answers at all.

God, I miss my friends.

I had tried to call my best friend, Mandy, shortly after everything happened. Since we had gone to the same grad program, we were the closest of the four women in our first apartment in Chicago. She's a writer, too, so I had kind of expected that she'd understand the pressure I had been under. The problem at the time was that it took her a while to get a publishing deal. She had just signed with a small press when I walked away from JMP, and on top of thinking it toxic to be associated with me, she was so jealous of the money I had been offered. She couldn't believe I had left that offer on the table. She called me names, shouted, and told me never to contact her again.

Ultimately, that interaction with her led me to block Ryan's number. She preyed on my vulnerabilities and burnout. She convinced me that I had cursed myself when it came to publishing and, in such a small industry, it was best for him that I disappear.

I shake myself out of the memory as I stand in front of the full-length mirror in my closet. I've settled on dark jeans, a green blouse, and black flats. Simple, understated, casual but not *too* casual. Good enough.

The restaurant is within walking distance of my apartment, and it's a nice evening. I opt to walk the ten minutes, leaving with plenty of time to stroll. I arrive early, but to my surprise, Charles is already sitting at the bar when I walk in. His golden hair is cast in a yellow glow from the overhead lighting, and he kind of blends well with the deep reds and browns of the restaurant. He's tapping furiously on his phone with an almost-full glass of beer at his elbow, and he doesn't notice me approach.

"Is this seat taken?" I flash a cheesy smile as I stand behind the empty seat next to him.

He looks up, sighing heavily and his hand clenching on his phone, but his expression clears when he sees me. Well, this is off to a great start.

"S.J.!" he exclaims, standing to embrace me in a bear hug. He crushes me so hard against his pecs that I can barely breathe. My face is smooshed against the same navy sweater from earlier today, and I suddenly feel silly for worrying about my own outfit.

I awkwardly pat his very broad back until he lets me go and I can breathe again. "Good to see you again, Charles." I have to wonder how he greets really good friends if that's how he says hello to someone he met hours ago. But instead of asking that, I dip my chin to the drink on the bar. "Am I late?"

"What? Oh, no. I was in the area, so I figured I'd just wait for you at the bar. Ended up having a conversation with my agent about my little meeting today. She doesn't seem to think it's a good move to switch to a smaller imprint, but I think the writing is on the wall, know what I'm saying? Anyway, you know how agents are. What're you drinking?"

Maybe I'm out of practice when it comes to having an actual conversation, but he spews out so much information all at once, I'm not exactly sure where to start. He must take the pause as me being starstruck again, because he claps me on the back good-naturedly. It causes me to cough, but he doesn't seem to notice.

"Wine? You look like a wine gal. Maybe sangria? They have a great sangria here," he blabbers as he pulls out the barstool for me to sit down.

"Oh, I don't really drink—"

"Red or white?"

"Neither," I say with more conviction this time. My meds don't mix well with alcohol, though I'm starting to wish I could drink just to make this guy more tolerable. The idea that *anyone* would consider this a date is already laughable. I've only been here a few minutes, and I can't get a word in.

"You're not one of those sober girls, are you?" He pulls a face. "Is it a health thing, or did you get into some trouble with the law? I know a few great lawyers if you need."

"I'll bet you do," I mutter under my breath. Fuck, this is going to be a long evening. Clearing my throat, I speak louder this time. "I just...don't drink. It's not that deep."

Charles nods pensively, studying me as if he's trying to tell if I'm lying or not. I'm not ashamed of taking medication to help with my depressive episodes, but I have a sudden feeling that the less he knows about me, the better. I'm happy to let him talk as if he's important for an hour or so and then be on my merry way.

The bartender gives me a small reprieve by coming to take my drink order, which is just a soda.

"Are you all eating here, or are you waiting for a table?" the bartender asks, pausing with his fingers over some menus that are piled off to the side.

"I figured we could eat here, if that's okay with you." Charles raises his eyebrows at me in question.

I'm so surprised he asked my opinion that I nod in agreement. It is already abundantly clear that this whole dinner was a mistake anyway. Waiting for a table would only draw it out. The bartender places menus in front of us, but I have a feeling I won't be needing mine. Sure enough, Charles orders some grilled octopus, empanadas, and curried chicken for both of us before checking if I have any dietary restrictions.

"Nope." I force a close-lipped smile. "All good here."

"Great. Those will do nicely for us, I think." He plucks my menu out of my hands and passes them both back to the bartender.

Charles takes a large swig of his beer, then plunks it down on the bar top with a satisfied *ahh*. "So, S.J. Your first book, huh?"

"Um..." I know what I'm supposed to say, especially since he hasn't recognized me. Not to mention Anastasios's warning from earlier is still ringing in my ears.

"You want to know how I got not one but two imprints trying to win me away from my current one?"

Not really, but I feign interest. "Two?"

He nods as if he is a wise sage and I am his lowly pupil. I'm surprised he doesn't ask me to take notes. "Anastasios and..." He pauses for what I'm assuming is some kind of dramatic effect. "JMP. You know them?"

My eyebrows shoot up at that, because that's not how publishing works. Imprints don't compete against their own. Is that why he didn't want me to tell anyone I saw him at Anastasios? Because he's secretly trying to pit them against each other? But luckily, I'm saved from trying to come up with an answer because Charles leans toward me suddenly. He's so close I can smell the beer on his breath. "Let me give you a little tip." He smiles, but it doesn't quite reach his eyes. "Don't trust anyone in this industry. They're all out to make money off you. They might say they're interested in your book or that they want what's best for the manuscript, but they don't. Not really. Everyone's always watching the bottom line—how much and what percentage and how many sales to get what in royalties."

He pauses to take another drink, so it seems like a good time to say something. "Sounds like you've been burned before."

"Me? Nah. I'm too cautious for that." He shrugs. "But I've seen it happen time and time again. You got a good agent?"

"The best," I say quickly.

Charles nods. "Good, good. And that guy who came to get you this morning? He's your editor?"

"Ryan. Yeah."

"He's being good to you?"

I snicker to myself. If this guy only knew. "He's been great. Really goes above and beyond."

"Don't expect that to continue. They've got plans for you right now, but once your book releases and they see what you're really worth, that's when their true colors will come out, mark my words. You excited about your release?"

Well, if I hadn't been through all of this before—and sold more copies than him, I have to keep telling myself—I would be terrified now. It's not that these things are untrue, per se. I've worked with my share of money-hungry people who had dollar signs in their eyes every time they looked at me, but what a thing to say to someone he thinks is a debut author. Is he trying to scare me away from publishing altogether?

"Yeah," I reply instead of telling him what I'm really thinking. He probably wouldn't hear me anyway.

"What's it about?" He takes another swig of beer.

"It's a coming-of-age story about a young girl." I could talk about my book all day, but he's not interested. Not really. All I had to do was mention "coming-of-age" and "girl" in the same sentence, and his eyes started glazing over. Suddenly, I'm wishing I were curled up with Ryan, talking about themes and words and structure. The ache for him is almost palpable, and it catches me off guard. I take sip of my soda, then decide to change the subject. "So, tell me. How does a writer have the time to work out as much as you clearly do?"

I had been banking on a hunch that Charles's favorite subject is himself, and boy, was I right. He launches straight into a lengthy overview of his workout plan. Our food comes somewhere between an estimate of how much he thinks he'll be able to squat tomorrow and his warning to me that sitting all day will surely cause cancer, so I'd better start working out, too.

Charles serves himself some of the food, so I do the same, though I avoid the grilled octopus because they actually look like little baby octopuses, and my stomach flips. As with everything I've done so far, he doesn't seem to notice. He's also oblivious to the fact that I'm just pushing food around my plate and not really eating.

I'm not even sure what he's talking about anymore because I'm not paying much attention. But a gentle hand between my shoulder blades wakes me up a bit. My spine straightens at the touch as a familiar voice croons into my ear.

"Imagine seeing you here," Ryan says, his voice smooth and soft—the exact opposite of the barking Charles has been doing. I turn my head to the left, and sure enough, he's standing there with his hand still resting almost possessively on my back.

"Ryan?" My voice is breathy. It's almost embarrassing how relieved I am. But the relief is short-lived because what the fuck is he doing here? Did he find out where we were going and when and follow us?

"I'm picking up takeout," he explains, as if reading my mind. "Charles mentioned tapas earlier, and I had a taste for it."

"This place is great," Charles says approvingly. "Good choice."

Ryan nods but doesn't really pay any attention to him. By the way his hand is still on my back and his eyes track my movements as I take another drink, it's clear that he's here to see me. I'm not seething about it, but I am annoyed. What is his purpose? Is he worried I'll lose my cool? Start crying? Engage in some risk-taking, after-dinner behavior?

And so what if I do? I'm not his anymore. Maybe Trina is right. Maybe it'd be good for me.

The bartender comes over, and Ryan gives him his name. He goes back to the kitchen to check on the order. Ryan's hand is still lying on my back, warming me. And as much as I want to lean into his touch—close my eyes and relish in it—that little voice at the back of my head won't let me forget he's full of shit. He has no right to crash this dinner, no matter how jealous he is.

I glare up at him. "You don't live near here."

He shrugs as if this doesn't matter. "I was passing through. Heard this place is pretty good."

"You seem to find yourself 'passing through' the South Loop a lot these days," I grumble. Ryan chuckles lightly.

The bartender returns with several to-go containers in a plastic bag. He hands the bag over the bar to Ryan, who takes it. I shiver at the cool air that meets my back at the loss of his hand.

Ryan looks back and forth between Charles—who has gone weirdly silent—and me. Apparently satisfied, he jams the hand not holding his food into his pocket. "Well, I'd better get going. Have a nice night, Sc—S.J. Charles." He nods at each of us, then turns on his heel and leaves.

Charles lets out a low whistle and shakes his head in dismay. "He's kind of a weird guy, huh? If you don't like working with him, you can always ask—"

"I like working with him a lot, actually." I cut him off. That might have been strange as hell, but the only person I'm not enjoying spending time with right now is Charles. I track Ryan's movements back through the restaurant and out the front door. "Can you...Wait here. I'll be right back."

Despite Charles's stuttering protests, I slide off the barstool and follow Ryan as quickly as I can. When I push open the heavy front door, I scan left and right, but I don't see him right away. It isn't until I hear a car door slamming across the street that I see his head pop up above the car. He looks around, waiting for traffic to subside before he can get into the driver's side.

"Ryan," I call over the noise of the cars passing between us.

His head whips toward me. It's almost dark out, but I could swear I see the ghost of a triumphant smile play on his lips.

That asshole. I knew it. He came here on purpose to break up my not-date.

"Hang on," he shouts. When there's a break in the traffic, he jogs back across the street. And then he's standing there, in front of me, hands yet again jammed into the pockets of his chinos and his shoulders creeping up against the slight chill in the spring air.

"What's up?" he asks, a little breathless from his jog across the street.

"'What's up?'" I spit back at him. "'What's up?' Are you serious? That's what you're going to lead with?"

His shoulders shrug the rest of the way toward his ears and come down again slightly. "Did you need something?"

"Did *you* need something?" I'm a writer. Words are my thing, so I'm not exactly sure why I keep repeating his incredulously. He's gotten me all flustered, and I don't like it.

Ryan laughs, but there's no humor in it. "Is there something wrong with wanting tapas?"

"From a restaurant that's a twenty-minute drive on a good day from your condo? On the night you knew Charles was taking me out for that exact meal in this exact neighborhood? Yes, I'd say there's something wrong with that."

"I'm sorry you feel that way," he deflects. "I will try to avoid wanting similar foods to your dates in the future." The last part comes out more bitter than anything he's said thus far, which is all the confirmation I need that he's lying about his sudden craving for finger foods.

"Dammit, Ryan. For the last fucking time, it wasn't a date!" I'm shouting now, and people are turning their heads to look at me as they pass on the sidewalk. I don't even care. I hope they get a good show.

"I'm sure that's not what he thought." Ryan's voice remains cool and collected. I hate him even more for his ability to stay perfectly calm.

I fling my arm toward the door of the restaurant. "If that man in there thought he was on a date...well then, I guess I know why he's single. The only person he was on a date with was himself."

I wait for Ryan's face to break into a self-satisfied smile, but it doesn't. Instead, he pins me to the spot with his dark eyes. They're burning with intensity behind his glasses, and he takes a step toward me as if he can't help it. My entire body heats as his gaze settles on mine.

"Why did you go out with him?" he asks, almost in a whisper.

"Because he asked," I reply honestly. "Because I'm lonely," I say a little louder, gaining momentum. "Because I cracked open one tiny little door to dip my toes into the publishing world again, and ever since, it's been a freefall with one thing after another after another that reminds me exactly how good I had it. Because instead of waiting for the other shoe to drop again, I want to take back a little bit of the life I had before, but better this time. I might not deserve it, Ryan, but that doesn't make me want it any less."

He pulls his hands out of his pockets, but he remains silent. His eyes never leave mine. The sidewalk is empty now, and I shift from one foot to another. A street light blinks on above us, casting a soft glow over the scene. The ring on his right hand shines.

"You deserve it." It's so quiet, I almost miss it.

"I don't. I walked away from the best thing I ever had and disappeared for five years. You don't just get a second chance after something like that."

His dark brows furrow together, and he shakes his head in confusion. "We signed you. You literally got a second chance. You're living it, Scarlett, and it's going to be great."

I laugh darkly. "I wasn't talking about the book."

Slowly—painfully slowly—Ryan's eyes widen. His jaw goes slack, and he leans a fraction of an inch toward me, then back again, like he's trying to talk himself out of something.

Me. He's trying to talk himself out of me. The realization hurts more than anything I've experienced in the last month. More than if he shoved the pages of my book back into my hands and told me it was shit. This is why it's safer to have dinner with guys who would rather talk about their workout routines than bare their souls. Charles Hall was never going to break my heart.

My gaze falls to the sidewalk. A couple tumbles out of the

restaurant, clinging to each other. Their laughter bubbles upward to be carried away in the night air. She sighs and rests her head on his shoulder as they fall into stride with each other and make their way down the street.

"I should go back inside."

I make it one step in the direction of the door before Ryan lets out a strangled, "Scarlett."

"What?" I face him again, dejected this time. "Look, we've been here before, Ryan. No matter how safe we think it is to toe the line between what we are and what we were, I can't ignore the fact that I ultimately walked away because you're better off without—"

Before I even know what's happening, Ryan crosses the distance between us and kisses me. It's frantic, his mouth covering mine as if he could stop my thoughts along with the words. His arms envelop me, and he presses his palms into my back, drawing me closer. Our bodies snap together in that old, familiar way. Muscle memory takes over, guiding hands and lips and tongues until we're completely intertwined.

I don't resist. How could I possibly, when every hope and word and dream I've ever had has always been so wrapped up in him that I don't know where I end and he begins? I melt into him, open for him, grab the front of his shirt and desperately angle my head for more.

He breaks away from me, panting, before I've gotten nearly enough. Without thinking, I follow his retreat. I've gone without him for far too long—a woman on a diet, trying to convince myself that apples are a good substitute for chocolate, and now that I've tasted his decadence again, I doubt I'll ever get enough.

On a moan, he indulges me, meeting my lips with his again, and any concern I may have had about whether or not he has been just as starved as I have is washed away with his kiss.

A whoop sounds from a group of guys passing by us on the sidewalk. Ryan and I both breathe out a laugh. He presses his forehead to mine, and when I open my eyes to look at him, his are still closed, his face calm and happy.

"I've never been better off without you," he says quietly. "I'm going to need you to delete that thought from your storyline and never bring it back."

I hum, rubbing my forehead gently against his. "Only if you admit you came here because you were jealous."

Ryan pulls away from me to run a hand through his hair. He rubs it against the back of his neck sheepishly. "Not only did I come here looking for you, I went to two other places beforehand."

"You *what*?" I tip my head back and cackle incredulously. "Ryan Whitlock, you are unhinged."

"I have a lot of tapas in my back seat. I could use some help eating it?" His voice tips up hopefully.

I half laugh, half groan. "I'm starving, and that sounds amazing, but Charles is still waiting for me. He probably thinks he's important enough to ruin the life of the poor little debut author-girl who left him hanging."

"Tell him it's an editorial emergency," he suggests.

"There's no such thing."

"Don't underestimate me, Scarlett." Ryan's eyes darken as he drags them over my face. "When I have editorial notes, the world stops for them."

I cock an eyebrow, unimpressed. "I've dealt with enough toxic male egos for the night, thank you. I don't need yours too. I'll just...tell him I don't feel well. Hang on."

As much as it pains me to leave Ryan's side, I walk back into the restaurant to say my goodbyes. I don't get more than two steps before I can see the bar where Charles is currently dragging his finger lightly over the arm of a giggling twentysomething. He leans in and whispers something into her ear that makes her practically turn into a puddle on the spot.

I walk right back outside. It seems we're both going home with someone else, which feels appropriate.

"That was fast," Ryan says as I grab his hand and interlace our fingers.

"He was occupied. Let's go." I tug him toward his car.

It doesn't take long to get to my apartment, but the whole way there, Ryan clutches my hand like it's a lifeline. We only let go to get out of the car, then we snap right back together again for the elevator ride up to my floor.

As he clings to me and I to him, I tell myself that I do deserve this. That, sometimes, people do get second chances. And even if there is more to say, now we have time to say it.

Chapter 24

Ryan

We're silent the whole way to her apartment. Scarlett fumbles with the lock on her door. She laughs at herself, but her hands are shaking as she brings the key back to the lock. I set the bags of food on the floor and gently take the keys from her. Those big blue eyes I fell in love with so many years ago lift to watch my face through her thick eyelashes as I put the key into the lock and turn.

The door pops open, but we remain where we are. Scarlett leans back against the doorframe, her eyelids hooded and her mouth parted.

"If I kiss you again, I'm not going to stop." My voice is low and rasping. My own heartbeat whooshes in my ears.

Scarlett licks her lips, leaving a shiny coating over the pink of them. "Okay," she breathes.

"The food will get cold," I warn.

"I have an oven." She flashes a lazy smile. "I'm pretty sure it even works."

I huff and rest my forearm above her head, unable to resist leaning into her and smelling her black-tea scent. God, it has been so long since I've smelled her, tasted her. I can barely concentrate. "You make a good point."

Her eyes trail over my skin, leaving warmth in their wake. "I know," she says. "Now kiss me."

Heat. Desire. Need. I'm reduced to these three basic elements as she looks up at me expectantly. But there's something else in her gaze that I hadn't seen before. I think it's doubt. As if she's asking me to make a move again in order to give me an out if I want it.

Doesn't she know I've been dreaming of the taste of her lips and the feel of her body next to mine for five long years?

As her eyebrows crease slightly, I realize that no, she doesn't. How could she when she said herself that she thinks I've been better off without her?

Words tumble around my brain—how beautiful she is, how wonderful it has been to have her in my life again, how I've never truly stopped loving her or worrying about her. I may not have thought about her every moment of every day, but she's been a constant white noise. I could ignore it sometimes, but not all the time, and it was always playing.

But now that she's here, it's silent again, as if that part of me has been sated. As if having her near me has turned down the volume on everything but her as she leans against the door, her body beneath mine, a battle between hope and concern playing out on her face.

There are no words for how I feel about her. There never have been. I'll just have to show her.

My gaze drops to her lips, and she lets out a little relieved exhale. I capture it as my mouth meets hers. I'm greedy for it. I want every breath, every sound, every word. They're mine now, and as she arches her back so her hips meet mine, I know she'll give them freely.

The tips of my fingers touch the waistband of her jeans, and I groan softly at the smooth skin above them as my hands work her blouse up higher. Somehow, in a way that is both messy and sexy and so *us*, we make it into the apartment with the food in tow and without losing contact with each other. But as soon as the door shuts behind us, I'm on her again with more searing kisses, devouring her whimpers and moans and fumbling with the buttons on her shirt.

She takes a step back, dragging her bottom lip through her teeth. Her fingers trail a seductive line from her collarbone down the V of her neckline before she starts undoing the buttons of her shirt one by one.

"Are you sure about this?" she asks as her fingers work another button free.

"I have never been more sure about anything in my entire life," I whisper as I track her movements. The fly of my pants presses uncomfortably against my cock as more and more of her silky skin is exposed. "Are you?"

She laughs a little, and if I could swallow that sound, too, I would. I'd keep it in a bottle close to my heart.

"Yeah. It's...um...it's been a while, though." Her fingers finally free the last button, and her shirt slides to the floor, exposing a simple black bra.

I step closer to her, unable to keep my hands to myself any longer. My palms meet the skin at her waist, and I grip lightly.

"I can be gentle if that's what you want." I'd do anything for her, but when I kiss her neck and taste the salt of her skin, I know that's going to be a difficult promise to keep.

"Maybe." She tilts her head to give me better access to her neck. "Right now, I want your shirt off."

"Hmm," I hum into her skin. "Seems fair." I tug my shirt over my head and let her drink her fill of my exposed torso.

Scarlett comes back to me, running her hands up my chest and tangling her fingers in my hair. "I missed you."

I clutch her close. "You have no idea how much I missed you."

Her gaze meets mine, the haze of her desire clearing a bit. "I didn't want to leave you, Ryan. I need you to know that. So much had happened, and I thought—"

I dip my head to capture her words with another kiss. There's more to say. I'm not fool enough to think that we've resolved everything that happened in the five years between us, but I'm also not fool enough to stop kissing her when my body and mind are screaming at me to make sure she knows I'll never let her go again.

"I know, beautiful. It's okay." I soothe her between kisses. "I promise. It's okay."

Whatever we need to figure out, it can be tomorrow's problem. Or next week's problem, for all I care. If we can find our way back to each other after five years apart, there's nothing between us that can't be fixed. I'm sure of it.

Kissing a line down my neck, her fingers find my belt buckle, but they pause before it comes undone. I've closed my eyes to enjoy the sensation of having her hands on me again, but she's gone so still. When I open them, she's studying my forearm.

"That tattoo." She almost chokes on the word. "Is that..."

I raise my arm so she can see. The tips of her fingers lightly graze over the ink, following the words underneath the torn-paper design. Her lips move as she silently reads, and when she drags her eyes to meet mine again, they're lined with tears.

"Those are my words," she whispers.

"*This was one of those moments when there was a clear before and after*," I quote. The passage is inked in my memory as much as it is on my skin. "*She was never going to be the same again. Those minutes and hours in the time before seemed to stretch out of reach now. She was never going to get them back. There was only forward. Only what was ahead of her. And she had to face it.*"

Twin tears fall silently down her cheeks. "Ryan..." She trails off, shaking her head.

I kiss one tear away, then another. "There has never been another woman for me, Scarlett." I cup her face in my hands and swipe my thumbs over the wetness on her cheeks. "If I couldn't have you with me, I wanted your words."

As if a dam has finally broken, she throws her arms around my neck and kisses me passionately, our teeth clicking together with the force of it.

Maybe this is one of those moments she wrote about, where there's a clear before and after. I knew it was when she left, and now that she's back again, I can feel it the same way. There's only what's ahead of us. We can face it together.

In a moment of strength I'm not sure I'll ever be able to replicate again, I grab her ass and lift her off the ground. Her legs squeeze around my midsection, and she rolls her hips against me. The moan that falls from her lips when my hardness meets her soft center is decadent. And it's all for me.

I carry her like this to the bedroom, then with all the self-control I can muster, I lay her gently on the bed. The more primal part of me wants to toss her around and show her who she belongs to, but she asked for tenderness, so I'll try.

Her dark hair splays out on the comforter, making her look like a mermaid or a siren or some other temptress, luring men to their watery deaths. Fitting, because I would gladly follow her under. I'm practically drowning in her as it is—those gorgeous blue eyes, her lips that are swollen from my kisses, her legs still wrapped around my waist, the velvety, black-tea scent of her—and I don't want to come up for air.

I lean close for a kiss, but she stops me, taking the corners of my glasses between her fingers. "You want to take these off?"

I shake my head, swallowing hard. "I've spent five years without being able to see your body. I'm leaving them on."

She drags her bottom lip through her teeth, suddenly shy. Her blue eyes skim over my face, then my shoulders. Her cheeks grow rosy, and I kiss them lightly. I can't help myself.

"What is it, beautiful?" I run my thumb over her lips where her teeth just were.

Her eyelids flutter closed. "I'm nervous," she whispers, as if saying it any louder will make it somehow more true. "Sometimes..." She trails off and swallows hard, still not looking at me. "I want this. I don't even think I let myself admit how much I wanted it until now. But my meds...sometimes they make it hard to...you know." A little, embarrassed laugh escapes her.

"Scarlett," I say, my voice low and rumbling. "Look at me."

She does, but her eyebrows pinch together with concern as she undoes the button on my pants. "I can just—"

Grabbing her chin with my thumb and forefinger, I draw her eyes back to mine. "Scarlett," I repeat, more forceful this time. Those blue eyes settle on me, and now that I have her full attention, I say more gently, "Is it difficult for you every time?"

"Um..." Her gaze skates away from me again, but I grip her chin harder to remind her to keep it trained on me.

"When I said I wanted to see you, I didn't just mean your body. I want to see your brain, too. All of it. The good, the bad, and the in-between. So, tell me, beautiful. Is there anything that works?"

Scarlett's eyebrows raise and her eyes widen, then she nods.

"Show me, then," I command, letting go of her chin.

She blinks rapidly. "You want me to..."

"I want to watch," I say, leaning back on my heels. "I want to learn so I can memorize the way you touch yourself, so I can touch you the way you like."

There's a slight pause—just a small one—before a look of determination crosses her gorgeous features. "Okay," she agrees as she undoes the zipper of her jeans and slides them off. Next, her panties hit the ground. Reaching around her back, she makes quick work of the hook on her bra, and that joins the rest of her clothes.

And then, she reclines back onto the pillows at the head of her bed, her skin glowing in the dull light of the room. Her dark nipples are peaked, and she bites her lip as she takes one between her fingers and rolls it. The fingers of her other hand glide between her legs, dipping inside of her. They come out glistening, and she uses the longest one to rub against her clit. Her eyes lock on mine, and she flashes me a coy smile.

Returning her grin, I palm my erection through my pants. The pressure isn't nearly enough for any relief, but I can't help it. I have to do something. "You like it when I watch you, don't you?"

"Looks like you like it just as much," she quips before pinching her nipple harder. She moans deliciously as she inserts one finger, then another inside of herself again. Her chest heaves as she works, increasing her pace. Little beads of sweat glistening above her breasts.

"Fuck, Scarlett," I grind out, rubbing myself uselessly as I watch her. "You are so gorgeous like this, working yourself into a needy mess for me."

Her eyes roll back in my direction, but they're hooded now. "I am a mess." She removes her fingers from inside herself to circle her clit again.

"A beautiful mess," I say on a moan.

She licks her lips and drags her gaze all over me, little bumps rising in its wake. "It might help if I could see you. If you..." As if she's lost the ability to talk, she trails off and tips her head back, her breaths coming even faster now. "Clothes off," she demands.

I practically leap off the bed and shimmy out of my pants and boxers. My cock springs free, and I groan as I circle it with my palm, pumping in time with the work of her fingers.

"Can I taste you?" she whimpers. "Please?"

I grow impossibly harder at the thought of her tongue on me, but I shake my head. "I'm supposed to be watching you and learning."

Raising an eyebrow in challenge, she smiles, then gasps as she pinches her peaked nipple again. "You can still watch."

How could I ever say no to this woman? I don't want to, that's for sure, so I step closer to the bed as she turns her head toward me.

"Open," I tell her, and she does. Gripping the base, I feed her the tip. Her hot, wet tongue works over me, and my knees almost give way.

"Fuck." I breathe out. "Is this what you like? Your mouth around me while you fuck your fingers?"

She nods, moaning around me. Her hips start to move, writhing erratically as her fingers go deeper. The hand that was playing with her breasts snakes down to circle her clit now, and it doesn't take long before her little sounds of pleasure grow louder. I step back, and she releases me with a pop as her skin flushes a stunning pink and her body shakes with the force of her orgasm.

I missed this—watching her come apart for me.

"Do you want to come on me?" she asks as she comes down

from her high, those blue eyes lazily making their way up to meet mine again.

"No," I say. "I'd rather be inside you, Scarlett."

She bites her lip and nods, a fire behind her blue eyes. "Do you have a condom?"

I lean over to take my wallet out of my back pocket. Sending a little gratitude up that I took the lesson about always having a condom just in case, I pull it out and toss it onto the bed. It lands next to her head, and the doubt vanishes as she lets out a little giggle.

The foil wrapping of the condom crinkles as I tear it open and cast it aside. Scarlett takes it and scrambles to her knees so she can roll it over me. Unable to keep my hands off of her while she strokes me sensually, I tangle my fingers into her hair and pull.

"Oh god," she moans, her hand working me between us.

"See? I'm a fast learner." I cup one of her breasts, gently at first, then pinch just like she did. "You like this."

"I do. I need—" She gasps as I pull her hair again. "I need to feel things everywhere."

Cupping my hand between her legs, I slide a finger inside her wet heat. "Like here?"

"Mm-hmm." Her eyes close as she rests her head on my shoulder.

"Here?" I drag my finger closer to me until it touches her clit. Still sensitive, she cries out.

Teasing her with small, little circles, I kiss down her jaw and over her breasts. When I pull her nipple into my mouth, she makes a sound that could only be described as pure desire.

"I'm yours," she promises. "I always have been."

You always will be, I want to remind her, but I stop myself before I say it aloud.

She lies back on the bed again, and I hover over her. We both take a moment to drink in the sight of each other, naked with our desire visibly written on our bodies. Mine, an aching and pulsing hardness. Hers, a slick wetness that coats me as I drag my cock through her heat. Her hand skates up and over my chest. It lands on top of my still-pounding heart.

I'm going to combust if I'm not inside her for one second longer. I rest my forearm next to her head, my hand nestled in the silky strands of her hair, as I guide myself to her entrance. In one desperate thrust, I'm inside her. She lets out a sound that's somewhere between a whimper and a sigh of relief.

I stop, trying to read her expression. "Are you okay, beautiful?" I ask, stroking her hair and kissing her jaw.

"Yes." She nods emphatically. "Yes. I forgot, is all. It's you."

"It's me," I reassure her as I press inside another inch. "This okay?"

"Mm-hmm." Her blue eyes meet mine, clear desire burning in them. "More." Her legs fall open even further, giving me the access I need. Unable to resist, I shift again so I'm fully seated inside her. The moan that falls from my lips is positively indecent.

Leaning back, I shift so I'm sitting on my knees. I cup under Scarlett's legs and bring her closer to me. She arches her back, giving me a perfect view of her breasts.

"Open your legs wider, beautiful," I coax her. "That's it. Perfect."

I touch her where we're joined, coating my finger in her wetness, then use that finger to circle her exactly the way she did.

"Yes. Oh my god, yes," she says as she rocks her hips back and forth.

"You're taking me so well, Scarlett." I tell her as I thrust inside her. "You are so beautiful like this." Another thrust. "So perfect." Another. With each movement, she writhes beneath me, and her walls start to clench around my cock.

"I need more," she says. "Harder."

Before she knows what's happening, I pull out, stand at the edge of the bed, and grab her ankles to drag her toward me. In one movement, I'm back inside her, deeper this time, using the added leverage to go harder like she asked.

"You can give me one more, Scarlett," I encourage her as I put more pressure on her clit. "I know you can."

"Mm-hmm," she moans again, biting her lip. "Almost."

"Come apart for me," I demand as I pump myself in and out of her. After a few more thrusts, she does, her powerful orgasm pulling me right over the edge with her.

We hold each other, sweaty and intertwined, until our breathing returns to normal. I pull out of her and go to dispose of the condom. When I get back to the bedroom, her lips stretch into a brilliant smile.

"Should we see if my oven works?" she teases. "I'm starving."

"We worked up quite an appetite," I agree.

She giggles as she scrambles off the bed to put on her underwear and an oversized shirt. She rummages around in a drawer and tosses me a rumpled T-shirt. When I unroll it, I realize it's one of mine.

"You kept this?" I ask, my voice strangled with sudden emotion.

Scarlett bites her lip. "You got a tattoo. I kept a shirt." She shrugs, but I can tell from the jerkiness of the movement that her emotion matches mine underneath her words.

"Mine's more permanent, I guess." I mimic her lighthearted tone as best I can.

Laughing softly, she nods. "You win."

She passes by me and into the kitchen to rummage through cabinets for baking sheets and plates. We warm the food and spread out a blanket on the ground, enjoying a tapas picnic in her living room in our underwear.

In between kisses and shared bites of food, I can't help but think she's right. I've been able to work on a book that has woken me all the way up, and Scarlett is back in my life in the way I've always wanted her to be.

I have won.

FOR TWO PEOPLE for whom words are our lives, we don't share many over the next few days. Instead, we spend our time exploring each other's bodies, savoring all the ways we still fit together.

During the day, Ryan goes to work. Every morning, he tells me he wishes he could stay with me, but he wouldn't get anything done. There are a few projects in addition to mine that need his attention, and he's been distracted.

When he's gone, I write. And while I still have trouble letting go of the work each night, Ryan interrupts, and the pull of his touch is enough to make me close the computer and focus on other things like eating, bathing, laughing, making love.

There's a voice in the back of my mind that says Ryan used to be enough to keep me grounded before, too, and look how that went. But it's still small enough that I can generally ignore it. Besides, last time it wasn't the writing that did me in. It was all the extras—publicity tours, endless book signings, JMP's constant need for more and more and more. And then the ultimate knowledge that my life could never look the way I truly wanted it to—slower moments, quiet mornings, maybe even a family...

That's not going to happen this time. Trina made sure of it.

Different book. Different Scarlett. Different outcome.

Ryan has been very careful not to ask me about my breakdown. There have been a few times when he's skirted around the issue but stopped himself short of asking. For some reason, he seems reluctant to talk about it. I'm not entirely sure if it's because he's worried that asking will remind me why I left in the first place or if it's because he truly doesn't want to know. There are so many things I want to tell him, but I decide to let him take the lead. If he keeps changing the subject before asking, he has his reasons. I'll respect those boundaries. Anything he wants to know, I'll disclose. But for now, at least, I want to give us a chance to look forward instead of back. It's what he seems to need from me, and I want to make him happy.

One night as we're lying face-to-face in his bed, sated but still unable to take our hands off each other, Ryan skates his fingers lightly over the curve of my hip. He's taken to touching me in small ways like this, ways that are full of both tenderness and awe, as if he can't believe I'm here with him.

"Five years." He says it like a prayer, like he's lifting his gratitude that we came back to each other up into the universe. It has been such a long time and also no time at all.

"Five years," I whisper back, hoping that if I add my prayer to his, it'll mean something more.

"What did you do all that time?"

This is the first time either of us have broached the subject. It feels like a carefully designed question, dipping his toes into the waters of the past, and I imagine he's working backward toward the day I left. Which is good. It gives me a chance to think carefully about how I want to tell that story when the time comes.

"This and that," I hedge.

He pinches me, and I giggle. Smoothing over the spot with his thumb, he smiles softly. "Were you alone that whole time?"

"Are you asking me if I slept with anyone else? Because if we're sharing that kind of history, you'd better be ready to fess up yourself."

"No," he says quietly, unwilling to play into my teasing. His tone quickly sobers my mood. His gaze drops to my lips, then back to meet mine. "I called everyone when you wouldn't answer me. Trina, Mandy, Ava, Katherine...anyone who would have had any contact with you. None of them knew where you were. I went to your condo more times than I'd like to admit that first year. No one had heard a word from you. When I saw your condo was for sale, I finally gave up."

"But you never stopped worrying," I finish for him.

"No. I never stopped."

He's not wearing his glasses, and his face looks somehow younger and more vulnerable without them. Ryan has always been expressive, but he's even more so now, without those dark frames to shield him. And the look on his face could break my heart.

"I'm so sorry," I say on a shaky breath.

Ryan runs his hand soothingly over my side. "No, beautiful. None of that. That wasn't what I meant. Of course I worried, but eventually, I lived my life. I'm just asking if you were able to live yours too. I wanted that for you."

"Well..." I chew on my lip, glancing at the wall over his shoulder. "Yes and no. At first, I left town. That's why I was never at the apartment. I thought traveling would be a good idea, but I guess I was actually running away." I take a deep breath and laugh humorlessly. "Shockingly, all my problems followed me wherever I went, and then some, because people would recognize me. I got very good at slipping out of places before anyone could talk to me. I can't tell you how many times I stopped for a coffee or something and someone said, 'You look like that writer. You know the one?'"

Ryan chuckles, and it gives me permission to smile, too, though mine is sadder than his.

"So then, I figured I'd come back, but I couldn't go to the condo. Too many memories." I finally look at him, then, wincing. "I gave up my old place, hired people to put a lot of stuff in storage, and moved into the place I'm in now."

"What about your friends?" He almost tiptoes up to the subject, as if he's afraid of what he might find.

I sigh, looking upward toward the ceiling and rolling onto my back. Ryan's hand doesn't lose contact with me as he rests his palm on my stomach. It makes me inexplicably uncomfortable to have his hand there, but its absence would be worse, so I let it go.

"Mandy had just signed her deal, as you know. She was...not happy with me." I swallow hard. That's all I can say about that; the rest is still too painful. "Ava and Katherine sided with her. My parents also couldn't believe I left that money on the table, and even before that, they didn't think writing was a stable career choice, as you know. I couldn't deal with their disdain...so I didn't. And everyone at JMP was only my friend because I had a deal there. Trina stuck by me. God knows why. I think it's because my royalty checks kept coming, so she was still getting paid."

Ryan moves his hand to cup my cheek and trails his thumb lightly over it. "That's not why."

I shrug as best I can with my body pressed into the mattress, staring up at the ceiling. "That might be why. But it doesn't really matter. Once I realized I didn't have anyone left, the full weight of what I had done sank in. I was probably depressed before, but the constant movement kept me going. A body in motion and all that..."

"But when you stopped, you really started struggling," he guesses.

"Pretty much. So then there was therapy, medication, a lot of trial and error. And then research. Plotting. Outlining. Writing. And now."

He studies me for a moment with those brown eyes. His eyesight is terrible without his glasses, but I'm close enough for him to see me clearly. I roll back to my side so we're almost nose-to-nose.

"I won't lie. That makes me feel slightly better."

I huff a laugh. "Why? Because I didn't mention sex with anyone else in my sad story?"

He chuckles. "No. Though now that you mention it..."

Scoffing, I smack him lightly on the arm which only makes him laugh harder. His laughter takes a little of the heaviness off my heart.

"I wasn't exactly celibate these five years, though no one ever compared to you," he says.

That hurts, but it's not a surprise. Ryan is a catch. "I wouldn't expect you to have been."

"But what I meant was I spent a long time wondering if I had missed something huge. Something I could have fixed. If I didn't take good enough care of you..." His emotion cuts him off.

It's my turn to hold his face in my hands. "Please believe me when I say there was absolutely nothing you could have done. All of this was so far out of our control. That was part of the problem. I didn't have a handle on anything." I almost continue on to the end of the story, the part I've tucked away and hidden from for years, but he's gone introspective now.

"I could have pushed them for less press or longer deadlines instead of more money. I was young and stupid—"

"We both were. Please, Ryan. I need you to understand that I don't blame you for anything that happened to me. I never did. It took a lot of work before I was able to stop blaming myself, and I don't want you to carry that burden either."

He watches me for a long time, and I try to convey as much genuineness as I can in my expression. Eventually, he closes the distance between us and kisses me gently.

"Okay," he says into my lips. "Thank you for telling me."

I kiss him back, letting my body once again show him exactly how grateful I am that we're here, together.

"I REALLY THOUGHT I was doing better than this."

I'm sitting on Dianne's couch, picking at loose threads on a throw pillow in my lap again. I'm surprised this thing doesn't have holes in it by now. Or maybe she replaces it every once in a while, like a parent swapping out a dead goldfish when their kid isn't looking.

"What do you mean?" she asks.

Ugh. She's going to make me figure this out on my own. I

hate it when she does that.

"Well, it took a while, but now I'm able to talk about this so easily with you. I thought that was it. Once I could talk it out, I'd be better." As soon as I say that aloud, I realize how stupid it sounds.

Luckily, Dianne doesn't laugh at me. Instead, she tilts her head and indulges me with a smile. "Is that really what you thought?"

"Not anymore," I grumble, face tilted down to the pillow.

She does chuckle at that, but it's motherly, not derisive. "You should be incredibly proud of yourself, Scarlett. You showed up here—"

"I was dragged here by my agent."

"Trina doesn't have the muscle to carry you. You walked through that door on your own two feet, and you've kept showing up and working hard to get to a place you feel good about. I mean, look at you. You're not only writing again, but you're publishing too. Two years ago, you didn't even want to consider that as a possibility."

"Ryan had to come over and remind me to eat. And bathe," I admit to the pillow.

"Progress isn't linear."

"It should be for me," I insist stubbornly.

Dianne's nostrils flare as she frowns at me. "I know you're deflecting, but I also know you hold yourself to an impossibly high standard. We've talked about that when it comes to your writing. It applies here, too. And look, you did eat when Ryan reminded you. That's improvement. And you bathed, I'm guessing, because you don't stink more than usual."

I raise my gaze to glare at her, and she winks. I roll my eyes. Somehow, I always end up feeling like a petulant teenager when I'm here. "So why can't I talk to Ryan about some of the things that happened? I feel like I clam up, or we end up taking about something else." Or making out, but that's probably too much information. I'm sure she's figured it out anyway.

"Has he asked?"

I make a noncommittal noise. "He never seems to want to know what happened before. Only after."

Dianne tips her head back and forth, considering. "That could be why. You're responding to him. Though eventually, you're going to need to be strong enough to bring it up on your own, if it's something you feel he should know."

"He deserves the full story," I say with more conviction than I feel.

She nods as if this were her assessment too. "Sometimes, when we're dealing with something alone, we do a lot of work, and we feel really great about it. But when we try to see it through someone else's eyes, it can be like holding up a mirror when you're under fluorescent lights. It shows all the imperfections."

"That is an oddly specific metaphor."

She shrugs. "I'm not the writer here. My point is that you're starting to let people in again. That's amazing progress. There are bound to be some growing pains."

"Person," I correct her. "I've let one person in."

"And your circle has doubled," she points out.

I'd be offended if it weren't true. Since it is, all I can do is nod.

"Be gentle with yourself, Scarlett. Everything will happen in time. And when that time comes, you need to remember that you're strong enough to work through it."

The only problem is that I'm not only concerned for myself. Now that I have Ryan again, I'm worried about him too. And us.

"WHAT'S GOING ON with you?" Casey suddenly appears at my office door. Or maybe he's been standing there for a while. Honestly, I have no idea. I've been so consumed by Scarlett's words on my screen that I've lost track of the outside world.

I blink a few times and push my glasses up on my forehead to rub my dry, screen-tired eyes.

"What do you mean?" I hedge, though I have a good idea what he's asking me about.

Casey takes that as permission to enter my office, and he folds himself into one of the chairs facing my desk. With a few forceful blinks, I try to make myself transition out of the fictional world Scarlett has created and back into the land of the living. If he's sitting, this is going to take a while.

"I haven't seen you that engrossed in something for a long time." He smirks as he crosses an ankle over his knee and settles in.

"It's been a long time since I've had something to be engrossed in," I fire back.

"Mm-hmm." He nods as if that was also what he was thinking but doesn't say anything else.

"Did you need something?" I ask. "Because if you didn't, I'm really swamped."

Casey uses his chin to indicate my computer screen. "What are you working on?"

I narrow my eyes at him and rest my palms on my desk. "Scarlett's manuscript. I'm almost done with this pass."

His smirk widens into a smile, and I pinch the bridge of my nose. This is starting to get really irritating.

"Say it, Casey."

"We haven't talked in a while, is all. You've been...busy." The way he says it has me bristling. "I wanted to see if you have anything new in your life."

"As a matter of fact, I do," I say. His eyebrows tick up with curiosity. "And I have you to thank," I continue.

He removes his ankle from his knee so he can lean forward and rest his forearms on his thighs. "Yeah?" Casey has always been an insufferable gossip. I'm not surprised he's interested, but it is way too easy to get him excited.

"Yeah." I eye him across the desk to draw it out a little longer. "For kicking this manuscript to me. It's really great, man."

Casey leans back in his chair so violently that I'm surprised it doesn't tip over. "Come on, Ryan. I know you're seeing Scarlett again."

"How could you possibly know that?"

That gets him flustered. His eyes widen slightly, but he recovers and clears his throat. "I have my sources."

"Who?"

"I can't disclose that."

I glare at him over the top of my glasses. "This is a publishing house, not a newspaper."

"And either way, you didn't deny it." He's changing the subject, but I can see I won't get his source out of him anyway.

Sighing, I nod silently. This must be all the confirmation he needs, because he chuckles darkly and shakes his head.

"Are you sure that's a good idea?" he asks, wincing.

I frown. "A second ago, I thought you were excited."

"I don't know how to feel about it. And it's not really my feelings that matter. You're the one who got your heart crushed so badly that it fundamentally changed who you are as a human being."

"That's a little dramatic," I grumble.

"It's not," he insists. "You've been pining for her for so long that you got her words tattooed on your arm." He rolls his lips together as if it could stop him from saying the next thing, but he takes a breath and barrels on. "If I had known that manuscript was hers, I never would have asked you to look at it. I would have told Trina she was out of her mind to come around here with Scarlett's work again."

I arch an eyebrow and laugh. "Are you feeling guilty or something?"

"Not yet, but I will if this goes south."

"What makes you think it will?"

"Aside from the fact that it's a conflict of interest to have a romantic relationship with one of your authors?" Casey twitches an eyebrow up in challenge.

"You think Martis gives a shit about that? We weren't together when she signed, and if it's that big of a deal, I'll step aside for the next book." It would have gutted me to let her work go if we weren't seeing each other, but now I suppose I could have the best of both worlds if it came to that.

Casey narrows his eyes at me. "She has kind of a fraught history with her mental health. And with you."

"She's different now," I say without thinking.

"Different enough that you had to bring her food to get her out of a tough spot? It feels like you're conveniently ignoring a lot of what she was like before she bailed on JMP."

"You've been talking to Trina," I accuse him.

He shoots me a look. "I will neither confirm nor deny that. Don't try to weasel out of this, Ryan. I'm concerned."

"Don't be," I say harshly, but I soften a bit as I chew on a corner of my mouth. "The more I hear her side of it, the more I realize that we were the ones who wronged her, not the other way around. She deserved better."

"Better than a seven-figure publishing contract?"

"It wasn't about money."

Casey shakes his head. "It's always about money."

I furrow my brow so hard that I'm squinting in disbelief. "That is fundamentally incorrect. Anastasios Press was acquired on the idea of better work-life balance after JMP took a hard look at their practices."

"It's still capitalism," he says with an air so casual, it seems forced. "We still have to sell books. If this book sells well—and I'm sure it will, especially when people find out who wrote it—they'll want more and more. The cycle continues. What are you going to do then, Ry? What if she disappears again?"

I don't want to admit it, but Casey is voicing something I've been thinking about off and on since she ghosted Charles at the restaurant a week ago. But every time I consider the possibility of her leaving again, I remind myself that things really are different now. She's more open about her feelings, and I'm there every night to make sure she shuts the computer down and recharges. Last time, I let her work herself to the bone. I was distracted by dollars and didn't see the harm in it. I won't make that mistake again. I know the signs now, and I also know what I need to do to help her.

Shaking my head, I reply, "She won't. I know what I'm doing this time."

Casey draws his eyebrows together and tilts his head. "You can't fix her."

"But I can help her. I want to help her. I want it more than anything." I pause, taking a deep breath and smiling to myself. "I'm so fucking happy. Maybe it doesn't make sense to you, but she...I think she's my soulmate. If you believe in that sort of thing, I guess. I don't know if I do, but if soulmates exist, she's mine. Nothing felt right in my life until she was back in it. Even before I kissed her again...just knowing she was here and she was okay...it settled something in me. Like a missing piece." The cliché makes me cringe, and I silently curse the English language for not having words to adequately express how it feels to hold her again.

She could walk away from me a million times. As long as she

comes back to me a million and one, I'll die a happy man.

Casey regards me as he rubs his chin with his thumb and forefinger. "You love her again."

It's a statement, not a question, but I answer anyway. "I never stopped." I've never known something to be true in my bones like I know this: I love Scarlett. I will always love her. Even if she left me high and dry again, I'd still love her. Probably forever.

Casey sighs, resigned. "I know." He smiles sadly. "I hope things turn out better this time."

"They will," I insist. They have to. For both of us.

PULLING CONTAINERS OUT of the bag, I announce each as it lands on the counter in front of me. "I got buttered noodles, mac and cheese, and pad thai."

"You sure know the way to a girl's heart," Scarlett calls from her seat in my bedroom. When she had come here the first time after we spent the night at her apartment, she squealed with delight that I had set up the desk for her again in there and ran to it, setting up to work.

I didn't tell her I never had the heart to take it down in the first place. That it has remained, unused and untouched, since the last time she sat there. I couldn't bring myself to move it. Not the place she sat when she wrote her second book or when she told me she loved me for the first time.

"Pretty sure the saying is about the way to a *man's* heart being through his stomach," I reply, shifting so I can see her from my kitchen.

"Same biology," she says distractedly, not moving her eyes away from the screen. She taps her lips rapidly with her middle and pointer fingers. Her eyes narrow, then she starts typing again.

I come up behind her and lean down so I can wrap my arms around her shoulders. "Hey, beautiful. Come eat."

Her typing doesn't stop, and I watch as the words fire

across the screen. "Almost done." Her voice is vacant, as if she's responding on autopilot. Scarlett has left the building, and in her place is a one-woman writing machine.

The urge to kiss her is strong, so I plant one on her temple. Not moving my arms from around her, I pull back enough to watch her. Those blue eyes trail along the monitor like one of those bouncy balls illuminating words on a children's sing-along video. She's not paying attention to me in the least. So, I wait.

There's a moment—one breath, that's all—when Casey's warning plays in the back of my mind. What if she dives in again and I'm not enough to pull her back out?

But her rhythmic typing becomes erratic, then stops altogether. She rolls her eyes and smiles to herself. "You're staring at me like a creep."

"A creep with food," I counter, meeting her grin with one of my own.

She lets out a sigh, but it sounds like it's more for show than out of irritation. "You said mac and cheese?" Her voice is bright. Scarlett is back in the building. There is no crisis here.

"Oh, so you were listening," I tease.

She turns her face to mine, and my lips buzz at our proximity. But she winks before I can act. "I always listen when you talk about cheese."

"Noted." I do kiss her then, because I can't stay away. She's so brilliant, so beautiful. And she's mine. I won't waste another moment not kissing her when I could be. Not again.

Scarlett moans softly, circling her arms around my neck. I angle my head to kiss her more deeply, teasing at her lips with my tongue. She gives me entry easily. Without separating myself from her, I fumble around with my hand to close her laptop.

Chuckling, she pulls away and rubs her nose against mine. "Message received."

I don't know if I'll always be enough to pull her out of her work, but my heart soars with the knowledge that I am now. Keep things manageable—I can do that.

She kisses me again quickly, then stands and makes her way to the kitchen. “Cheese first, then dessert.”

I follow her out of the bedroom, adjusting myself as I walk. “I didn’t get dessert.”

Flashing me a devious smile, she retrieves a fork from the drawer and opens a container. “Not what I meant.”

I just about tear my clothes and hers off right then and there, but I restrain myself. This woman is going to be the end of me, and now that she’s back in my life, I’m going to enjoy every delicious moment.

THE NEXT WEEK is a whirlwind of Ryan, edits, writing, publicity emails, rinse, and repeat.

The draft for my cover comes in, and I have to check the calendar to make sure it's not April first, because there's no way it's not a joke. It's just a blue bicycle on a black background with *BECOMING* in big, bold letters at the top and *S.J. FALMOUTH* in smaller, bold letters at the bottom. Before my brain can even process the email, my phone rings. It's Trina, thank god.

"I don't know whether to laugh or cry," I say by way of greeting.

"It's not good."

"'Not good' is an understatement," I correct her. "Please tell me this is concept art and not the real thing."

Trina makes a little *ehh* noise that tells me I'm not going to like what she's about to say. "They labeled this as final."

"The bike in the book isn't even blue! You cannot possibly be serious."

"Listen, this is your boyfriend's doing, not mine. He's the one who handed the info off to design."

She keeps talking, but my mind snags on the word *boyfriend*. Is he my boyfriend? Do I want him to be? We've been spending time together, but we haven't been together again that long. Or do we count the time before? Between? Never mind that it's been the best week of my life, with publishing updates and Ryan almost finished with this round of edits and him coming here or me going to his place most nights to read and talk and touch like we've both been starving without one another.

At least, it was the best week of my life until this disaster landed in my inbox.

"Hello? Earth to Scarlett?" Trina's tinny voice cuts through my thoughts.

"What? Sorry. I was distracted."

"You don't say," she deadpans. "I was just saying I'll call who I can, but you might have better luck going straight to Ryan. Unless you want me to contact him for you?"

I can tell from her tone that she's fishing for information. I haven't told her we've been spending time together again, but she knew he brought me food, so she probably has an idea.

Groaning, I rest my forehead on my palm. I do not need an existential crisis on top of a design one today.

"I'll call him," I say simply.

"Uh-huh," Trina intones.

"I don't know what that means, but I'm hanging up now." Even though I can hear her spewing off a string of words, I end the call. I'll deal with that later.

There's still a giddy feeling about seeing Ryan's name in my phone. I never deleted his contact information even though I blocked him, but I didn't go looking for it either. Honestly, I hardly even touched my phone after everything happened. There was no one calling me anyway, and every time I logged into my social media accounts, there were more and more angry messages from fans who had tickets to meet me and wanted their money back, as if I had anything to do with their ticket purchase. Once I deleted those accounts, blocked Ryan, and lost most of my friends, there wasn't much for me to look at on there, so I just...didn't. After a year or so, I noticed messages disappearing. One by one, they all vanished into technological oblivion. Not that I had been pining over old messages or anything.

Sighing, I push Ryan's name and put him on speaker so I

can wring my hands as I stare at the blue bicycle on my computer screen. He answers on the third ring.

"Hey, beautiful." There is such tenderness in those two words that I almost do an about-face on the spot. They can have whatever cover they want if it means I get to be greeted like that when I call my editor.

No. Nope. This cover is bad, and I have to deal with it. "Did you see it?"

"See what? I've been knee-deep in your gorgeous book all morning. I should be sending it back to you tomorrow at the latest."

"Well, this gorgeous book has a cover..." I trail off, hoping he can put two and two together.

"Oh no," he groans. "Hang on."

There's some clicking and then silence.

Out of nowhere, he practically growls. "I will fix this."

The sound is so out of character for him that I devolve into a fit of giggles. I'm laughing so hard that I fold in half at the waist, and my head hits the table.

"This isn't funny, Scarlett. This is awful," he says, but I can hear the edge of laughter in his voice. It's so easy, the way we fall in sync. The way he knows exactly why I'm calling without me having to say it. The way we make each other laugh.

He always could make even the most serious problems seem lighter. It occurs to me that he could maybe make sense of everything that has been circling in my head since my last therapy session. I want him to.

But...one disaster at a time.

"It's pretty bad." I wipe at the corners of my eyes where tears have started to leak out.

"Pretty bad? The bike in the story isn't even blue!"

I take a few calming breaths to stop myself from cracking up again. "I guess I should feel vindicated about fighting for the bike to stay in if they thought it important enough to put on the cover."

"Yeah, well, it's the only thing they thought to put on the cover," Ryan grumbles, which draws a snort out of me. My shoulders shake with restrained humor.

"Okay. I'll leave you to take care of it." I close out of the image on my computer so I don't have to look at it anymore as I try to get ahold of myself again. "You said you're almost done with edits?"

"Yes." His voice softens. "Scarlett, I don't have words for how wonderful this book is. You have captured something so important—so universal. I know Meri's publicity is targeted to a mostly female demographic because of the subject matter, but... damn." He sounds almost reverent.

"So I won't have much to do?" I tease.

He chuckles. "I didn't say that. There are definitely a few passages that could use some work. A few things I'd like to see added, too, just to flesh out some of your themes a bit. Now that we've kept that godforsaken bicycle, we should do even more with it."

I pause for a moment as his excitement becomes mine. I know a lot of authors get nervous about the editing process, but that has never been me. Even before Ryan was my editor, I always thought there was something magical about taking raw words that I had written just for me and polishing them, refining them, into something beautiful for the world to see. But now that Ryan is working on it, it's even more special. It's something beautiful we've made together.

"We?" I ask through a new emotion rising inside me. I can't name it, but it feels close to fear. Trepidation. Everything unsaid between us is staring me in the face, telling me it could ruin this tenuous happiness we've started building again.

He goes quiet again, as if realizing what he's said. "Sorry," he says finally. "I got carried away."

I clear my throat. Now is not the time. But soon. It has to be soon.

"No, not at all," I reassure him. "It's ours. I like that."

He goes quiet for a minute again before cursing quietly. "Listen, I have to get going. I've been putting out fires all day, and another one just landed in my inbox. Dinner tonight?"

"I'd like that."

We say our goodbyes. I sit cross-legged at my kitchen table with my laptop in front of me, staring at a blank screen for a long time. I should be writing. I want to write. But I can't concentrate.

Maybe it's having Ryan back in my life. Our banter, his kiss, the way his body feels against mine—it's all so familiar. When he calls me beautiful with such ease, it's almost as if he hasn't missed a beat. Like there aren't five years and a whole lot of heartbreak between us. And the way he talked about "we" and "us" and "our book" just now—that's familiar too. My words have always been his and his mine to the point where I've never been exactly sure who suggested what.

The familiarity is comforting. But it also wakes something else up inside me as I stare at the blinking cursor on my screen. The memories of what this all felt like five years ago when I was burnt out keep pestering me, almost like they're trying to tell me not to get too comfortable. *You were happy last time, too,* they seem to whisper. *You had everything you thought you wanted, until you realized that wasn't what you wanted at all.*

That was it, wasn't it? It wasn't that I couldn't handle the fame or the work that came along with it but that I simply didn't want it. I wanted something else. The rustling of pages, the click of a keyboard, the scratch of Ryan's pen. Not the squeals of excited readers or the voices in my head screaming that I'd never be good enough.

A quieter life. A life with Ryan.

And when I closed the book on us, I put it on the shelf and told myself I wasn't enough for that story either.

I truly did think I had dealt with this. That it was done, and the only thing I had left to do was conquer my fear of publishing again, and I'd be healed. All that therapy, unraveling the story piece by piece. It was almost like editing, the way it happened. Dianne would listen to my first draft, then she'd poke at it, unearthing layer after layer. She'd ask me questions and make me think. It helped, obviously, but I've been alone with it for so long. Like she said the other day, the true test is letting someone in.

There's no question about what I want now. I still want that quiet life with Ryan. But there's only one path to it. We can't have our second chance if he doesn't know what happened with our first.

Chapter 28
Scarlett

Five Years Ago

TIRED. So, so tired. It's the only word my overworked brain can focus on when I'm not writing or interviewing or signing. There are probably more accurate or descriptive words to express my condition—stronger words, as Ryan might demand—but I'm too tired to think of them.

Every day should feel new and exciting, but it doesn't. If I sleep at all, I wake up, write, prepare for whatever event is on my calendar, write more, talk to Ryan, then write even more. Eventually, someone from my team reminds me I need to get on a plane to fly to the next thing.

Four days. I'll be home in four days. Ryan can hold me. I can eat something that isn't in a takeout container. I can rest.

Sort of. Trina told me JMP is very interested in signing me on for more books, and I need something to show them.

I love writing. If writing were the only thing, I could probably do it forever. Maybe I'd even be able to write something that wasn't absolute shit if I weren't stretched so thin. Yet as I stare at my screen, trying to make sense of whatever I typed at three in the morning, that doesn't seem to be happening anytime soon. In a fit of desperation, I highlight the entire chapter and hover my finger over the Delete button.

My phone chirps from the nightstand in my hotel room, and

I blink rapidly. Where am I? New York? A glance outside at the gorgeous view of the Empire State Building that I haven't been able to appreciate confirms my location. *In the Time Before* was a book club pick for a huge daytime talk show—one of the ones where five women sit around a fake kitchen table and talk. I'm slated for an appearance with them today, then a late-night show in two days. Then home.

The chirping sounds again, and I realize that's my ringtone. "Saved by the bell," I tell the jumble of highlighted words on my screen as I make my way over to my phone to answer it.

Great, now I'm talking to myself.

"Hello?"

"Good morning," Trina says rather loudly.

I pull the phone away from my ear to turn the volume down. "Hi."

She cuts right to the chase. "Got any pages for me to look at today? JMP is very curious what you've got up your sleeve, and honestly, so am I."

"I did," I grumble, poking around in the cabinets in the kitchenette for some coffee. "I read through it just now, and it's garbage."

"Scarlett, we've talked about this," she admonishes. "You are a best-selling author. Your books have won awards. You are about to appear on two major television shows because your books have become pillars of contemporary literature. Your writing is not garbage."

"No pressure," I snipe, finally finding a coffee pod and tossing it into the machine.

"There is some pressure," she singsongs. "JMP wants something to look at. Send me what you've got. I'm sure Ryan and I can put some makeup on it or something."

"Terrible metaphor." Apparently, my exhaustion has reduced me to responding in two-word phrases.

"Well, fine. I won't be the one fixing it up. But send it. Please?"

The coffee machine burbles to life, dripping weak-smelling

liquid into the nondescript mug below it. "Fine," I say, but only because I'm too tired to argue.

"Great. I look forward to seeing those soon. Gotta go, but let's do dinner when you're back, okay?"

"Sure," I say before we both hang up.

No sooner has the coffee finished brewing than my phone rings again. I'm filled with relief at just seeing his name on my screen. Somehow, that makes me even more tired, as if I've been a house on the shoreline held up by twin stilts of anxiety and desperation, and the flood of relief has washed them away.

I press the phone to my ear. "Hi." Even I can hear how happy I am to talk to him.

"Hey, beautiful." His deep voice is a balm, soothing over the debris in my heart. "Three more sleeps until I can hold you."

Every day that I'm gone, he greets me with how many nights until I'm his arms again. I love it for its simplicity, for the way it anchors me in space and time. I'm here now, but soon, I'll be there.

"I'm ready to be home," I sigh as I curl myself up on the hotel bed with my mug of coffee. "Ready for some time off."

"Three months," he says, and I love him even more for memorizing my schedule. "I hope you know I'm not letting you out of my sight."

I laugh, the sound foreign to my ears. "For three months? So you're not going to work either?"

"It was hyperbole." He chuckles, then puts on what I imagine he thinks of as a professor voice. "An extreme exaggeration."

I roll my eyes good-naturedly. "I know what hyperbole is."

"I know you do. Look, I have to get going, but I wanted to wish you luck today. I can't wait to watch it."

Ryan still watches every televised interview. He reads every review and article and sends me snippets of all the good ones. He's one of the first people to like every one of my social media posts. If there were an entry for *Most Supportive Boyfriend* in the dictionary, his picture would be the definition.

He's in my corner. That's what matters. Or at least, that's

what I tell myself when things get particularly difficult to manage.

A sudden emotion takes hold of me. This perfect man has chosen my imperfect self to love, and he loves me in the most perfect way. "Thanks, Ryan," I choke out.

"I'm so proud of you, beautiful. You're going to be great. I love you."

"Love you, too," I say, still holding back tears. We hang up, and I'm left alone once again.

I finish my weak coffee as I stare blankly out at the view beyond my window. One of these days, when I have time, I'd love to actually see some of the cities I visit for press. For now, the view will have to do.

After I dump my coffee mug in the sink, I send Trina what I've been working on before I can think too much of it. But not before I delete whatever that shit was that I wrote last night.

I SHOULD LOOK at the questions, but every interview is the same. Arrive, green room, seating area offstage, smile and wave while I walk on, answer the questions, leave while they break for commercial. The questions are always the same, too. Summarize the book, talk about my process, flash an apologetic smile when I can't tell them anything about what's up next for me. That last one is in my contract not to spill the beans. Not that I have any beans to spill since it's all garbage anyway.

"Oh, wow," says Kathy or Kelly—I can't remember which—her blonde hair teased as high as it can go, and her pink lips making a little O shape. "You are just living the dream of every little girl who carries around a notebook to write about her imaginary worlds, aren't you?"

"I sure am." If every little girl's dream is to live in a constant state of stress and exhaustion.

"And you have a looker of a boyfriend, too," says Janice or Janie from the other side of the kitchen table set. Where is this coming from? God, I should have looked at the show notes more carefully before leaving the hotel this morning.

Taylor chimes in. "She's got it all." I know her name for sure. I think.

I flash a tight smile and nod, forcing myself not to look off-camera to the director. Where the fuck is this going?

"We found a picture of you two on your social media. Can we show it?" Kathy-or-Kelly asks someone with a headset. "Oh, there it is."

The studio audience coos as a picture from six months ago flashes on a screen behind us. It's a sunny day. My hair is in a thick ponytail, and my sunglasses are on top of my head. I'm squinting up at Ryan who has his arm around my shoulders. He's looking down at me with absolute adoration all over his face. He looks so happy. And so do I—happy and healthy. I added the tank top I'm wearing in that picture to the donation pile before I left for New York because it started to hang off me.

Because the picture is behind me, I have to twist uncomfortably to see it, and I'm glad I'm not facing a camera when I do because my smile falters. Was this in the show notes? I feel like I'd remember this.

"Ohh, you're so cute," Janice-or-Janie croons. Fuck, her name is Jackie. "He looks about ready to propose here. Don't you think?" The other women hum and nod in affirmation.

"Thanks." I fix my smile back on my face and turn around so I don't have to see that picture anymore. It's a nonanswer, but I'm frozen, completely unsure of how to proceed. Of course I see myself married to Ryan, expanding our family, reading and writing and loving each other forever. If only I could find the time to start that chapter of our lives.

"Is it true he's your editor? How romantic," Taylor swoons.

"Uh, no. Sorry." Why am I apologizing? I blink a few times, giving myself a moment to recover. "He works with my publisher but not officially on my books."

"I bet he works on them unofficially." Jackie elbows me

playfully.

Is that some kind of innuendo? "He reads every word." I grin harder, hoping this segment is almost over. Talking about my personal life is almost never allowed, so I'm not sure how this slipped past everyone whose job it is to approve interview questions.

"So lucky," Kathy-or-Kelly says. It's unclear if she's referring to me or Ryan.

"And with that, it's time for a commercial break. We'll be right back." Taylor smiles into the camera. We all pause for a moment until we get the all-clear. They usher me off-camera, remove my mic, and I'm free to go.

Three more sleeps. Then three months off. I can do this.

After that interview, I task Trina with making sure I won't be ambushed with any more personal questions. She assures me I won't. Ryan calls, and he laughs a bit about the whole thing, but I can tell he's uncomfortable. He didn't sign up to be in the limelight, though I guess it's at least a little inevitable. Then, I write some more and end up passing out in my clothes sometime around one in the morning.

The next day, I write and write and write. I have a rare day between interviews with no obligations, and I intend to use it. JPM wants pages, and I'm determined to give them something that isn't absolute shit. I don't realize I've forgotten to eat until my phone rings yet again. A brief glance at the clock tells me it's past two in the afternoon. My stomach rumbles.

Pushing myself up from the table, I look around for my phone, but it's nowhere to be found. The ringing stops, then starts up again from the other side of the bed. Right. I put it in my purse so I wouldn't get distracted.

I flop onto the bed and grab my purse to rummage through it. Wallet, lipstick, tissues, a couple of mints, pads and tampons, a granola bar I was saving for later. Phone. There it is.

In the span of a few seconds, the phone goes silent, and I go still. My stomach drops.

Pads and tampons.

I brought them with because I was supposed to start my period almost as soon as I got to New York a week ago. Frantically, I dump all the contents of my purse onto the bed until I find my packet of birth control pills. I've never been good at remembering to take medication, but with the exception of those stupid placebo pills at the end of the month, I'm usually pretty good about taking these. Because there is absolutely no way I could handle a baby right now. Not with this schedule. Not with this pressure. No matter how much I want a kid somewhere down the line.

But sure enough, I missed a few pills this month.

It's hard to fill my lungs, almost as if the air in my hotel room is suddenly thin. *Okay, Scarlett. Don't panic*, I try to tell myself. There's nothing to do but make sure. It's probably nothing. Stress can cause you to miss a period. So can weight loss.

I shove everything into my purse and hurry out the door.

Two lines.

Two fucking lines.

My phone rings yet again as I'm standing in the bathroom, holding the positive test. Instead of the relief I usually feel when I see Ryan's name, my heart starts racing. Am I supposed to tell him I'm pregnant over the phone? How is he going to react? Is this something he wants? Is this something I want?

Yes. With him. Eventually.

Not now. I can't right now. This is going to change everything, and not in a magical way where everything will be fixed. In an awful way where I will have a baby and still need to fulfill my contracts with JMP.

With a shaky hand, I answer the phone and bring it to my

ear. "Hey, you." My own forced cheerfulness makes me wince, but Ryan doesn't seem to notice.

"Hey, beautiful."

Two words.

Two lines, absolute panic, and two words have me bolstered. It's Ryan. This is what he does for me, to me. He gives me strength to keep going without even knowing I needed it. Maybe without even knowing he's doing it.

Could we do this? With him in my corner, the impossible feels possible. And it's something I want eventually. Janice-or-Janie-or-Jackie's unapproved question made me realize that earlier. Maybe it was a sign.

I don't know what kind of mother I'd be, but I know without a doubt that Ryan would be an incredible father. I wouldn't be alone in this. I'd have him. *We* would do it.

Bolstering myself to get it over with and tell him right now, I suck in a deep breath, but he speaks before I get a chance.

"I've been trying to get ahold of you all day. I have some amazing news."

That breath leaves me like a deflating balloon. "Oh yeah? Well...I have news too."

"I want to wait to tell you in person, though."

In person. Yes. That's the best way. That will give me some time to figure out what I want to say, and I'll be able to gauge his reaction better. No one wants to have a conversation like this over the phone.

"Same."

"Okay, I have to go. I just wanted to hear your voice." He sounds rushed, and there are voices in the background. "Two more sleeps. I love you."

"I love you, too."

Two lines and two more sleeps. I close my eyes and try to breathe deep.

ANOTHER GREEN ROOM. This time, there is a bouquet of flowers waiting for me with a note.

One more sleep. I'm so proud of you. I love you.

Another fake smile. Another round of questions. I don't really hear any of them. I don't really know how I respond, either, but it must be okay because no one seems to be looking at me like anything is wrong.

If only they knew everything is wrong.

But I smile through it. Answer the questions. Go to commercial. Leave.

One more sleep, and I'm no closer to knowing what to say.

I ACTUALLY FALL asleep when I get back to the hotel, but it feels more like my brain is shutting down than anything restful. Sometime in the middle of the night, I'm jolted awake. For a moment, I'm not sure what woke me. But then, pain lances through my lower abdomen. I double over, waiting for it to pass. When it does, I stumble to the bathroom.

There's blood everywhere. Much heavier than a period, and it *hurts*. It's so painful that I sit on the toilet and cry. I clean up as much as I can before bundling up my satin pajamas and shoving them into the tiny bathroom trash can.

I call the after-hours number for my doctor's office. They explain what's happening. Words like "miscarriage" and "pain management" and "watch out for excessive bleeding" float through the phone, but they only half register. I thank them and hang up.

I want desperately to call Ryan, but what am I supposed to say? *I was pregnant with your baby. Now I'm not. And to top it off, I'm not sure which of those sentences I'm supposed to be happy about?* No, I can't do that. And besides, it's late. He's definitely sleeping.

A hot shower. That would feel good. I run the water as hot as I'm able to stand and step in. As the water splashes over my flushed skin, relief comes with it. I lean my forehead against the cold tile. I couldn't have had a baby right now.

But right on its heels is a rage hotter than the water running over me. Why shouldn't I have a baby if that's what I wanted? I'm in a stable relationship. I have plenty of money. There should be room in my life for the family I want. Yet if things keep going the way they are, I'll never have that. Where is a baby supposed to fit between writing, editing, and endless press?

The next day, I pop some painkillers, wrap myself up as best I can, and board the plane. But it's not the relief that comes home with me. It's the rage.

"I THOUGHT RYAN was going to pick me up," I tell Trina as she tries to play Tetris with my suitcase and the boxes of books she has in her trunk.

"He's at the JMP offices waiting for us." She flattens her bright red lips. With a grunt and a shove, the suitcase finally slides in. "We've got news."

"Yeah, I heard." I get in the passenger side and try to swallow my disappointment at not having Ryan here as Trina jogs around to drive. I had hoped for at least a few minutes with him before this meeting Trina had scheduled. Though maybe it's for the best. I wouldn't have been able to tell him anything in a short car ride.

She drives the twenty minutes to JMP in silence, but I can feel her excitement practically vibrating off her. This is always what she does when she has something she wants to say but can't for some reason. But somewhere over Ohio, my rage gave way to numbness, and I'm having a hard time pretending to give a shit about whatever Trina and Ryan have been evading. I'm still bleeding.

We pull into the parking garage next to the building housing JMP's offices. Trina leads the way to a conference room, and when she opens the door, there are six other people sitting around a large table. Ryan is to my left, and I almost run to him before I remember we're in his place of employment and that would be inappropriate. Next to him is Lori, the publicist I've been working with. Then the two editors who worked on both my previous books. And the CEO and publisher, Mark.

Holy shit. There are a lot of really important people in one room. They're all smiling at me, so I must not have done something too terribly wrong.

"Please, sit." Mark waves at the two empty chairs in front of us. I slink into the one next to Ryan, my heart beating in my ears. Trina sits on the other side of me, and for some reason, I feel like I'm being flanked by soldiers, ready to go to battle.

"Hey, beautiful," Ryan whispers.

I glance sidelong at him. "What is this about?"

He just smiles at me and winks.

Mark draws my attention away from Ryan by clearing his throat. "Welcome back, Scarlett. We trust you had a productive trip."

Productive. Not *nice* or *fun*. Because that's what it's about, right? Writing and selling and selling and writing. All work and no play...

"Yes," I say tersely. Trina kicks me gently under the table in what I'm assuming is an unspoken reminder to be more personable, but I'm not giving anything away until I know what the hell is going on.

Mark raps his knuckles on the table. "Good. I'm sure you're wondering why we've asked you here today, so I'll go ahead and say it. We want to sign you on for three more books in two years." He slides a small stack of papers in our direction.

Trina takes them and skims, nodding approvingly as she does. "This all looks in order." She hands them to me, beaming.

I pretend to look, but my ears are ringing, and the walls feel like they're closing in on me. Three more books. More than one per year. I can't handle the two I have out and the one I'm working on. In what world could I do this three *more* times? We knew they'd make an offer. Trina was confident about that, but only for one, and then we figured I could leverage my success for more time between releases. Three is unfathomable.

The words "one-point-five-million dollars" cut through the buzzing in my ears.

I shake my head, trying to clear it to no avail. "I'm sorry, what?"

"They're offering you seven figures for three books!" Trina exclaims quietly, though there's a terse edge to her voice as if she's willing me to get it together.

"The money is reflective of the work you've been asked to put in," Ryan says a lot more calmly.

My gaze slides to him. "The work I've been asked to put in, or will be asked to put in?"

The room goes quiet. One of my editors cracks open a bottle of water and gulps it loudly.

Lori is the first to speak. "We'd like to do another comprehensive press tour for each book, as outlined in the contract."

Once she breaks the silence, people start talking rapid-fire. It's hard to believe anyone is listening to each other with how fast they spit out questions and answers. Trina interjects a few times. No one asks what I want. They all just assume I'm on board.

And why wouldn't I be? A million and a half to write books is a dream.

My pain killers must be wearing off because a cramp builds low in my abdomen. I can feel the color drain from my face.

"Hey, beautiful." Ryan's voice is so close to me. So soft. I want to curl up inside it and stay there until it's all over.

"Hey," I whisper.

"Are you okay? I thought you'd be happy about this."

I turn my face toward his, like a flower seeking the sun. Only, his expression is stormy. Pinched. Concerned.

"This was your idea?" I ask. No one else is listening to us anyway.

He nods, but his brows stay tightly knitted together. "You've been working so hard. I thought maybe if you were actually compensated for that, it could help—"

"No." It's so quiet, even I can barely hear myself.

His heart is in the right place, but mine is currently crumbling into pieces in my chest. A million dollars can't fix it. Not even Ryan can put the pieces back together this time.

"No," I say again, stronger this time. I press my palms into the table and stand on shaky legs. I suck in a breath as pain lances through me. "I don't want this," I say through gritted teeth.

"Scarlett," Trina pleads through nervous laughter. "Please, sit back down. What's going on?"

"I told you. I don't want this. I want to go home"—my voice cracks on the word, knowing already that I won't allow Ryan to come with me—"and sleep."

"Oh, honey." Trina clicks her tongue. "I'm so sorry. I know you're tired after that trip." She looks around the table, wincing in apology. "We should reschedule."

"No." The more times I say it, the easier it becomes. "I won't sign this. I'm done."

And then I turn on my heel and walk out the door before anyone can persuade me otherwise.

I DON'T CRY. Not one tear as I make my way home. Ryan tries to follow me, but I tell him I need some time alone. He calls, but I ignore it. Instead, I call Mandy. She just signed her deal with a smaller press a few months ago, so I'm sure the pressure is on. She'll get it. She has to.

But when I get done explaining everything to her, there are no reassurances. No condolences. Only silence.

"Mandy?" I ask, my voice trembling.

"I don't even know what to say." The anger in her voice could cut me in two. "Do you know how many people would kill for a deal like that?"

My mouth gapes open, then closed, then open again. "Did you miss the part where I am having a miscarriage?"

"You said yourself you were relieved."

I throw up my hands, then let them smack on the couch next to me. "That's the point. I shouldn't have had to be relieved. I should be able to do this job and have a relationship and kids if I want."

"Poor you. You can't handle a seven-figure deal and a perfect relationship. You made a choice, Scarlett. I guess you'll have to live with it."

"What the fuck, Mandy?"

She scoffs. "I can't feel bad for you. You had everything offered to you on a silver platter—"

"I worked hard. Too hard. That is the point." I spit the words out of my mouth like they taste bad.

"I've been working hard, too, and what do I have? A low five-figure advance and a promise that my paperback will be in a couple of stores. Certainly not a perfect boyfriend who is going to rush in and fight for a deal. And I'll tell you what—if I did what you did, I'd do him a favor and never speak to him again. He's going to be in deep shit with JMP for talking them into this."

Admittedly, I had been angry at Ryan for suggesting this deal, but Mandy is right. He'll likely get it from both sides now. We were never super private about our relationship, but if Mark puts two and two together, they might assume he was taking a risk that he wouldn't have if I weren't his girlfriend.

"You really fucked up, Scarlett," Mandy is saying. "This could be damaging for anyone who is connected to you."

She's talking about herself now. Clearly, she thinks I'm in the wrong here, even though I don't know how I could be. I didn't get myself knocked up, I didn't cause the pregnancy to end before it could even really start, and I didn't ask for this deal.

So much for my best friend.

"Yeah, message received," I snap at her. "Sorry I called. I won't make that mistake again."

I hang up and throw the phone angrily onto the couch. But I lie there well into the night, contemplating what she said. Ryan is going to be in deep shit, and he loves me. That's a dangerous combination. He loves me enough to give up his career, and I can't let him do that. And as my abdomen contracts painfully, my old friend rage returns. No one is strong enough to deal with all of this at once. If he had asked first, I would have told him everything.

No one asked. They all assumed I'd take the money, shut up, and sell more books. Ryan included.

In my research for my second book, I read all about the stages of grief. It's comforting to know that I can settle into this anger for a while. But eventually, there's acceptance, and the sooner I can accept that Mandy is right, the better. They're all better off without me for now. It's better if I just disappear.

That's when I do cry. Through my tears, I block Ryan's number. If he calls again, I'll answer, and I know he'd do anything for me, including commit career suicide. I can't let him do that, no matter how angry I am. I love him too much.

But there are so many memories of him in this place. I can't stay here. So I pack a duffel bag, then call a ride to the airport.

Chapter 29

Ryan

"GOOD NEWS," I call out as I enter my apartment laden with grocery bags. "The design team is mocking up a new cover, and they're sending it over to us tomorrow morning to approve."

After the cover debacle yesterday, I invited Scarlett over for dinner to make it up to her. Thinking it might be nice for her to get out of her apartment for a little while, I had told her where I leave my spare key, and she had texted me a few hours ago telling me she was headed to my place for a change of scenery.

I dump the bags onto the kitchen counter before I realize that the whole place is kind of dark. The shades are drawn, there aren't any lights on, and it's silent. I don't even hear her telltale keyboard tapping from the bedroom.

That's strange. Her car is parked outside, so I know she's here.

"Hello?" I call, coming around the counter to peek in the bedroom to see if maybe she fell asleep or something. The bed is empty, but she's sitting cross-legged on the chair, her hands in her lap, and her eyes fixed on a black computer screen.

My heart thuds in my chest. She's so still. The rhythmic rising and falling of her chest is the only reason I know she's not a statue. Casey's warning rings through my consciousness, but I shake my head to dispel it. She seemed fine on the phone. There's nothing that could have put her over the edge, as far as I know. The cover issue was inconvenient but not insurmountable, and she told me she didn't have any difficult scenes coming up.

"Scarlett?" I ask cautiously from the doorway. "Is everything okay?"

She takes in a shaky breath, then lets it out through pursed lips. "No."

In an instant, I'm on my knees in front of her, my hands resting comfortingly on her thighs just under the hem of her shorts. Now that I'm close to her, I can see her cheeks are shining with tears. "Beautiful, what's wrong?"

Scarlett presses her eyes closed, her face still turned to the screen. Why won't she look at me? What the hell is going on?

"There was a baby," she says finally, not opening her eyes. "Not a baby. An embryo, probably. They're called embryos for the first eight weeks. I looked that up because I was trying to feel better about it. I thought that if I didn't call it a baby, it wouldn't be as confusing for me, I guess. I don't know. It felt like something one of my characters would have done, but it didn't really work. How could I be upset about a cluster of cells? But I was, even though I didn't want to be."

She's rambling, her eyes still pressed closed. Is she trying to work out a scene? Is she so lost in her words that she doesn't know I'm here? That wouldn't be unlike her. Maybe I misunderstood what this new book is about.

I rub her thighs with a little more pressure, trying to draw her out of whatever trance she's in. "Scarlett, look at me."

She furrows her brows and squeezes her eyes shut further. "I can't."

Okay, so she does know I'm here. I can work with that. "Why not, beautiful? Is this about your story?"

"No. It's about me. Us? I've been alone with it for so long, I don't even know anymore."

My hands go still on her legs. I blink a few times, trying to get my brain to catch up to her words.

Alone with it for so long...

Baby...Embryo...

"You were pregnant?" I whisper, afraid that speaking it aloud will make it more true than it already is. My stomach drops as a pit of anger forms like dead weight in my belly. Is that what kept her away for all those years? "Whose?"

She finally looks at me, her blue eyes flying open, her frown intensifying in her own offense. "Yours."

I jump to my feet and move away from her. Right away, I know it's a mistake, but I can't think. I can't breathe. Space. I need space.

Running a hand through my hair, I pace a few steps, then stop. "When?" I manage to choke out.

"I miscarried in New York." Unlike her earlier ramblings, she says those words plainly. They're flat. Factual. As if she is familiar with these. She must be, if she's lived with it for five years.

Realizing my hand is lodged painfully in my hair, I drop it to my side with an angry slap. "You went to New York pregnant, and you didn't tell me?"

"I didn't tell you because I didn't know. I found out in New York when I realized my period was late, and then I wanted to tell you in person."

There was a phone call. It comes rushing back to me, the memory of it weakening my knees enough that I sink to the edge of the bed.

I was barely able to contain my excitement. The ink wasn't even dry on the draft of the contract yet. But the desire to see the look on her face when she saw it was stronger than my need to tell her. "I've been trying to get ahold of you all day. I have some amazing news.

"Oh yeah? Well...I have news, too." She sounded more nervous than excited, but that was okay. I was nervous, too.

"I want to wait to tell you in person, though."

A pause. Was she disappointed? But then she said, "Same."

I try to fill my lungs with oxygen, to no avail. "You had news."

She twists around in the chair so she can face me, and she

presses her chest into the back of it as she nods. The position is so similar to the one she took the first time she told me she loved me that my heart aches at that memory too.

So many memories between us. They're almost unbearable.

"I didn't know how you'd feel about it," she says. "It was an accident, obviously. So I wanted to tell you in person. I was so tired. I couldn't think."

She had been exhausted. Every time I saw her, the purple under her eyes was more prominent. Just before she left, we had gone through her closet to donate some clothes that had gotten too big. We joked about it then, both of us too uncomfortable with the fact that she was wasting away to talk about it. I had tried to cook for her when she was home, but there was only so much I could do when she was on the road. And she always seemed to be on the road. But a few weeks before she left for New York, we had spent almost every minute together. Then one more set of interviews, and she was supposed to have months off. Trina and I protected that time off for her, even as the book club and appearance requests kept rolling in.

I was so fucking stupid. Why the hell did I think more money would have made any of that better? Of course it wouldn't have. The love of my life was drowning in the middle of an ocean, and I sent her what I thought was a lifeboat but was actually a measly piece of wood.

And she was pregnant on top of it all.

Rubbing my aching eyes under my glasses, I huff incredulously. "Why didn't you tell me?"

"When, Ryan?" She sounds irritated. When I look at her again, her expression confirms it. "I sat in that room, actively bleeding while people talked over me. No one asked me what I wanted. No one bothered to check in with me. I had gone from a flight to a conference room with no time in between. I was still *bleeding*. How long was I supposed to be paraded around like a commodity? In perpetuity? Until my books stopped selling? No one was worried about anything but dollar signs." Her eyes fill with tears again, glittering in the fading light filtering in through a crack in the curtains. "Not even you." She whispers that last part, like it hurts her too much to say.

"I didn't tell you to leave me." I fight to keep my own irritation out of my voice. It seems like we're going to have it all out right now, so I might as well say it. "You didn't have to be alone with this. I tried calling, messaging, stopping by."

She makes a pained noise, and her nostrils flare. "In retrospect, I know I made a huge mistake. I was young and stupid and confused as fuck. But in my defense, why the hell would you want me anymore?" Almost shouting now, she stands and leans forward, almost on her toes. "I couldn't hack it. I blew up your deal. I got myself blacklisted from JMP. And I couldn't even have your baby." Her voice cracks on the last sentence, as if it can't hold the pain anymore.

Involuntarily, I reel backward. "Is that how you think of it? That you did something wrong? That you caused it?"

Her shoulders curl into herself, and she drops her gaze to the ground. "I didn't want it. Not at first. I didn't see how it would fit into my life. And as soon as I started to warm up to the idea, it was over."

I sit on the edge of the bed again with my head in my hands. She can't think this way. I won't allow it. "That's not how it works," I tell her. "You don't cause a miscarriage by not wanting a baby."

She gives me a half shrug, her gaze still trained on the ground. "The rest of it is still true."

"I never cared about any of that. I only ever cared about you. Why didn't you let me help you?"

The anguish is apparent in her eyes as they slide to meet mine. "There wasn't anything you could do. You can't fix everything for me, Ryan."

Her words echo Casey's, but somehow it hurts more coming from her. I might not be able to fix everything, but I can help. I wish she'd just let me help. Standing again, I walk to the window and throw it open. If only I could get some air, maybe I could think.

But gulping in the fresh, spring air does nothing to clear my mind. And when I turn around to face Scarlett again, hoping that seeing her face will help me find the right words to say to her, the space she had been occupying is empty.

She's gone.

Chapter 30

Scarlett

As soon as Ryan opens the window and starts taking big, deep breaths, I know it's my time to go. I have no idea what any of this means for us, but he deserves the space and time to process it all. I've had five years; he's had about five minutes. And while I wish he had rushed to me and held me and told me that none of it mattered, deep down, I knew that was never going to happen.

If I'm being honest with myself, I buried the loss. Yes, I had talked to Dianne about it, but after the initial few meetings, we focused much more on my writing than anything else. That's how I wanted it.

When I started writing again, I had a vague thought that if I had been able to have that baby, he or she would be in preschool. It felt fitting that I was getting back into it then. There are plenty of stories of mothers going back to work when their kids go to school. I read a lot of them in my darker, lonelier moments on the internet.

But when you didn't actually have a kid, it gets tricky. How much time is enough to have mourned something you didn't even know you wanted until you lost it? Was I mourning the loss of a pregnancy, or writing, or Ryan? Did I spend too much time away? Is there a time limit on these things?

Right now, it hurts so badly that it feels like even five more years wouldn't have been enough.

I'm almost to my car when I hear a door bang open behind me. No sooner do I rest my hand on the door handle of my car than I hear Ryan's voice, shouting.

"What the fuck, Scarlett?"

Red-faced with hair mussed from running his hands through it, he's jogging down the steps that lead to the entrance of his building. My heart doesn't get the message that his body language is giving off. He's pissed as hell, but it still soars with gratitude that he came after me.

Breathless, he slows to a stop in front of me. He's so tall, I have to turn my face up toward his, and the waning sun casts a glare in my vision. Squinting, I shade my eyes with my hand.

"You left." He spits the words out. "Again."

I wince at that. It's fair, but that doesn't make it hurt any less. "I didn't think you wanted me there."

He throws his hands in the air in a gesture of pure frustration. "What the hell gave you that impression?"

Swallowing hard, I put all of my energy into remaining calm. It's not his fault I dropped a bomb on him today. He has every right to be upset. "You seemed agitated."

An incredulous huff escapes him, and he runs his hands through his hair again. The need to fold myself into him and sob into his chest rises so violently within me that I stagger back. My ass hits the door of my car, and it takes all my strength not to slump to the ground.

His dark gaze locks on mine, so intense, it warms me far more than the sunlight. "I'm not agitated with you." Something unreadable crosses his face. "Well, I am now. You can't keep running when things get hard, Scarlett."

"Jesus, Ryan," I yell. Apparently, I've reached the end of my ability to remain calm and understanding. "Twist the goddamn knife, why don't you?"

"And why shouldn't I?" His voice is deceptively calm and measured. But there's a storm brewing there. I can see it under his dark glasses. "Fuck, Scarlett. I can't keep watching your back as you walk out when things get hard. If I have to throw a knife at it to get your attention, then I will."

I blink rapidly, not sure if I want to laugh or cry. What comes out of me is some kind of cackle-sob combination that sounds more like an animal dying than a human emotion. Which actually feels appropriate. I am just an animal, and I feel like I'm dying. Surely even death doesn't hurt this bad.

"How dare you," I say when I can find my words again. "I admitted I made a mistake. I said I was wrong. I've said it a million times since I saw you at Anastasios, and I guess I'll say it a million more if that's what it takes. But if you think for one second that I did any of this for me—any of it—you've lost your mind. Do you think I liked being alone for five years with only my agent and my therapist to talk to? Do you think it was fun for me to bleed while watching men in expensive suits with dollar signs for eyes make major decisions about my career without my input? Do you think I laughed as I blacklisted myself, lost my best friends because of it, and had to come to terms with the fact that you loved me so much that you'd throw your own career away just to be with me? I walked away for *you*, Ryan. So you could at least have one thing left when the dust settled." I'm screaming now, tears streaming down my cheeks again and landing on the pavement in front of me.

I want him to explode back at me. For some reason, I think it might be cathartic to scream at each other again, like we did outside of that tapas place. But he doesn't. Instead, he nods.

"You're right," he says simply. And with those two words, I can physically feel my heart breaking in two. I'm right. I was right that he'd end his career for me, and I was right to walk away.

It takes all my effort not to crumple into a ball right there on top of my tears on the pavement and sob. I was never a crier before this. I think I can count on one hand the number of times I cried before Ryan came back into my life. And yet, now it's like all of those emotions have burst out of wherever I buried them and are lingering right on the surface, ready to take over at any second.

But Ryan rests his hands on my shoulders, dragging them down my upper arms. Goose bumps come to life under my sleeves at his touch, and when he rests his forehead on mine, I let out a relieved breath. I didn't even know this is what I needed, but he did. He always knows.

"You're right. I would have given up everything to be with you," he whispers, his breath tickling my lips. "I would have done it then, and I'd do it now, and I wouldn't regret it for one single second. You're worth far more than a job, Scarlett. I wish you had let me show you that."

And just like that, the weight of it is gone. I hadn't even realized how much I was carrying until he took it from me. Maybe it really is going to be okay.

Ryan folds me into a hug, cradling my shoulders with one long arm and my head with another, his fingers weaving into my hair and holding my head against his chest. He smells so good, like almonds and vanilla and paper. And that's what does me in, that scent that feels at once so old and so new, like one chapter into the next. I clutch at his back as I wrap my arms around him and let go of every tear I had been holding back. He just holds me through it all.

By the time I've let it out, the sun has almost dipped behind his building. Everything is golden and beautiful and warm. I tip my head up to look at Ryan, and even though I must look like a goblin, he smiles down at me and rubs a gentle thumb against my cheek.

"I have to admit, this is a plot twist I didn't see coming." He purses his lips against a smile.

"Ryan Whitlock," I say on a disbelieving laugh. "Was that a pun?"

"I thought you'd appreciate the dark humor."

If only he knew how much. This is the furthest thing from funny, but if he can joke about it, maybe there's hope for us. For me.

"But that's all it is. Just a plot twist," he continues. He kisses my forehead. One of his hands snakes its way into my hair again so his fingers can massage the nape of my neck reassuringly. "I spent five years without you, Scarlett. I'm not letting you go again. We can both be sad about this and still love each other. We can talk about babies..." He raises a questioning eyebrow but laughs at the face I make. "Or not yet. There's space and time for all of that and more, if you'll only stop running away from me."

Filling my lungs with the spring air, I let the mix of sharp, cut grass and delicate, new flowers reawaken something inside me. Something new, reborn, perfectly symbolic. It was winter, and now it's spring. Everything is starting over, both new and cyclical. Even me. Even us.

"You still love me?" I ask.

A soft smile tugs at his lips, and he shakes his head slowly. "*Love* isn't a strong enough word."

"Show me, then," I demand. And he does. His lips meet mine in a kiss at once passionate and unhurried, like he has all the time in the world to kiss me in any way he wants.

When he pulls away, he laces his fingers through mine and leads me back into his condo where we spend the rest of the night showing each other how we feel, over and over again.

Chapter 31

Ryan

I LIE AWAKE long after Scarlett has fallen asleep. Her dark hair is splayed out on the pillow, and her face is peaceful. Maybe more peaceful than I've ever seen it.

Her hand is resting on my chest, and I bring it to my lips to kiss her fingers before laying it gently next to her so I can get up. The rhythmic rising and falling of her back doesn't change, which tells me she's deeply asleep. As quietly as I can, I tiptoe over to my dresser and slide the top drawer open. Using my phone as a light, I rummage under the clothes until I find the small box I'm looking for. I take it with me out into the living room, closing the bedroom door behind me so I can turn on a light and sit on the couch.

The box is a soft, navy velvet that has been worn down over the years. I haven't taken it out to look at it in a while—not since I got my tattoo, actually—but this box has been well loved, first by my parents, then by me. I used to hold it all the time even though I'd never open it. I haven't opened it in five years.

My hands almost dwarf it, and my fingers shake slightly as I take a deep breath and crack it open. The hinge squeaks and pops open to reveal a ring. The band is gold and flares where it meets a single, small diamond solitaire. It was my mother's ring. My dad had bought it for her on a limited budget. To hear her tell it, he always said he'd get her a new one—a better one—but she wouldn't have it. "This is my ring," she'd say, and that was that.

I use my thumb to spin his matching gold band around on my

middle finger. His hands were always so much bigger than mine. Where he was bulky and solid, I was always thin and spindly. When he gave it to me before he died, it slid right off my finger. I wore it on a chain on my neck until I was an adult. Even now, I have to wear it on my middle finger.

My mom gave me her ring years after he died. She said she wanted me to have it just in case I ever met a woman I loved as much as my dad loved her.

That day in the park, as we ate our tacos and read our books in the Chicago summer sun, I knew I'd give this ring to Scarlett someday. It was too soon then, but I knew all the same.

I was carrying it with me the day Scarlett turned down JMP's offer. I had thought we'd celebrate her signing, and I'd give it to her over dinner. Maybe I'd even have ordered tacos. I hadn't really thought about it, but I knew I wanted her to have it that day. I wanted her to be my wife.

Carefully, I remove the ring from the box and turn it this way and that. It glints in the yellow light from the single lamp next to the couch. The band is worn on the underside because my mom wore it every single day for almost twenty-five years—well after he died. She didn't take it off until she started dating again. The diamond is a little cloudy, but none of that ever seemed to matter. This was the ring, and Scarlett was the woman. She still is. She always will be.

But now isn't the time, either. We're just starting to find each other again, learning all the new ways we fit together. Someday, though. Soon. Because if we can make it through this, I'm confident we can make it through anything.

I put the ring back in the box and snap it shut. For some reason, I had needed to see it, to reassure myself it was still there. Of course it was. Right where I left it.

Turning off the lamp, I find my way through the dark to my bedroom. I place the box in the drawer and carefully climb back into bed. Scarlett shifts this time, then sighs in her sleep. Her hand finds me again, cold against my skin. I hold it in mine and place it back over my chest, where it belongs.

WHEN I LEAVE for work the next morning, Scarlett is still half-asleep. It's almost unheard of for her to sleep longer than me, but I'm glad. She needs it. So I kiss her temple, whisper to her that she can stay as long as she likes, and head out the door.

The one drawback of working at Anastasios Press is the commute—I drive about an hour each way now that the offices are in the suburbs, though if I took public transportation, it would have taken me that same hour to get to JMP on a good day. Even all of the traffic in the world has been worth the move, though. It's such a better environment. And it brought Scarlett back to me.

If that's not fate, I don't know what is.

And that's how I find myself musing about fate and soulmates and marriage as I distractedly make my way through the hallways to my office, my mind occupied by my own contentment.

I've barely set down my bag and powered on my laptop when a small knock comes from the doorframe of my open door. My intern, Margie, pokes her head in.

"Oh good, you're here," she says breathlessly. If I didn't know any better, I'd think she sounded nervous.

"Come on in, Margie." I motion for her to sit. "What's up?"

She takes a step into the room, but lingers by the doorway, wringing her hands in front of her. "Mr. Martis was looking for you."

"Really?" I ask. Then I snap my fingers when it dawns on me. "It must be because of that cover. There was a mistake. I'll find him in a little while to explain—"

"I don't think it was about the cover," Margie interrupts, her eyes wide with worry. "He said you should meet him in the conference room right away when you got in. Miss McBryde is there with him, too, and Mr. Endersen and the publicity team. He did not seem happy."

Trina, Casey, and Publicity? That's strange, but this couldn't be anything too terrible about Scarlett. She is currently either still snuggled underneath the covers in my bed or drinking my coffee and getting ready for her day.

"I'll head over there right now. Thank you, Margie."

She nods once and leaves quickly, as if staying anywhere near me is dangerous.

I walk quickly down the hall to the conference room where everyone Margie named is, indeed, sitting around the large table. When I walk in, they all look at me in unison and the room goes silent. A quick glance at Casey has me officially worried, because he looks about as panicked as he can get. Trina's eyes are the only pair not on me—they're downcast as she stares at something on the table in front of her.

"Mr. Whitlock," Anastasios booms. "Thank you for coming. Have a seat."

"Good morning, everyone," I say as I sink into the chair in front of me. "What's going on?"

Anastasios leans forward and folds his hands together on top of the table. "We have a very serious problem."

"If this is about the cover—" I start, but he interrupts with a hand raised, palm out.

"This isn't about the cover. Somehow, JMP found out that Scarlett Frye has signed with us, before we were ready to alert them. And even though we've assured them we were planning to disclose the information, they're still very upset. So upset, in fact, that this does not bode well for my position here."

"What?" I ask, still trying to process this information. "How the fuck did that happen? All external communication has only had her pen name on it."

Anastasios gives me a pointed look. "That is what we are here to find out."

Suddenly, Casey's panicked look makes sense. And so does Trina's expression. She's sad. Like she's been disappointed, and she's not sure how she's going to break the news.

"Wait." I close my eyes and shake my head as if my willpower alone could make this all stop. "You think I outed Scarlett to JMP?"

"Everyone who knew about her identity is in this room, and you're the only one who we haven't talked to yet," Anastasios says. "And you have to admit, your motivations are questionable." He's outwardly calm, but his voice carries an undertone of a disciplinarian. He's ready to punish me if he doesn't like my answers.

"How, exactly, are my motivations questionable?" I am also trying to remain calm, but it's proving difficult.

"This was posted to social media this morning," Casey chimes in, sliding his phone across the table to me. I look at the post. Sure enough, it's an old picture of Scarlett and me at a coffee shop downtown. I'm pointing at her computer and saying something, and she's watching me with wide eyes. Underneath is a caption that reads, *Scarlett Frye is back with a new book, this time at JMP's imprint Anastasios Press. Rumor is that JMP is none too happy one of their imprints snapped her up. She and her new editor were caught cozying up at a coffee shop to work. Will this book actually be released this time? Only time will tell.*

"Who wrote that?" I mumble. "The caption is garbage. You can't possibly think I put that together. At the very least, I would have used a lot less repetition and put the commas in the right places."

"This is not a laughing matter," Anastasios warns, though his expression shifts as if he hadn't thought of that.

"Oh, I'm not laughing," I assure him. "This could destroy Scarlett in more ways than one." The image of her sobbing against my chest yesterday works its way to the front of my mind. "I don't understand why you think I would have done this. Aside from Trina, I'm the one person in this room who has the most to lose professionally if JMP makes you rescind your contract." No one has said that's where this is going yet, but I can assume it's on the table. We might have a lot of autonomy here, but JMP officially runs the show. They can do what they want.

Anastasios clears his throat. "Did they offer you a higher position over there for this information, Ryan? They seemed very interested in this book and whatever she was going to do next—"

"No, they did not offer me anything, and even if they did, there's no way in hell I would have taken it."

"Revenge, maybe?" he suggests. "I know you were involved in her deal at JMP."

My gaze flies to Casey, who has the good sense to look sheepish. I shake my head. "I would never want revenge on Scarlett. I..." I trail off. It's not against the rules for editors to be romantically involved with authors, but I could get taken off this book if they found out. It reeks of bias.

As my eyes meet those of everyone in the room in turn, I make a decision. Fuck it. I made her a promise, and I intend to keep it. If Scarlett goes down, I go down with her.

"That picture is from six years ago. I don't know how anyone got it. We had done an impromptu photo shoot for her social media, but all of that has been deleted." I take a deep breath to steady myself before continuing. "Scarlett and I had been in a romantic relationship at the time. It was why I was so involved in that deal with JMP. When Trina submitted *Becoming* here, I had no idea it was hers. I hadn't seen or heard from her since the day she left."

"I can attest to that," Trina chimes in, looking wide-eyed at me.

"Being a spurned lover doesn't exactly make your case for not wanting revenge," Meri offers matter-of-factly.

Is everyone just out to clear their own names by implicating me? I shoot daggers in her direction, but I manage to calm myself before speaking again. "That's true, but Scarlett and I recently rekindled our relationship." Looking squarely at Anastasios, I add, "I loved her then. I've loved her for the entire time she was gone. And I love her now, sir. I would never hurt her. Not knowingly, and certainly not like this."

Casey slumps in relief. I can't believe he or Trina ever thought for a second that I had something to do with this, but I'm going to have to deal with that later because Anastasios runs a hand through his graying hair and grumbles.

"That's a bit of a problem, Whitlock." He sounds tired.

"I know, sir. But it's not this problem." I indicate Casey's phone, which has gone dark on the table.

"No, it's not," Anastasios agrees.

"Did JMP hear about this from that post?" I ask.

"The caption on that photo would suggest no," he says. "And it didn't sound like it when they called this morning, but there were a lot of words. Most of them were unkind and vaguely litigious."

"They don't have a legal leg to stand on," Trina says vehemently. "I checked. They never sued Scarlett. They couldn't. She never signed anything. She walked away from that deal like any author has a right to."

"Doesn't mean they won't tie us up in red tape until we fold," Casey points out. "They're technically in charge here, even if they do leave us mostly alone."

"At any rate, we're going to have to get Ms. Frye in here to see if any of this can be salvaged," Anastasios says. "Our best bet is probably to release the information ourselves, rush a release of the book, and make sure it makes enough money that JMP doesn't have a choice but to let it go."

I don't like the sound of that one bit, but I sense that I'm still on thin ice because of our relationship, so I don't speak up. Everyone starts talking at once, but I remain carefully quiet. Patting my pockets to look for my phone, I think that maybe if I can at least warn Scarlett of what's coming, she'll be prepared when she walks in here, but I must have left my phone in my office in my haste to get here.

Trina catches my eye and reaches a hand over to cover mine where they rest on the table. "I called her," she says quietly. "She's on her way. It'll be okay."

"How do you possibly know that?" I mumble.

"Because we're on her side this time." She shrugs and places her hand back in her lap. "I'm optimistic."

I'm not. But the only thing I can do now is wait.

Chapter 32
Scarlett

"I NEED TO tell you something, but I don't want you to panic."

My coffee cup—well, Ryan's since I'm standing in his kitchen—stops halfway to my mouth as Trina's words sink in. She's speaking quietly, almost whispering, and she sounds exactly as panicked as she's telling me not to be.

"That is not how you get someone to remain calm." I indulge in a long sip of coffee. If shit is going to hit the fan, I may as well be caffeinated.

She makes a noncommittal noise, then comes right out with it. "Someone outed you to JMP, and they're super pissed Anastasios let you sign with them. I got called in this morning for damage control, and they want you to come in, too."

I check the time on the microwave clock. It's barely nine in the morning. "How did you get there so fast?"

Trina makes another noise—this one sounding like it's accompanied by an epic eye roll. "Scarlett, focus. This is very bad. They could force Anastasios to rescind your deal. This is already on social media. Ryan could lose his job—"

"Wait. What does Ryan have to do with it?"

She's uncharacteristically silent for longer than I would like. Just when I *am* about to start panicking, she speaks. "Very few people knew about this. You didn't out yourself. You're dumb, but you're not insane. Martis was waiting to tell JMP for obvious reasons. Your publicity team has been working overtime to figure out how to release the information within the constraints we set out for them, so there's no way they'd want to undo all that work. It wasn't me. I actually care about you. And it wasn't Casey. He left JMP for a lot of the same reasons you did." She stops there, but she doesn't have to say what's next.

"Ryan didn't do this."

"I don't know if he did, honey." Oh, great. Now she's placating me. "But you didn't see him when you left before. He was...beside himself."

"And you haven't seen him with me now. There's no way," I insist, but my mind is working overtime. I left him high and dry. To hear him tell it, I took his love of literature with me. I disappeared from his life for five years. And yesterday I told him I lost our baby, which I had kept from him for so long. I did think I heard him get up in the middle of the night last night. Could he have been secretly so angry that he plotted some kind of revenge?

No. No. That's not like Ryan at all. If he had wanted vengeance, he wouldn't have brought me tacos or washed my hair or held me while I sobbed in his parking lot. He would have let me fester in my own depression. Or he would have gone to JMP straight away.

"Listen, he's on his way in," Trina is saying. "We're going to talk to him and hopefully set this whole thing straight. Can you get here quick?"

I sigh heavily, wishing I could jump in a time machine and go back five hours to when Ryan and I were snuggled up together, our skin touching at every point of contact we could manage, his leg possessively intertwined between mine as I rocked back to feel him against me.

Scratch that. I wish I could go back five years and do literally everything differently to save everyone from this mess.

"Yeah," I say, dejected. "I'll be there as soon as I can."

I'M LED INTO the conference room at Anastasios by a sweet-looking college kid. She introduced herself as Maggie or Marlee or something like that. And not for the first time in my life, I wish I was better at remembering people's names in the middle of crisis moments.

The minute the door opens, Ryan practically jumps out of his seat. Distress is etched all over his features. "Scarlett, I'm so sorry," he says.

I don't know what he has to be sorry for. I won't allow the little seed of doubt Trina planted earlier to take root. Ryan couldn't have done this. Not after everything he said yesterday.

"Mr. Whitlock, sit down," Anastasios says, his voice even but edged with frustration. "Ms. Frye, please, come in."

There isn't an open seat next to Ryan, though I wish there were. The only chair available is on the other side of Trina, sandwiched between her and Anastasios. It sure feels like this placement is by design, though I can't imagine why. No one knows about my relationship with Ryan. Unless...

"Thank you for coming," Anastasios interrupts my thoughts as I sink, shaking, into the open chair. "I'm sure Ms. McBryde has apprised you of the situation?"

I nod, resisting the urge to gulp audibly. The tension in the room is almost tangible.

Careful not to look in Ryan's direction, I ask, "Do you know who did this?"

"We do not," Anastasios says, not unkindly. "Unless someone in this room is lying, it was someone on the outside. But rest assured, Ms. Frye, we have a plan to get out in front of this thing and mitigate the damage."

My guess is that he's talking about mitigating the damage done to the imprint—and to him personally. They are likely not talking about the damage they're going to do to me. I know how this works. In cases like this, more publicity is inevitable. I'm going to need to tell my side of the story over and over again until my narrative becomes the accepted one.

A glance in Trina's direction confirms it. Her red lips are pressed into a thin line, and she's clutching her hands together on top of the table so hard that her knuckles are turning white. She fought for me before I got here. That, I'm sure of.

Just like my first meeting here—and my last at JMP—everyone seemingly starts talking at once. Phrases filter in and out of my consciousness as if the words themselves were floating in front of me, out of reach.

"We can get her on at least a couple major talk shows..."

"No guarantee about book clubs until the book is out, but we'll start asking around..."

"Anything we can do. The more popular this thing is, the more JMP will look the other way..."

"Rush the release. Get it out while people are paying attention..."

"What about that daytime show with those women? They seemed to like her last time..."

My gaze shifts to Ryan. He's staring at me intensely, almost as if he has been willing me to look at him. When I do, he blinks, and his face crumples. He shakes his head slightly, but all I can do is look away. I don't have the energy for the depth of emotion he's displaying. This all feels so familiar that I can feel myself shutting down as they all talk around me.

"People would probably show up for signings again out of curiosity..."

"We could put a call out for people who had tickets to her last tour. Let them come for free..."

"Six weeks. Maybe ten. A break to write the new book, then back for another five..."

How am I possibly going to write and edit and do all this press again? Not to mention people showing up potentially still angry about the canceled tour last time. Can I take being shit on to my face by angry readers who don't know any better?

I understand what this team is trying to do, or at least I think I do. From the snippets of conversation, it's clear they think selling a ton of books will appease JMP. It's not a bad plan, actually. JMP has always been all about the money. It would probably work, if it weren't for one thing.

I can't go back to that grueling schedule. I can barely handle writing, and if it weren't for Ryan forcing me away from the work each night, I wouldn't be able to handle that either.

But I also can't walk out of here right now. If I did, it would only serve to show that I didn't change, that I'm not different. It would put the nail in the coffin of my career. There wouldn't be any coming back from this.

No, I need to let them talk over me and about me like I'm not even here, and then I need to take all the information and figure out how to make it work. That's all I can do if I ever want to write again.

So I sit there for the next thirty minutes as they come up with a plan. Trina asks me questions every once in a while, but all I can do is shrug. Ryan continues to stare at me as if he could hold me together with his eyes, but I can't look at him. He would have ruined his career five years ago, and I believe that if he saw even a hint of doubt in me, he'd do it now, too. And I can't let him.

As soon as they wrap up, I stand on shaky legs and silently make my way toward the door. I need to get somewhere where I can lose my shit in private, and I need to do it fast.

"Scarlett—" Ryan moves toward me at almost lighting speed, taking my hand in his.

"I just want to be alone," I say quietly, looking ahead and not directly at him. "I'm okay. I just...need some space."

Out of the corner of my eye, I see Trina stand and lay a hand on his shoulder. "Let her go," she whispers. "Today has been a lot."

Ryan pauses but ultimately drops my hand and steps back. Now, I absolutely cannot look at him because if I do, I'll see how much it hurt him to do that. But it doesn't change the fact that right now, I need to get the fuck out of here. Fast.

Putting my head down, I push the door to the conference room open. I make it all the way to the elevator but then decide to take the stairs. A small space would feel confining right now, and I don't need that on top of everything else. As if a little Dianne is sitting on my shoulder, her voice stops me before I can rush down the stairs and outside. *Take your time*, she reminds me. *Use each step as a way to ground yourself. Don't shut down. Use your emotions.*

What do I have to lose? Nothing, I guess, so I start my descent carefully, noting the feel of the hard tile under my flat shoes, the cold metal of the railing, the way my steps echo against the walls. And with each step, I do come back into my body. It almost feels like my heart is there, waiting for me, opening its arms and welcoming me back.

And with each step after that, I have questions. Who would do this? Why? Is there someone out there who hates me that much—who is that angry at me—who also knew I was writing again? Why do these things keep happening to me? Am I just meant to be Scarlett Frye, best-selling author and a commodity for my publisher to throw around as they see fit?

Dianne also often asks me to name my emotions. She says that when I shut them out and don't talk about them, that's when they grow into unmanageable beasts. So by the time I hit that last step on the ground level, I try to give what I'm feeling a name.

Confusion. But also anger. I don't want to do this again. I wasn't supposed to have to do this again. When does it all fucking *end*?

That's where I find myself when I open the door to the stairwell and two things happen at once. First, the elevator door across the lobby opens and Ryan steps out. Second, Charles Hall and his annoying swagger passes between us.

Just my luck, Charles turns his head to me and smiles, though it's really more of a sneer, and it takes all my power not to sigh in exasperation. The last thing I want to do right now is make small talk with this asshole, but he stops to face me fully, his back to Ryan as if he didn't see him or he doesn't matter.

"Hello, Scarlett." He curls his lip when he says it. It takes a second, but something about the way he emphasizes my name—my real name—stokes the little flame that sparked in my belly on my way down the stairs.

The realization slams into me hard enough that I take an involuntary step back as I gasp. "It was you."

Charles folds his arms across his bulky chest and chuckles without any humor whatsoever. "What? Did you think I was too stupid to figure it out?"

Ryan takes a few steps forward as if he's going to come to my defense, but he stops when I tilt my head and blink at Charles a few times, considering what to do next. I could do the demure thing and walk away. Considering everything that just happened upstairs, that's definitely what I should do—smile, play nice, take it on the chin. But as it turns out, I'm pissed, and I left the last of my fucks in that conference room.

"Honestly, I didn't think you were paying enough attention to come to the obvious conclusion," I say, thanking everything that is and ever was holy that my voice is even and cool. And then, because I just can't help myself now that I know exactly how much of a jackass this guy is, I add, "It's not like my best-selling face hasn't been all over the place in the past."

Charles narrows his eyes at me, and his biceps flex a bit as he tenses. He doesn't say anything, which isn't a surprise. He's not quick enough to come up with something witty or cutting.

"Why did you do it?" I have to know, and if I know anything about his type, I know he's just dying to tell me anyway.

Sure enough, his lips curl into a sinister smile again. "I've been secretly meeting with JMP, too. Remember? I thought they might be interested in the information that their imprint signed an author who fucked them over. Turns out I was right. They were very interested." He removes one of his hands from where it's folded in his arm and rubs his thumb and fingers together. I take that to mean they offered him a lot of money for his book in return.

"Hmm." I nod slowly. "Turns out I was right, too. You are exactly as self-centered as I originally thought."

I could swear I see Ryan's jaw drop, but Charles scoffs.

"Whatever gets me the money, sweetheart. I was just here in a meeting to see if Anastasios would counter. Seems like they might."

Oh, gag me. I have to force myself not to physically lose my breakfast at his demeaning nickname. "Fine." I shrug. "I'll bite. If you got the money, why'd you put it on social media?" I saw that caption. Only someone who can't string a sentence together with his two remaining brain cells would have written that garbage.

"Ahh." And that insufferable smile is back. "That one was extra because you left me high and dry at that restaurant. For your editor boyfriend, no less. God, I hope you both are in such deep shit for that."

"Oh, please." I laugh at his audacity. "You were sucking face with some young thing when I came back. Maybe if you had given a shit about anything I had to say, I would have stuck around until a polite time to leave."

"Nah, Scarlett." He makes an expression that tells me he thinks he's won. "Leaving is kind of your thing."

A knife. That's what his comment feels like. Ryan would mock the cliché, but there's no other way to describe it. It fucking hurt. Because he's right.

And yet, I can't let him have the last word. I lick my lips and narrow my eyes at him. "You know what, Charles? You're right—that is my thing. And you're lucky it is. You're the kind of trash that takes itself out, so I *am* going to leave now so I can stand by and watch it happen."

With that, I turn on my heel and walk right out the door and to my car, pulling out of the parking lot and putting as much distance between myself and Charles and Anastasios Press as I can.

Chapter 33

Ryan

"Don't follow her," Trina says as soon as Scarlett is out the door of the conference room. "She said she needed space." Everyone filed out quickly after the meeting was over, so Trina, Casey, and I are the only ones here.

"I can help her," I say. I feel like I've been saying that a lot lately, and I wish people could just see that I'm good for her. We make a good team.

"She doesn't need help. She needs space," Trina reiterates. "And besides, you have to transfer all the files to Casey so he can finish this job as fast as he can. You're done with it, Ryan. I should have insisted on it from the start." The last part she says mostly to herself, but it still stings.

Casey claps a hand on my shoulder. "I'm sorry, man. I had my reservations, but I was rooting for you. This book...Scarlett...I wanted it to work out."

"Anastasios may have insisted I transfer the manuscript to you, but I haven't lost Scarlett," I insist.

To his credit, Casey does try to hide his skepticism, but I've known him long enough to see it. And that's all it takes to have me running to the elevator, trying to catch Scarlett before she leaves despite the protests of these two. Because if she walks out of this building and disappears like last time, I'll never forgive myself.

She's nowhere to be found when I get to the elevator, so I get in as fast as I can and go to the ground level. Maybe I can see her before she gets to her car. Uselessly, I push the button about ten times before the door closes and I start my descent.

But when the elevator door opens on Scarlett and Charles Hall standing in the lobby, I pause. When he sneers at her, using her full name no less, I see red. Even though I know he would murder me if I were to try, I still want to wipe the floor with him. I want to tell him to get her beautiful name out of his filthy mouth.

Her name. He knows her name. Of course he does—I used her real name when they met in some kind of power move to try to prove to him that I knew her better than he ever could and she was mine.

And suddenly, I know exactly who did this to her. It was this piece of shit with his back to me, probably trying to make some kind of statement like I don't matter.

I take a couple of tentative steps forward to try to step in but stop myself short. If this is my fault, I should fix it. But Scarlett gives him a look like he isn't fit to wipe the scum off her shoes. It stops me in my tracks, that look. The last time I saw it, she was calling me pedantic in a noisy bar. Except then, it was edged with a bit of humor. Now she looks like she's going to squash him in exactly the way he deserves.

Scarlett owns him. She's cool and calm and collected in a way I haven't seen in a long, long time. It's amazing. Inspiring, even. It's a privilege to watch.

Even when he says that leaving is kind of her thing, she shows no weakness. I know that must hurt like hell, but she just narrows her eyes and says, "You know what, Charles? You're right—it is my thing. And you're lucky it is. You're the kind of trash that takes itself out, so I *am* going to leave now so I can stand by and watch it happen."

And with that, she's gone. Charles is left standing there, gaping after her like a fish out of water before he, too, walks out the front door without even a glance at me.

I should follow Scarlett. I know I should. But I also can't help but think I caused this, and I have to do what I can to make it right before I talk to her again.

So, I get back in the elevator and go right back up to the offices. Casey and Trina are still in the hallway outside of the conference room, talking with their heads bowed toward each other. When I burst past them, they both look up, wide-eyed with shock and almost looking a little guilty. But I don't have time for that right now. I march right up to Anastasios Martis's office door and knock loudly.

"Come in," I hear from inside. But when I open the door and he sees it's me, he stifles an exasperated sigh. "Whitlock, I think you and I both have had enough of this today—"

"All due respect, sir, I know who outed Scarlett."

His chair creaks as he sits up straighter. He leans his ear toward me slightly, as if he isn't sure he heard me right.

"What? Who?" Trina says behind me. I hadn't realized I had an audience, but when I turn around, she and Casey are standing there. Margie is lurking in the distance, too, but close enough that she can hear me.

"Charles Hall," I say, still breathless with excitement. "He's been in talks with us and JMP for his new book."

"Last I heard, JMP wasn't interested in his book at all," Casey said.

I raise my eyebrows. That figures. He likely panicked when he told his publisher he was shopping around, only to not have any deals waiting for him at all. "Well, they're interested now. I just overheard him telling Scarlett he had been secretly meeting with both them and us and planned to leverage bids without anyone knowing our fellow imprint was the one in talks with him. They offered him a deal for his book in exchange for the information he had."

Casey snorts with a shrug. "They can have him. Why would we want to work with him after something like that?"

"Does the man have an agent?" Trina asks. "What reputable agent would agree to this?"

Casey eyes her. "Like attracts like."

"To hear him tell it, he was being secretive. Lying to us and them. Using the deal with JMP as leverage to try to get us to offer more." I direct this to Anastasios. If I'm reading the room right, he's just as angry as any of us because he's also in hot water for signing Scarlett in the first place.

Sure enough, his hand is on his phone in two seconds flat. "The fuck he is," he mutters under his breath as he violently punches numbers on the keypad.

"Get me Mark," he grumbles into the phone before looking up at the three of us with a glare.

I linger because I want to make sure this is handled, but Casey puts a hand on my shoulder. "Come on, man. He'll take care of it."

Nodding once in Anastasios's direction, I pull his door shut behind me as I exit his office.

Chapter 34

Ryan

Four Years Ago

It has been exactly one year since the last time I saw Scarlett, almost to the minute. I've been counting. Scratching the days off with unhinged tally marks on the wall like a prisoner. It's an exaggeration, but sometimes I feel like I might as well be. Every day feels like torture. Long and arduous, each one more bleak than the last, because with each day, I'm more sure she's not coming back.

I used to dream of her showing up at my apartment unannounced. I'd take her into my arms and tell her everything was okay, that as long as we were together, everything would be fine.

I was angry, but not at her. Never at her. I just couldn't understand what made her just disappear, as if she had never been there in the first place.

But she never showed up. Never answered my texts. Never sent a single word to anyone—not me or Trina. I even called Mandy and her other friends, but they hadn't heard from her and didn't seem like they wanted to. Mandy sounded a little upset, maybe even guilty, but wouldn't tell me why. She just said she hoped I found her, and that was that.

I make a habit of walking by her condo every so often. Not in a creepy way. But I want to see her. I *need* to see her. On the anniversary of her disappearance, I take one such walk, glancing upward toward her windows as casually as I can.

Scarlett isn't up there. Of course she's not. But there is a red sign that makes me trip over my feet. My knees hit the concrete sidewalk with a painful smack, but I don't even feel it.

CONDO FOR SALE, UNIT 406

Unit 406 is Scarlett's number. She put her condo up for sale.

Is she back? Did she come back and not tell me? Has anyone heard from her? Surely someone has if her condo is for sale.

With shaking hands, I find Trina's number in my contact list. I must look like I've lost it, kneeling on the sidewalk in the middle of the day, trying not to cry, but I don't even care.

"Ryan?" Trina answers, her cheerful voice coming through the speaker pressed to my ear. "It's been a while. How are you?"

"Was Scarlett back? Is she back?" I don't even try to keep the desperation out of my voice. Even if she didn't call me, if I can just find her...

"Not that I know of," she says cautiously. "Why?"

My heart drops to the bottom of my chest. "I'm outside her condo. It's for sale."

Trina curses quietly. I hear muffled voices behind her, then a scraping noise as she covers the phone and says something, then it's quiet again. "Oh, Ryan. I'm so sorry. I swear I haven't heard from her. I would tell you if I had. I know how you felt about her."

"Feel," I grind out, trying desperately to hold back angry tears. "How I feel about her."

There's silence for a moment before she sighs. "You didn't ask for my advice, but I'm going to give it to you anyway. It's been a year, Ryan. I know it's hard. I'm hurting, too. I lost a friend, and I know that's not the same, but...it sucks, okay? Still...if I were you, I'd try to move on. If Scarlett wanted to be found, we'd have found her, you know?"

I like to consider myself a rational, adult man. But there is nothing rational for me when it comes to Scarlett. My love for her is so deep and so ferocious that it has only grown in her absence. Giving up on the idea of her coming back to me is unfathomable.

The tears burst free then. I crumple forward, curling into myself as if I can wrap my body around my heart and protect it. The noises escaping me sound inhuman, even to my ears. The desire to punch something rises so violently within me, but there's nothing around but concrete and steel. I can't imagine what Trina is hearing over the phone, but she waits it out. I don't even know how long I kneel there, crying.

"I know," she croons when my sobs have subsided. "I fucking know. God, this is awful." She sniffles as if she's crying too. "Do you need me to come get you?"

I wipe my nose with the back of my hand and take a trembling breath. "No. I think I'm going to walk. Clear my head."

"Okay. It was good to hear from you, Ryan. Call me if you need me, okay?"

"Sure," I say before hanging up.

Getting myself off the sidewalk is one of the hardest things I've ever had to do. The last time I felt this way was when my dad died. Grief is heavy. Loss is a familiar weight, but it still wants to drag me down until I'm lying prostrate on the sidewalk, unable to move or breathe or think.

As wonderful as it sounds to become one with the Earth, I need to get up. This is not a good look for me. People walking by are starting to give me a wide berth and clutch their children closer to them. And if I don't move, I might actually drive my fist into the sidewalk. A different kind of pain might feel good for a second, but the only real result would be a broken hand.

I force myself to my feet and start walking aimlessly. I don't know how long I walk. Half an hour, maybe? I find myself passing by a tattoo parlor. The three guys inside are all sitting around, chatting. They don't look very busy.

Tattoos have never really appealed to me, but something tugs at me to go in. Maybe if this internal pain could be external for a little while, I'd feel better. And this is a way to do that without breaking my hand. It could be cathartic. Without giving it too much thought, I pull the door open and enter.

"What can we do for you?" one of the guys asks. He's a big, burly man, and almost every inch of his skin is covered in intricate designs. On a normal day, I might actually be intimidated by him, but not today. Today I'm too pissed off and sad to feel anything else.

"I'd like a tattoo, if you have an opening."

The man eyes me up and down, assessing. I'm sure they have a policy about not tattooing people who look like they're in the wrong state of mind to make permanent decisions, but he must see something in me that makes him give a sharp nod. "Sure. What did you have in mind?"

I don't have anything in mind. The only thing I have in mind is Scarlett, but it would look far too desperate to tattoo her face on my arm. Besides, I don't know if I could look at that every day.

Words that are as much a part of her as they are of me rise up from my heart. I close my eyes as they wash over me. I'm sure I look delirious as I recite them in the middle of a tattoo parlor to three of the biggest men I've ever met, but I don't care.

"*This was one of those moments when there was a clear before and after. She was never going to be the same again. Those minutes and hours in the time before seemed to stretch out of reach now. She was never going to get them back. There was only forward. Only what was ahead of her. And she had to face it.*"

Silence falls over the shop. When I open my eyes, they're all staring at me. But instead of telling me to leave and come back when I'm in my right mind, every one of them nods as if they completely understand.

"That's nice, man. Where did it come from?" the burly guy asks.

"A book." I clear my throat. "I'm an editor."

"You got a design you like?"

I shake my head and huff a laugh. "No. Honestly, I didn't

even know I was doing this until I walked in."

He narrows his eyes pensively, then motions for me to come back to his chair. "I got you," he says.

And for the next several hours, he does have me. He takes such care to do the passage justice, and as he inks Scarlett's words permanently onto my skin, I can't help but feel this is also one of those moments with a clear before and after. I won't walk out of here a new man, but giving my internal pain an external outlet is freeing in a way. I can see why people do this.

When I cry, he lets me. He must sense it's not about the pain from the needle, because he doesn't stop after the first time he asks me if I'm okay. When he's done, he wipes away the blood and extra ink and assesses his work.

"She'll always be with you," he says, clapping me on the shoulder. "This is just a reminder."

"Yeah," I say, choking back more tears. "Thanks."

After I pay the guy and leave, I expect to feel different, and I do in some ways. But in others, everything is exactly the same. Scarlett left. She's not coming back. And now, somehow, I need to find a way to move on.

"I FEEL LIKE I should be wearing dark sunglasses and a giant scarf to hide my features," Trina quips as she sits down in a chair next to me.

"What do you mean?" I don't have the energy to play around or figure out what the hell she's talking about. I'm amazed I even got myself to this coffee shop, but when she called and asked me to meet her, I also didn't have the heart to say no. After that meeting and my encounter with Charles, I'm completely out of steam. If only someone could tell me what to do next. Maybe Trina has a plan.

"I don't know." She shrugs, clearly a little sad her joke didn't land. "Are we going incognito or something? Should we be hiding from the paparazzi?"

Frowning at her, I take a sip of my latte because, in typical Trina fashion, even though she asked me to meet here, she was late. "I've never been famous enough to be followed by paparazzi."

She sighs and droops her head so low that it almost hits the table. "I'm just trying to keep this lighthearted, Scarlett."

"Why?"

"Ohmygod." She groans it all as one word, her face now tipping upward. "I don't know. This is kind of uncharted territory for me."

"Because I stuck around this time?" I ask plainly. While I may have tried to hide how much Charles's last insult hurt me, his words buried themselves deep and pulled me right back down to a dark place I haven't inhabited in a while. Even in this coffee shop, nothing feels right or looks right. Everything is just a bit too loud, too bright, and I can't quite make sense of what I'm seeing. It's like I'm living in a movie of my own life when I want to hide in my apartment under a blanket and never come out.

Which I'm sure is exactly why Trina insisted we meet here instead of just coming over.

She covers my hand with hers and squeezes. "Honey, no. I got a little worried there when you went all statue on me in that meeting, and I'm glad you're still here, but I know all the work you've done. I didn't doubt for one second things would be different this time. I'm proud of you."

A sudden ache blooms in my chest, and it pushes a knot of emotion up into my throat. I swallow hard and try to blink it all away, but the damn thing sticks there. I'm not used to experiencing this many feelings in such rapid succession. I wish they'd all just go away and leave me to wallow in peace.

But between Ryan's unconditional forgiveness yesterday and Trina's pride today, I'm starting to realize I've buried some things pretty far down. Suddenly, a lot of Dianne's mantras are starting to make sense. *Emotion needs motion. Name the beast. You can't heal until you face your demons.* So many clichés I had passed off as lines she had pulled from various therapist textbooks and regurgitated at me. But she has always been convinced that my depression has been triggered by a need to bury my true feelings and hide from them, that I wouldn't find real healing until I faced my issues head-on.

I hate to admit it, but I think she might have been right. Because as much as these past few days have hurt, I'm starting to feel lighter. More capable. Like I could take the next problem and deal with it instead of running away, like Charles said. Even if I desperately don't want to.

"I had a miscarriage," I blurt out.

Fuck, I need to get better at doing that. For a person who

deals with words for a living, I sure don't know how to talk. Yet this time was somehow easier. I'm getting used to saying it aloud. Maybe that's part of the healing, too.

Trina's eyes go wide, and her hand clutches mine on the table. "What? When?"

I clear my throat, determined not to be an awkward mess about the rest of this conversation. "Five years ago. In New York."

Her entire expression shifts from shock to horror, and I'm suddenly wishing I could melt into myself again. But I take a deep breath and watch her carefully, readying myself to take on whatever emotion comes next.

"You were *having a miscarriage* when we handed you that deal." She states it like a fact, then uses her free hand to cover her red-painted mouth. "Holy shit, Scarlett. No wonder. Why didn't you say anything?"

I shrug. I don't have an answer for that. Words escape me yet again.

Trina must realize I'm not going to respond because she drops her hand from her mouth to the table. She still hasn't let go of mine with her other hand. "Ryan's?"

I nod.

"Does he know?"

"I told him yesterday."

"Well." She laughs without an ounce of humor. "You've had quite a couple of days, then, haven't you?"

The smile that breaks my lips open feels like a rainbow after the rain. I should have known a long time ago Trina wouldn't blanch at this. She is as steadfast and supportive as they come. But I didn't think I could trust anyone back then. I'm glad I can now.

"Second time in my life that's been true." It's a dry joke, just like hers.

Trina nods thoughtfully, her warm hand still resting on top of mine. "Lots of parallels, I suppose." When I blink at her in surprise, she winks. "I can be literary, too, you know."

I laugh, then, and it sounds crackly, but it feels good. Swiping at my eyes, I realize I've been crying. When did I turn into such a weeper?

"So, what are you going to do about it this time?" she asks. And here we are, at the precipice of the question she probably called me here to ask. She knows I don't want to do this again. Our terms were to never rush a release or have another press tour like that.

Chewing on my bottom lip, I meet her gaze and hold it. If I'm going to say this, I want to be looking her in the eyes when I do, facing it head-on.

"I don't think I can do it."

She studies me for a moment, then her red lips twist into a sad smile and she nods slowly, as if she knew already. "I'm so sorry."

I flip my hand over so I can squeeze hers. "Me too."

"I came here with a plan to wiggle out of your contract with Anastasios and pitch this book to a bunch of other houses, but...do you want to hear it?"

Another editor and another campaign and another risk? I shake my head. "I don't think I'm in the right place for that right now." I watch Trina try to hide her disappointment for a minute, then I add, "That's not a *never.* It's a *not right now.*"

"That's fair," she begrudgingly admits. "What will you do?"

Sighing, I look out the window in front of me. People walk back and forth, laughing and enjoying the sunshine. Spring in Chicago is wonderful like that. All of a sudden, the cold breaks and everyone sheds their outer layers. For months, people talk about how nice the weather is and how wonderful it is to be outside again after the bitter cold of winter. I want to be those people. I want to walk in the sunshine and talk about simple things and be happy.

Can I be happy without writing?

"I don't know," I say honestly. It's an answer to both of our questions, and it's the best I can do right now.

"You'll figure it out," Trina says.

I hope she's right.

TRINA AND I chat for another hour or so. The door is open now, so she asks me more about everything that happened five years ago. I tell her some things, but she reads me pretty well and changes the subject when I get uncomfortable. It's nice having a friend to talk to. I guess that's what we are now—just friends. Even if my royalties still pay for her groceries.

When we finish our coffees, we part ways. I check my phone on the way back to my apartment to see four missed calls and no voicemails. Three are from Ryan, but one is from a number I haven't seen in a long time. I stop in the middle of the sidewalk and stare at it for a minute until someone bumps into me, and I move nearer to a building so I'm out of the way.

It couldn't have been a mistake. She hasn't called me in five years, whether on purpose or otherwise. I never thought I'd hear from her again, and suddenly, I desperately need to know why she called. With a heaping dose of false confidence in my own ability to keep it together, I touch the number and bring the phone to my ear. It rings once before she answers, like she's been waiting for me to call back.

"Scarlett?"

"Mandy?" Her voice is unmistakable, but I still can't believe it. That feeling of watching myself live my life is back because it doesn't seem real that I could be talking to my former best friend after five years of silence.

"Holy shit," she breathes out. She sounds relieved. "Are you okay?"

Where was this concern years ago when I was going through the absolute hardest part of my life alone? If I had any energy left after the day I've had, I'd shout all of the creative obscenities I've been saving up over the years. But right now, the best I can muster is curiosity. "What do you mean?"

She launches into her questions at about a mile a minute. "I saw that post and all the comments. You're publishing again? Was this some kind of marketing ploy? I'm guessing no because it's not like you. Were you supposed to use your name? Who outed you? Did Ryan find you?"

"Whoa," I interrupt her. "Slow down. Where is this coming from?"

Taking a deep breath, she starts again, calmer this time. "That post of you and Ryan at that coffee shop. It's all over social media. But it felt weird, you know? I took that picture. I remember going with you guys and taking a bunch for you to use and you posted that one. So, I guessed something wasn't right, and I wanted to..." She trails off.

"You wanted to what, Mandy? Get a front-row seat to the show?" Even I can hear the bitterness in my voice, but I decide to lean into it. If everyone who has ever wronged me wants a piece of me today, I guess they can each have a small one until there's nothing left.

"No." She sounds frustrated. "Listen, you're not going to believe me, and that's fine. I wouldn't expect you to. But after the last time we talked, I thought a lot about our conversation. It haunted me, you know? I was wrong. Ryan called looking for you, and that was when I realized you'd left. I wanted to apologize but...I didn't know if you would have answered."

"I wouldn't have. I really needed you, and you acted like a bitch." I hadn't meant to say it quite so bluntly, but no matter what I had said, the sentiment would have been the same.

"Yes," she admits, though it sounds like it pains her. "I did. I'm sorry. I think..." She trails off, then makes a frustrated noise. "I was so jealous of you. There I was, after two years with a book on submission, signing with a small press. And you...well, you know what you had. It never even crossed my mind that you weren't happy. How could you not have been?"

"It would seem a lot of people had that exact same question," I say drily.

"Right. But you get so scared when you sign that first deal, you know? It all feels so tenuous, like it could fall apart at any minute. You get people telling you to behave, watch what you say and who you're with—"

I let out a low growl and start walking again. Something about standing still and rehashing old shit feels unbearable. "I don't really need to hear all over again about how my life was perfect and I had no reason to be upset, Mandy. I've spent years unlearning all of that."

"I know," she interrupts. "I know. That's why I finally called you. You were never the problem. The industry is the problem. JMP was the problem. I..." She coughs. "I was the problem. And I get it if you never want to talk to me again. But please believe me when I say the only reason I called was to see if you're okay."

A beat of silence passes while I walk and think of what to say. When I come up to my building, I open the front door and get into the elevator. "I was, eventually. And now I'm not. But... the darkness doesn't get to take over anymore, you know? I will be okay again."

That's all I can give her. As lonely as I've been and as much as I want my friends back, the hurt she caused is still very real. It's going to take time for her to earn my trust again.

When the elevator doors open on my floor, I peer down the hallway. A figure is sitting across from my door, silhouetted by the afternoon light coming in from the window at the end of the corridor. He's leaning his head against the wall and resting his arms against his legs, which are bent at the knee and folded up near his chest. The sunlight glints off his glasses, but as soon as he turns his head to see me, he folds his long limbs under him and jumps up to face me.

"Hey," I say into the phone. "I have to go."

"Okay." Mandy sounds defeated but maybe also a little hopeful. "Can we...talk again sometime?"

I could lie. I could reject her outright and say something hurtful so she can get a taste of her own medicine. But despite what people might think, I never wanted to hurt anyone. I only ever wanted to protect myself.

"Yeah, maybe," I say as Ryan locks eyes with me from where he stands. "I'll call you." I don't wait for her to say goodbye before I hang up. But it isn't long before I break eye contact with him and walk up to my door to unlock it.

"I'm kind of peopled-out today," I tell him as I open my door. He follows me inside, and I sigh as I close the door behind us. Suddenly unbearably tired, it takes a lot of effort to face him, but I do.

He looks haggard. His dark hair is standing up at all angles, which is clearly the work of his worried hands. His glasses are smudged, so he's probably been rubbing his eyes. His clothes are rumpled, too, which makes me wonder how long he's been sitting on the cold floor of my apartment hallway.

"I needed to see you."

I walk past him to toss my keys and purse on a chair. "Why? Figured I flew the coop again?" God, when the fuck did I get so angry? If anyone had asked me even two days ago, I'd have said anger was never my primary emotion—at least it hasn't been since I was bleeding in a hotel room in New York—but it sure feels like it is now.

Ryan steps closer but doesn't touch me. I don't know what would hurt more, having his hands on me or not, so I stand right where I am and decide to let him make the first move.

"Are you going to leave again?" He whispers the words as if speaking them any louder would summon a repeat of the same curse that came upon us last time.

I huff and look to the side, unable to meet his eyes again. "Depends on what you mean by 'leave.'"

Like a switch has flipped, his long fingers circle around my biceps as if holding on to me could keep me from disappearing before his very eyes. "Scarlett, no—"

"I can't do it, Ryan." I also can't listen to his pleas. If he begs me to keep writing, I might give in. For this man, who has seen the worst of me and loves me both in spite and because of it, I'd do anything.

"Don't leave me again." His voice is deep, husky. It's a command and a prayer, and he's looking at me like I'm the goddess who could answer both.

"I couldn't," I say. "But I can't see any way out of this with all the pieces of me intact either."

He drops his hands and takes a step back from me, and the loss of contact is so unexpected, I gasp. But the look on his face is one of pure devastation. He shakes his head slowly as he says, "You're pulling the book."

Straightening my spine, I feign the confidence I need to get through this. "I have to. I won't survive another round. And please don't tell me it'll be different this time. It doesn't matter."

Ryan's expression hardens, and fear settles deep in my gut. Despite all the reassurances—that I am more than my books, that he loves me for who I am and not what I write, that he'll stay by my side no matter what—my books have never truly been off the table. When words and souls and bodies are so wrapped up that you don't know where one ends and the other begins, what happens if one of those is untangled? Does the whole thing unravel?

"The world needs this book." His voice is firm. "You're not going to let some asshole win, are you? This won't last forever. They'll convince JMP that signing you was a good move, and then it'll be over."

"It's more than just what Charles did." I sink into an empty chair. "You and I both know that once they realize how much they can make if I play along, they'll never let me rest again. We like to tell ourselves that it's about the art, not the money. And that's true to some extent...until someone makes a bunch of the latter." I turn my gaze up to meet his again, needing him to understand. "I loved writing all my books, Ryan. They're all pieces of me, and the fact that each one of them has gone through you in one way or another only makes them more special. But I can't take part in another money-making scheme that involves these books I love so much. It won't make me happy. I want to be happy."

I turn my eyes to him, internally pleading for him to understand. All I've ever wanted was to exist with my words. With him. I can't do that with so many other people in the mix. And I certainly can't do that when I'm not actually with him, when I'm traveling the country living for phone calls and counting sleeps.

Ryan falls to his knees in front of me. He cups my face with his hands, and I have no choice but to look right into his brown eyes. "You're a writer. You're the best damn writer I've ever worked with. You cannot let Charles Hall take that away from you."

"I'm not letting him take anything," I counter. "I'm making a very conscious decision to keep it for myself."

He shakes his head again, narrowing his eyes. "Then don't let him take it away from the rest of the world who needs it."

"From the rest of the world? Or from you?"

Ryan flinches, and his fingers go stiff where they rest at my temples, but he doesn't say anything.

"I'm not leaving you. I already told you that. But I think you need to decide if you can be with a different version of me. One who isn't a best-selling author. One who is messier than maybe you even thought, given everything we talked about yesterday. Because that's all I have to offer." I take a deep breath. "This is me, and this is what I need. And I know now that I'm worth more than my job, but instead of supporting this decision, you're yet again ignoring what this is going to do to me and begging me to make the best of the cards I'm being dealt. For what? For some anonymous audience who might feel something when they read my books? Or for you? Because this stopped being about me the minute they mentioned book clubs and tours and saving their own asses, and you know it."

"It's not about me," he says, but I'm not convinced. "Where is the Scarlett who told Charles where he could shove it earlier today? You're stronger than this. I know you are."

"This *is* strength, Ryan. I need to be strong enough to recognize that no matter what I do, this is going to keep happening. And then, I need to be strong enough to walk away and stay away."

"No," he says quietly, disappointment stretching the word and making it linger in the space between us. He rocks back on his heels and drops his hands to my knees. "I don't believe this is what you truly want."

I throw my hands up. "Of course this isn't what I want!" I exclaim. "All I've ever wanted is to write my little books and live my life and love you. Things just keep getting bigger and bigger without any input from me. I can't write myself out of this one."

Ryan jumps to his feet. "Yes, you can." He punctuates each word with a point of his finger at me. "I saw you take Charles down about five pegs today. I was going to jump in and help, but you didn't even need me. You weren't going to let him have any satisfaction. I saw a fire in you that I haven't seen in so long. But it's still there. You still have it. Stoke those flames, Scarlett. Take the life you want. Grab it and make it yours."

I stand too. Somehow, it seems better to be standing when you shout at someone. "That's not how any of this works! This doesn't have a happy ending. I might have taken him down a peg, but Charles got what he wanted. And one way or another, Anastasios will get what he wants too. Because I'll either go along with his plan or I'll be out of his hair. The only agency I have here is to choose between two bad options, so I'm going to choose the one that saves at least a part of *me*"—my voice cracks on the word—"not the words I wrote on a page."

He stiffens suddenly and runs a hand through his hair. Letting out a forceful breath, he drops his arm back to his side. "You are more than your words," he says quietly. "I've told you that before, and I meant it. I'll love you forever—I meant that too. But this isn't how it ends, Scarlett. Charles won't win. He doesn't deserve it." His eyes meet mine, and I can't help feeling like it seems final. "But you do. Be strong enough to take it back."

Without another word, he stalks to the door, opens it, and leaves.

Walking away from Scarlett has to be the hardest thing I've ever done. But between the miscarriage and the book, I don't know where my head is at anymore. She doesn't need my confusion right now. She's already making stupid decisions based on a couple of bad days, and it didn't seem like anything I was saying would change her mind. So, I left.

Once I get a chance to collect my thoughts, I'll go back to her with a more rational argument about why she's doing the wrong thing. Maybe I'll devise a plan for her. I'll title it *Ten Steps to the Life You Want*. No, too close to a self-help book. More like *Why the Bad Guy Can't Win*. I'll even put together a presentation. What the hell else am I doing? Not editing her book. That was yet another thing ripped out from under me today.

Charles fucking Hall cannot have the last laugh here. I won't allow it. I don't care if life isn't a book with a happy ending. It simply cannot happen. Even if he gets to keep his deal, he shouldn't get to make Scarlett give up hers in the process.

I check my phone before starting my car, but there aren't any messages. After Anastasios kicked us out of his office, I left before I heard any news about whatever phone calls he was making in there. Casey told me he'd update me if he heard anything before practically shoving me out the door. He could tell how nervous I was about Scarlett. I couldn't lose her again.

And yet, here I am, driving away from her apartment instead

of folding her into my arms and telling her everything will be all right.

When I pull up to a stoplight, I call Casey. I'm sure he doesn't have news about Charles, but I'm already sick of sitting alone with my own thoughts. His phone rings a few times over my speakers before he answers.

"How is she?" he asks by way of greeting.

"She's thinking about pulling the book." I don't tell him she's already made her decision. She can do that herself if she really wants to.

"I can't say I'm surprised." Casey sounds as if he's shifting in his chair. "That meeting was intense, and we're basically telling her she has to do a bunch of stuff she made very clear she was never going to do again. I'm actually kind of proud of her for sticking to her boundaries."

"How are you not more worried about this?" I shout as I hit my steering wheel in frustration.

"Whoa," he says, his tone one of warning. "Isn't the goal to keep Scarlett here this time? With you? You really want her to have to go through all of that again—"

"It's temporary," I interject, though now I'm not sure who I'm trying to convince—him or myself. "It's a few months of a tour, and once the dust settles, she can renegotiate."

"But..." He draws the word out. "Why would you want the woman you love to go through that again even for a few months when she doesn't want to?"

When he puts it that way, it sounds like I'm the asshole now, and I don't like it. "The world needs her books," I say adamantly. "And I need her."

Casey hums. "It's kind of wild how you don't even hear yourself."

"What do you mean?" I ask, flicking on my turn signal and pulling into the left turn lane.

"Wait, are you driving? Didn't you go to see her?"

"We had a fight. Sort of. I needed a minute to think. I don't know, man. It's been a long couple of days."

"Oh my god," Casey groans. I can picture him with his elbow on his desk and his head in his hands. "You are a moron."

"Fuck off," I say, but there's no venom behind the words.

"I'm serious," he insists. "You say you're so worried about her, but when it comes down to it, you not only don't think about what this is going to do to her, but you leave her alone—"

"I've done nothing but think about her *since we met*," I spit out.

"Okay, fine. Maybe you're too close to it. Back up a minute and look at the big picture." When he's only met with my obstinate silence, he prods me again. "Come on. You can do this. You're an editor. Look at the whole story. Pretend you're both characters. What is your character doing here? What is his purpose?"

"My—"

"His," Casey corrects. "Back up."

I shove out a frustrated sigh. "Fine. *His* purpose is her and her words. It always has been."

"Okay. So, is this his big hero moment? Where he tells her she can do it all this time despite multiple protestations and evidence to the contrary? Despite her clearly having trouble keeping herself on this side of depression already? Is he going to have her repeat the past? Is that what our hero would do?"

"No. He'd make sure it was different this time..." I trail off. It's a weak, tentative response. And it's wrong. I can feel that.

You can't fix her.

Casey hums. He's probably smirking, too. "I think you're almost there."

You can't save her either.

I swing my steering wheel around and pull into my parking spot, but I leave the car running. The back of my head hits the headrest in defeat. "What do I do?"

"I can't do that part for you," he says. "But I think it starts with taking a hard look at what she actually needs versus what you think she needs. Maybe turning off your optimism and realistically thinking about what the past tells you about your future. If this were a book, you'd want it to end realistically, not in some fantasyland where everything works out with sunshine and roses. Start there."

Using my thumb to rub my ring, I nod. My dad would have known what to do. He always did right by my mom. Always.

I sigh in defeat. "Let me know if you hear about Charles, okay?"

"Will do. And Ryan?"

"Yeah?"

"I know you're well aware of this, but Scarlett is really special. And so fucking talented. This book...I get why you don't want to let it go. But I have to believe that by supporting her now, you'll see more from her later—you know what I mean?"

I'm starting to get it. Lightly running my fingers over the tattoo on my forearm, I say, "Yeah. I hope you're right."

But what I don't say is that I also hope it doesn't take another five years to get there.

Chapter 37

Scarlett

Ryan doesn't want to be followed. I know because I've been there, and I recognized the look on his face when he left. So, I stay right where I am.

Left alone, I stare into space in silence for a while before ultimately turning on a baking show to at least try to quiet my racing thoughts. When it gets dark, I change into my satin pajamas, put my hair in a messy bun, and curl up under a blanket to watch some more.

I tell myself I'm not falling back into any kind of depressive episode. I'm just watching television like a normal person. Everyone binges shows, right? This is a totally mundane thing to do on a weekday evening when I don't have work to do in the morning.

No work in the morning. I actually think, for normal people, that would be fun. A reprieve from the grind. But writing was never a grind, even if it was hard to shut it down at the end of the day. It was all the people-facing stuff—the travel, the interviews, the signings. Even those wouldn't have been so bad if there weren't so many of them.

Can I really walk away from the magic of bringing characters and scenes to life using only words on a page? That's what it is—magic. A little kernel of an idea starts in my mind, all tiny and fuzzy at first. It grows bigger and bigger until it solidifies and intensifies to the point where if I don't get it out, I start to feel like I might crawl out of my own skin. That's when I pull out the laptop and type like a mad woman late into the night and early in the morning. And when I'm done, there it is—a living, breathing story on the page.

And then Ryan comes in. He tugs and tweaks and asks *Why?* and *What if?* He suggests stronger words. He makes it a stronger story. I take it back and respond. It's a beautiful conversation where we weave thoughts and ideas, we give and take, we help it expand—and it wouldn't happen if it weren't for that little fuzzy kernel of an idea. If I never let it grow.

Words on paper. Ink on pages. A whole new world where there wasn't one before.

Magic.

Always more magical because he was part of it. If I stop now, that piece of us will wither away. That piece of *me* will, too. There's no way around it. Can I really let that happen?

We could replace it with a different kind of magic. I press a hand to my abdomen, remembering another tiny thing. It never got to grow, but we could try again. Maybe. If he wants to.

But not tonight. Tonight I'm pretending to be normal. I'm resting. No work in the morning. Ryan and I will talk eventually, when he's ready. I don't have to figure everything out today. Which was another one of Dianne's mantras. I'm starting to realize I haven't appreciated her enough. I should get her a gift or something.

For a few hours, I watch bakers create beautiful, intricate treats out of disparate ingredients, the flickering light of the screen the only brightness in the room, before my phone dings with an incoming message.

Trina

Thought you might find this interesting.

There's a link included, so I click on it. When it loads, it's a social media post about Charles Hall, which is strange. I didn't mention anything about Charles when we were out for coffee. I had figured his role in this was ultimately unimportant. In the story of my life, he might be a catalyst, but he's still always going to be just a side character. Nothing was going to change if she knew about it or not, so I didn't bother bringing it up.

But she's right. I am interested. Scrolling down a bit, I read the caption.

Charles Hall's anticipated Midnight on Main Street *will be delayed indefinitely. We know this is a hard blow for his fans, but after months of trying to find the right home for it, there doesn't seem to be a publisher that is the right fit. Alas, we will not give up the fight, dear Charlatans. Onward and upward.*

"Does this idiot write his own social media captions?" I mutter to myself as I type out a response to Trina.

He calls his fans "Charlatans"?

Trina

You read that whole post and that was your takeaway?

It means someone who deceives others.

Trina

Seems appropriate to me.

I pull the corners of my lips down and nod. She's not wrong. But before I can tell her that, she messages again.

Trina

No one is publishing his book.

Yes, I can read.

Trina

That isn't the least bit interesting to you?

Smiling softly to myself, I glance up as one of the bakers pours batter into a cake pan. Maybe Ryan was right. Maybe the bad guy doesn't get to win this time.

Wait...

I blink rapidly a few times, trying to convince myself that this is a coincidence. But how could it be? Not twelve hours ago, Charles Hall's smug-ass face was telling me he got an amazing deal for that book by selling me out. Why did it die today of all days?

Pushing the Call button, I lean forward to mute the television as I press my phone to my ear. It only takes one ring for Trina to answer.

"There it is," she says, self-satisfied.

"You knew about Charles."

"Yes."

"Ryan told you."

"Also yes."

"You didn't say anything today."

"Neither did you."

"You got his deal pulled? How did you do that?" I can't help myself—I'm practically giddy. My knees are bouncing up and down with a sudden energy, and I can feel my body vibrating.

"I didn't do anything."

"But then how—"

Finally, Trina jumps in. "Dumbest smart person I know, I swear. Come on, Scarlett. Ryan ran up after seeing you two go at it in the lobby and marched straight into Anastasios's office. Pretty big deal, if you ask me, since he's already in some shit for dating one of his authors, or didn't you notice?"

I did notice, but it wasn't my biggest concern at the time. "So, what? In some grand gesture, he told Anastasios, who called JMP, and they both decided that they weren't going to get played by some prick?"

"Pretty much."

"JMP already gave him a deal for information about me. They wouldn't just pull it. That's not how publishing works," I insist.

"Maybe Anastasios made a good case that some average man thinking he can use an extremely talented woman to further his own mediocrity wasn't the narrative either of them wanted." Trina sounds like she's shrugging nonchalantly, but I can tell this is exciting for her.

"Wow." I lean back on my couch. All the bakers are putting their cakes in the oven now. "So, what does this mean for me?"

"Nothing," she says simply.

"What do you mean nothing? Why would you send that to me if it means nothing?"

"You said you were done publishing. Sounded pretty final. This is just interesting information, that's all."

This isn't how it ends, Scarlett. Charles won't win. He doesn't deserve it.

Ryan's words echo in my mind, repeating, growing, gaining purchase. Solidifying.

But you do. Be strong enough to take it back.

I take a deep breath, laughing softly on the exhale. "I need a win, Trina. Can you help me?"

"Fuck yes." She sounds like she's punching air. "I knew you'd get there. Let's do this."

Chapter 38

Ryan

I WAKE UP the next morning with dread pooling low in my belly. There's only one certainty in my life right now: I fucked up. Badly.

Last time, I had no way of knowing that pushing for that deal wasn't what Scarlett needed. I truly thought I was helping—that if she were adequately compensated for the work she was putting in, it might feel more fair, more motivating. And then she was gone, and I couldn't fully grasp the ramifications of my actions until she was here with me again.

But I'm not the hero of this story. I think that's what Casey was getting at with his little "be an editor" exercise. The hero would learn from the past. If yesterday is any indication, I haven't learned shit. Instead of being different this time, I tried to convince her that things outside of our control would be different. And she was right. They won't. Not really. Not in any important way. Not in the way she needs.

I try to call her when I wake up, but she doesn't answer. If I didn't have to go into the office, I'd stand outside of her apartment with a boombox over my head, blasting love songs until she came outside to me. But I'm on thin ice as it is, so I head to work.

"Hello," Margie singsongs as I walk into my office. "Your phone rang a few times this morning."

Glancing at the clock on the wall, I frown. "It's only just after nine."

She shrugs. "All I know is that it was ringing. I don't think anyone left any messages, though."

The voicemail light isn't on, so she's right. Strange. I don't know very many people who would call my office line before nine, and certainly no one who would do that and not leave a message. Maybe it was Anastasios and I'm in deeper shit than I thought. Maybe it was about Scarlett.

"Thanks, Margie. What do you have on the docket today?" I ask as I sink into my chair and try to shake the feeling that something is very, very wrong.

"Mucking through the slush pile, as usual." She tilts her head and presses her lips together. "I suppose you probably need a new project now."

My shoulders fall as I sigh. The thought of going back to business as usual is the nail in my coffin this morning. "Yeah, I guess I do."

Just as the depressing realization that I'm back to editing works that can't hold a candle to Scarlett's is sinking in, Trina appears in my doorway in a flurry of orange skirts and jingly jewelry. Her red lips are twisted into a mischievous grin.

"Don't you ever answer your phone?" she asks.

I'm out of my chair in a second, walking toward her. "I just got here. What happened? Is Scarlett okay? Why didn't you call my cell?"

"Down, boy." She raises her eyebrows, but that smile is still plastered on her face. "She's on her way here. Last I talked to her, she was a few minutes behind me. I thought you might want to...I don't know. Meet her in the lobby or something."

She's on her way to tell everyone she's not publishing her book. I do my best to fight the dread. This is what she needs, and I will support her, even if I'm disappointed. But Trina is right. I can see her. I need to see her.

Nodding once, I rush past her out my door. But before I can even hit the button for the elevator, Trina's voice follows me down the hallway.

"Hey, Whitlock," she calls. "Let her do this, okay? Trust her."

Swallowing hard, I nod again. The elevator doors ding open behind me, and before I know it, I'm descending. My heart is in my throat, and my hands wiggle at my sides as if some of my nervous energy could be shaken out through my fingers.

There wasn't any real part of me that thought she'd disappear again, but I'd be lying if I said the possibility hadn't crossed my mind last night while I was busy thinking about how much of an idiot I had been to walk away from her in the first place.

But now she's coming here. She's on her way. And I guess I didn't realize how afraid of never seeing her again I truly was, because the relief I feel when the elevator doors open just as she's stepping into the lobby is palpable.

Scarlett has always been beautiful, but today she's radiant. Her dark hair is shining in the sunlight as it cascades in soft waves down her back. She's wearing a loose-fitting cream blouse that has been tucked into navy linen pants that cinch her waist and flow outward toward her brown ballet flats. And when she turns her blue eyes to me, they sparkle.

The icing on the cake is the luminous smile that expands her pink lips when she sees me.

"Hi," she says, and with that one word, I can tell she's happier than she's been in a long time. It's a casual word, relaxed. I don't think I even realized how stressed she had been and for how long until seeing her now, put together and smiling and glowing, tossing me a "Hi" in the lobby.

The weight of publishing was pulling her down, and it happened so slowly, so quietly that I missed it. Not only did I miss it, I helped it happen. Now that she's about to let it go, she's free.

I won't stand in the way of that freedom. Not anymore.

Ten. I count the steps it takes to get to her, and it's ten. Ten too many, if you ask me, but when I'm standing in front of her, watching her face tip up toward me, smelling her black-tea scent, I can't imagine being anywhere else with anyone else ever again.

Professional workplace decorum be damned. I thread my fingers into her silky hair and tug to angle her face just right so I can devour her lips with mine. She opens easily for me, and I slip my tongue in to dance with hers, capturing her small moan for myself. As she presses her body closer to mine, we lock together, all of my angles meeting her soft curves. Exactly how we should be.

I break the kiss well before I want to, trying to restrain myself a little in my place of work. But when I open my eyes, hers are studying me softly, and that smile is back on her now swollen lips.

"Hi," I say back, and we both laugh. God, it feels so fucking good to hear her laugh.

"Listen, I want to explain—" she starts, but I cut her off.

"No. You don't have to explain anything. I'm the one who needs to explain. Scratch that. I need to grovel at your feet for the rest of eternity."

"Cool it with the hyperbole, oh Wise and Witty Syntax Sorcerer, Wielder of the Red Pen, and Master of Manuscripts." She giggles. She actually giggles.

I blink in surprise. "You...You remember that whole thing?"

She tilts her head and pinches her brows. "Of course I do," she says quietly, the words full of emotion. "They might not be tattooed on my arm, but they're right there in my heart. I never stopped loving you, either, you know."

Tears sting at the corners of my eyes, and I breathe a little huff full of awe. "Scarlett, I'm so sorry. Whatever you need to do now, I'm with you. One hundred percent. Forever. Okay? I promise."

That smile is back, and it's stunning. I kiss her forehead for the only reason that I can't keep my lips off of her for long, and I also want to watch that smile for a few more minutes.

"I'm glad to hear you say that." She reaches out her hand and interlaces her fingers with mine. "Come with me?"

"I can try," I offer. "I doubt they'll let me in."

"They will," she says, and she's so sure of it. Her eyebrows tick up as she raises her chin in a challenge. "They'll do what I want."

It's hard to argue with that, so hand in hand, we go back upstairs and right into the conference room where the team is, indeed, waiting for her. Trina is already seated, a smug smile curling on her face. Casey is there, too, trying unsuccessfully not to look confused. Meri is representing the publicity team. And Anastasios Martis sits tall in the center of it all, his face giving nothing away.

"Good morning, Ms. Frye," he greets her before turning his gaze to me. "Mr. Whitlock, thank you for walking her up here, but you're no longer needed."

"Ryan stays," Scarlett states, her voice powerful and clear. Those blue eyes, glittering a few minutes ago, are now cold and unmoving, trained on my boss across the conference table.

Just when I think he's going to double down, he nods once. "Fine."

Quickly, I sink into the empty chair in front of me before he can change his mind, but Scarlett remains standing. For a second, I think about standing again, holding her hand and helping her get through this, but I stay where I am. I have to trust that she can do this on her own.

She clears her throat and meets the eyes of each person in the room in turn. "Thank you for meeting me on such short notice."

"We are glad you called this meeting, actually." Anastasios motions to one of the others for some papers. "There are a few finer points of your new contract that we'd like to go over—"

"All due respect, Mr. Martis," she interrupts, "but I'd appreciate it if you would let me talk."

The entire room goes still. Anastasios sets the papers down with the control of someone who is not used to being talked to like this. But he must also know that his hold on this entire situation is flimsy at best because he folds his hands on the table in front of him and says, "Of course."

"Thank you." Scarlett takes a big breath. "Originally, I was coming here today to tell you that I will not be signing a new contract, that I was pulling *Becoming* from publication. I even had Trina draw up a plan to reimburse you for the resources you've already spent on this project so there would be no hard feelings, unlike last time." Her lips twitch against a grin at her own dry sarcasm, and little bubbles of pride start to rise up in my chest. Even in giving up on this book, she's not going to let them have any reason to fault her.

Everyone in the room collectively stiffens, but they must read the determined look on her face because no one says anything. She takes a sip of the water on the table in front of her before she continues.

"I know you are aware of Charles Hall's involvement in all of this. I also know that you, sir"—she addresses Anastasios—"had a major hand in ensuring that the deals he thought he'd get out of his information were rescinded. Thank you for that."

He nods at her again, this time a small smirk twisting his lips. He must have enjoyed taking that asshole down. I can't blame him.

"But you never would have known about any of that if it weren't for Ryan." Scarlett doesn't look at me when she says it, but I can't take my eyes off her. She's standing tall and powerful, and even though she shifts uncomfortably on her feet, her words are true. She knows what she's doing.

"I'm not the type of person to say anything when I've been wronged. Or, at least, I wasn't. I hope one day, I can be. But Ryan...he won't let people like Charles Hall win, and I think that's admirable. If there were any questions that he has always had not only the best interests of this book at heart but my best interests as well, I would think his willingness to tell you everything that happened despite the fact that you're unhappy with him should dispel them."

My brows pinch as I stare up at her. She's setting something up here, but I don't know what. Is she trying to save me this time? If that's the case, I want to jump up and tell her she doesn't have to.

Anastasios flicks his gaze to me, then back to Scarlett. "I won't argue with that," he says.

"Good." She shifts her feet again and rests her hands on the back of the chair in front of her. "In the interest of full disclosure, Ryan and I were involved when we were both at JMP. Any relationship between us was established long before I signed with you, and I agreed to work with him because I knew he was the best person to work on my book. He only felt the need to disclose our relationship because you accused him of leaking my identity. I need to make it clear that I am not the only one who lost something because of Charles Hall. Ryan did, too. He loves this book as much as I do, and I think Casey would agree that his edits so far have been spot on."

Casey nods, but my frown deepens. What the hell is she doing here? I take a breath to chime in, but she splays the fingers of the hand at her side closest to me in a signal to keep quiet, so I close my mouth and try my best to stay out of it.

"Ryan went one step further yesterday. He reminded me that men like Charles Hall shouldn't win. Yes, his deals were rescinded, but if I don't publish my book, he wins in a different way. I cannot let that happen." She pulls the chair out and finally sits down, folding her hands in front of her in a move that mirrors Anastasios's exactly.

My eyes widen in surprise. She's not pulling her book. Those little bubbles of pride grow so fast, I'm afraid they might burst. And as I look around the table at the eyes trained on her, I know I'm not the only one feeling this way. Trina's clearly in on this—her smug satisfaction makes sense now. Casey is trying to cover a smile with his hand. Even Meri looks impressed.

She's going to do this the way she always wanted.

"You want this book." She says it with a well-earned arrogance. "It will sell. We all know that. Everyone will love—or, at least, be interested in—my comeback story, even if we don't shove it in their faces on every major network. In fact, people might be even more curious if we leave a little to the imagination, right, Meri?"

"It could work," the publicist admits.

"It will work, because I'm good at this." She flashes her sparkly interview smile with a sassy tilt of her head. Casey stifles a chuckle, and Meri huffs, amused. Scarlett turns serious again. "So,

I am here to present my terms. They are nonnegotiable. First, we will not rush the release. You have free rein to publish any teasers or reveals you want or do whatever preorder campaigns you think might work, but the timeline remains. We take my pen name off the cover and use my real name from the start. No sense in playing that game anymore. And make it a good cover this time. I'm not an inexperienced author you can push around. Leverage my name in whatever way you choose. I will do one month of pre-release events and one month of post-release events. Two per week, sixteen total. Whichever events, wherever you want, but that's my limit. After that, I'm coming home"—her voice cracks on the word, but she straightens her shoulders and carries on—"to write the next book. We can see how this goes and negotiate press for that one, but I have to tell you upfront that I won't be willing to do much more than this." She looks at me then and smiles. "I have other things I need to focus on."

"I think we can work with that," Meri chimes in. "In this case, if we pick the right events, more might not necessarily be better."

"You've made your terms clear, Ms. Frye," Anastasios says with no little amount of irritation. "We will need to discuss this."

"Oh, I'm not done." Scarlett flicks her gaze back to the rest of the table. Trina ticks up an eyebrow, clearly unaware there was more, but Scarlett lifts her chin in determination. "Just one last thing. If you want this book, you'll let Ryan continue edits. You can kick the next one to whomever you feel is appropriate, but Ryan started this, and I want him to finish it with me."

Anastasios's nostrils flare and his eyes narrow. "We'll talk about it and get back to you."

Trina's eyes bounce back and forth between Scarlett and me before she reclines in her chair and folds her arms over her chest. "You know this book will do exactly what you were expecting it to before. It'll be good for your imprint and make you a ton of money. With Scarlett Frye's name on it from the start, you're in an even better position. I don't think you understand that she almost quit entirely. As of yesterday afternoon, she was done. You've already broken your first contract with her. Someone else will scoop this book up in a heartbeat. She wants to stay here. Do not let her walk out of here without an answer."

The silence that falls over the room is deafening. My heartbeat roars in my ears. Scarlett reaches over and grabs my hand under the table. She doesn't look at me, but she squeezes once, and I squeeze back.

Whatever happens, she did exactly what I had hoped she would. She saw the life she wanted, and she reached out and took it.

It seems impossible, but I love her even more now than I did before. And whatever comes at us now, we can handle it together.

"Okay," Anastasios finally says. "We will draw up a contract with your terms and send it to your agent to review later today."

The desire to jump up and whoop into the air is so strong that I have to physically grab the bottom of my chair to keep myself seated. With all the professionalism in the world, Scarlett thanks him, and we all stand to file out of the room.

In the hallway, Casey shakes our hands. Trina gives us hugs. They go back to his office to talk about another writer or something that I am too distracted to remember. I walk out to the parking lot with Scarlett, where I pull her to the side of the building and kiss her senseless. It feels like the perfect outlet for the giddy pride in her that started building while I watched her in that room. Lucky for me, she seems more than willing to kiss me right back.

"You tricked me," I say into her skin when we come up for air.

"I didn't want to interrupt your groveling," she teases.

I nip at her ear. "You're amazing. I love you."

"*Love* isn't a strong enough word," she reminds me with a soft smile.

"No," I say. "But you're strong enough. We're strong enough. And that's really all that matters."

"I like that." She locks eyes with me, and we stand for a moment in the warm sunshine, smiling at each other like fools in love because we are. She may have won today, but I'm the real winner here. This brilliant, beautiful, strong woman is mine.

Eventually, we part ways—me back to the office to finish the edits on her book, and her to my condo to write until I get home. And when I do, I take her in my arms to kiss her and hold her. We eat tacos and make plans for all the things we want to do together, and when words inevitably fail us, as they are known to do, we spend the rest of the night showing each other exactly what it means to love.

One Year Later

I SIT CROSS-LEGGED on the chair in front of my desk in my newly renovated office, typing and deleting, typing and deleting. My hands are shaking so badly that I keep making stupid mistakes. Every few seconds, I glance at the timer I set on my phone. The numbers are moving slower than normal, I'm sure of it. Something must be wrong with it. Ryan's going to be home any minute, and I can't wait.

It didn't take very long after signing my new deal with Anastasios Press for me to move in with him. I spent practically every night at his place anyway, so it only made sense. When *Becoming* came out, he had the cover—a much better one than the first—framed and hung it in the office, telling me it was my room now.

"Bestselling authors need offices, not desks in bedrooms," he had said, and that was that.

The press tour was short. I know other outlets wanted to have me, but Trina fielded those calls expertly. And when it was time to pitch another book, she took that on as well. She's been exactly the kind of agent I always needed—making sure I get breaks and keeping Anastasios in check when they get overeager.

Ryan isn't my editor anymore, but that's okay. He still reads every word, and when I turn in drafts, I'm never quite sure what's mine and what's his. It's ours, which is exactly the way I want it.

I take comfort in all of that as I keep watch on the timer. It ticks so slowly.

When it finally rings, I shut it off and rush to the bathroom on shaky legs. And, of course, at that moment, Ryan comes in the front door.

"I brought food," he calls. I hear him put a crinkly bag down on the counter, then toss his keys aside. "And I have something for you." He sounds almost giddy, like he can't wait another minute either. The parallelism of us both being excited to share something important at the same time scratches a literary itch in my brain. We're in sync, even when we don't mean to be.

"Yeah?" I shout back, trying to keep my voice steady. There's a little kernel of emotion building in me. Joy? Fear? I'm not sure, and it seems too soon to name it. "I have something for you too."

I step out into the hallway, and his dark eyes find me immediately. "Hey, beautiful," he says, and it settles the anxious part inside of me. He comes around and hands me a small, rectangular package that's been wrapped in newspaper. "I can't wait. I picked this up today, and I was going to plan something special but..." He shrugs helplessly. "Me first?"

Laughing lightly, I start to carefully open it at the edges. "You got me a book?"

"For part one." He ticks an eyebrow up, then motions me on impatiently. "Open it."

"Okay, okay." I tear the paper off to reveal a hardcover book. The title reads *Stories and Second Chances*, and underneath is a beautifully illustrated picture of Ryan and me, lying on a blanket in a park with books and open takeout containers of tacos strewn about.

"Oh," I breathe as I delicately run my fingers over the image. "It's us." Looking up at him, all nervousness forgotten, I bite my lip. "What is this?"

Ryan smiles stiffly, like he knows this is a big fucking deal but doesn't want to admit it. "I'm not the writer here, but I know good stories. I thought ours was a pretty good one. So, I wrote down some of it and hired an illustrator and got it printed. Look inside."

I have a hard time taking my eyes off him, but his eagerness drives me to crack the book open. Each chapter starts with a beautiful illustration of us, and as I skim through them, I can see all of our best stories are there. Some of the tough ones, too, but that seems right. We've been through a lot, and each word has made us—even the hard ones.

When I get to what looks about halfway, I flip a page and am surprised to see a little part of the rest of the book hollowed out. Inside, there's a gold ring with a single diamond. I take it out of the book, and when I look up, Ryan is on one knee, right there in the middle of his living room.

"Marry me, Scarlett," he whispers.

"Oh my god," I breathe. "Are you serious?"

He nods, taking the book from my hands and placing it to the side. He gently takes the ring from my hand, and he slides it onto my ring finger. "This was my mom's. I want you to have it. I have always known I would marry you, but I kept waiting and waiting for the right time. I can't wait any longer. Please say you'll marry me, Scarlett."

"Of course I'll marry you," I say, and in a heartbeat, he's on his feet, kissing me and laughing.

"I love you." He presses a kiss to my neck, and my knees go weak. "I love your brain." Another kiss to my forehead. "I love your body." Another kiss on my jaw. "I love everything you are." Another kiss on my lips. "I love everything we'll be."

"Speaking of..." It's now or never, probably. "Can I give you my surprise now?"

He grumbles in protest as I try to extract myself from him. Reluctantly, he lets me go, and I go back to the bathroom. When I emerge again, holding the stick in my hand, Ryan is standing still, gaping at me as if words have failed him.

"Um..." I start, suddenly uncertain. "I know we weren't planning this. Again." I roll my eyes to the ceiling, feeling like I might actually cry. I'm happy—I think—but I need him with me this time.

"Scarlett..." He trails off, and his voice cracks. "Is that...?"

I wave the stick back and forth. "Surprise." And then I grimace at my own inability to do this right. "Ugh. Fuck. You gave me a whole-ass book, and all I can do is pee on something and wave it around like a moron—"

"You're pregnant," he says, his voice so full of awe it somehow erases every feeling of doubt I had.

Daring to give him a small smile, still a little afraid that if I let this bliss take hold, it'll be torn from me again, I nod. "Yeah." Biting my lip, I will the tears building at the corners of my eyes not to fall. "I'm happy. Are you happy? I really fucking want you to be happy."

Like a fire has been finally lit under him, he closes the distance between us and sweeps me in his arms. He twirls me around, then sets me on the ground and kisses me passionately.

"Happy?" he asks as he pulls back. He cups my jaw, his long fingers brushing gently against my cheek. "No." He smiles, his dark eyes crinkling at the corners as he looks down at me. "Elated, maybe. Overjoyed. Jubilant. Ecstatic." Each word comes louder and more ridiculous until we're both laughing, breathless and weightless with life and love and joy for this new little thing that's ours.

He kisses me again, until he finally pulls back to say what I already knew was coming, but I needed to hear it anyway.

"*Happy* isn't a strong enough word."

"Maxwell."

Scarlett stirs some cereal with the spoon in her right hand while rubbing her swollen belly with her left. She lifts her delicate fingers to turn the page of the book that lays open on the table next to her cereal, then returns her hand to her abdomen, stroking absent-mindedly.

I turn my head to cough into my shoulder before lifting my mug from the kitchen counter and carrying it over to join her at the table. She spares me a glance with an arched eyebrow before dropping her gaze back to her page.

"You don't like that one either," she states, resigned.

"It's not that I don't like it..." I trail off. She eyes me again, and I shrug. "Yeah, I don't like it. What would we call him?"

"We'd call him Maxwell," she says as if it's obvious.

I shake my head, taking a sip of coffee. "Everyone would want to call him Max. Three letters are too short for a name."

Scarlett squints at me, her hand going still on her belly. "As opposed to the four that make up Ryan?"

"I didn't pick my name, okay? I just think our boy deserves a good, strong name that lends itself to a good, strong nickname."

Her blue eyes tip up to the ceiling, but her features soften at the mention of our boy. In all honesty, I still can't quite believe it. Not only is Scarlett here with me, but we're about to welcome our baby boy in a few short months.

The early days after we learned of her pregnancy were fraught with worry for her. She tried not to let it show, but she had difficulty sleeping. Each night, I'd hold her as she drifted off, and in the middle of the night she'd jolt awake and run to the bathroom. At first, I thought it was morning sickness, and I started leaving crackers and ginger ale on her nightstand, but she eventually told me how she discovered her miscarriage in the middle of the night, alone in a hotel room.

My heart ached for her, and I tried to remind her of what her therapist had said—different pregnancy, different outcome. Ultimately, her doctor adjusted her medication which seemed to help, but Scarlett remained almost concerningly focused on her work, only talking about the pregnancy in short, disjointed bursts and clinical terms. I was the one who downloaded the app, knew what fruit the baby compared to, started adding baby things to my online cart.

After deciding we didn't want to know the sex of the baby at the halfway mark, I walked into her office one day to find her chewing on her nails and staring at the wall.

"It still doesn't feel real to me," she had said. When I asked her what would help her connect with this experience more, she blurted out, *"I want the baby to have a name."*

We went to the doctor a week later and found out we were having a boy. And now, with two months left, we still haven't come up with the right name.

"This shouldn't be that hard." She shovels a spoonful of cereal into her mouth. "Naming people is literally part of my job."

I push my glasses up my nose as I study her. "How do you pick character names? I don't think we've ever talked about that, now that I think about it."

"The characters name themselves," she says around a soggy mouthful. "I never have to work for it. It just...comes to me."

"Okay," I shrug. "Maybe his name will come to you."

"*Maxwell* came to me," she mumbles. "You didn't like it."

I chuckle into my coffee, shaking my head as I take another

sip. If there's one thing I trust, it's that we'll figure it out. We always do.

"BENJAMIN," SCARLETT CALLS from the bathroom after spitting her toothpaste into the sink.

"Ben," I counter. "Three letters."

"Oh my *god*," she groans. "You are insufferable."

I peer at her over my glasses from where I sit on our bed, legs stretched out in front of me as I balance a stack of papers on my knees. She's dangerously close to waddling as she makes her way over, grunting quietly as she swings her legs up and lays on her side, facing me. The satin maternity pajamas I bought her ride up just enough to show a strip of skin, new stretch marks on display like the pattern light makes on rippling water—fluid, clear, beautiful.

"You're gorgeous," I say softly, unable to keep myself from smiling.

"Don't change the subject." She frowns, but there's no malice in it.

"We've been at this for weeks. Let's give it a rest."

Sighing deeply, she stretches an arm out to turn off the light on her side of the bed. "Fine. How much longer will you be working?"

Flipping forward a couple of pages to see where the chapter ends, I say, "maybe twenty minutes."

"Okay," she breathes, but her eyes have already drifted closed. Her hand rests on my leg, warmth seeping through my sweatpants. My heart skips a beat at the way she still always anchors herself to me, and I send up a silent prayer that I'll always be able to steady her in this small way.

We're silent for a moment, but her breathing hasn't evened out, so I know she's still mostly awake. "Julius," I say under my breath.

"Oh, fuck no." She blinks one eye open. "Next you're going to say Odysseus or something."

Shaking my head, I stifle a grin. "Real historical figures only. Nothing fictional."

Both her eyes are open now, pools of blue sparkling with mirth. There's the Scarlett I love the most—fiery and sure of herself. Strong and ready to fight. "We're going historical now?" she taunts. "Fine. Abraham."

"No."

"Alexander."

"You're going to go down the alphabet, now?"

"Edgar."

"Oh, literary. I like it."

That makes her pause, her brows knitting together. "Really?"

"No," I say on a laugh.

The relief on her face is clear as day. "Oh, thank god." She shudders. "I was kidding."

My train of thought is lost, so I stack the papers neatly on my nightstand, laying my pen and glasses on top of them. We shift so we're under the blanket, and I wrap my arms around her, kissing her forehead. "I love you, Scarlett."

"I love you too."

Her voice is blurry at the edges as she starts to drift off, but I can't help shimmying down to kiss her belly.

"Good night to you too, little Napoleon." I nuzzle the skin of her abdomen with my nose.

"I'm not even going to justify that with a response," she murmurs into my neck as I fold her right back into my arms where she belongs.

A WEEK LATER and we're still at it. She must have done some searching, because she's started taunting me with every single name that could have a three-letter nickname. Robert, James,

Thomas, Timothy, Joseph, Samuel.

I tease her right back with older names—Sebastian, Jason, Philip, Orion.

"Wait, seriously?" she pauses on the last one, her fingers pausing over her keyboard. "That would be kind of cute."

"Orion?"

"Yeah." Her eyes light up. "Because your name is Ryan. It's like a little play on words."

I press my lips together to keep myself from laughing outright. There's no way we're naming our son Orion, but she seems excited about the idea, and I don't want to crush her.

"We can add it to the list of maybes," I say slowly.

"Really?" She bounces forward on her toes, but her eyebrow gives her away by ticking up a fraction of an inch. She's fucking with me.

"Yeah, absolutely." I nod emphatically, gaining momentum. "It would be really cute. And it's a strong name. The hunter—a constellation of stars. Little tiny lights, just like this little guy." Pressing my palm to her belly, I feel a thump. "Oh, he likes it."

Scarlett holds out for a second longer before she cracks, her lips curling up in disgust. "He's protesting. He hates it."

I try desperately to hide my smirk. "How can you tell?"

"I'm his mother. I know."

It doesn't escape me that this is one of the first times I've heard her refer to herself as our baby's mother, but I don't want to make a big deal about it. And yet, my heart swells. I had been worried that our inability to settle on a name would further disconnect her from this pregnancy, but it seems to be doing the opposite.

Solemnly, I nod. "Mother knows best."

Scarlett scoffs. "Damn right, she does."

A FEW DAYS later, we're each working at opposite sides of the couch—Scarlett with her laptop sitting precariously on top of her thighs and her feet resting on my lap. My own computer is perched on the armrest of the couch to give her feet room. It's not the most comfortable position, but I like to think we both need the contact so I'm not complaining.

It's moments like these when I have to stop and take stock of my blessings. Scarlett has shared so much with me already, from her beautiful brain to her perfect body. And now she's chosen to share even more. A child. A life. Two things I never thought I'd get to have with her after she left.

I don't know what I did to deserve her, but I'm grateful every single day.

The click of her keyboard goes silent, and it's another few seconds before I realize she's looking at me, her eyes reflecting the light of her screen as they settle on me. Her head tilts and she blinks a few times.

"What?" I ask, one corner of my lips tilting up in a soft smile.

"Lucas," she whispers.

I go still, my jaw slack. The ring on my finger becomes a weighty presence, and I rub at it with my thumb.

"That was my dad's name," I manage to say when words come back to me.

"I know." Scarlett bites her lip. "I had thought about it before, but...I didn't know how you'd feel about it."

Hot tears prick at the corners of my eyes. I swallow hard, resting my hands on her feet and idly rubbing the arches with my thumbs. "He was the strongest man I knew."

She nods. "And his name means *bringer of light.*" A small smirk plays at her lips. "Which I did actually like about Orion."

Laughing wetly, I snap my laptop shut, then hers, moving them both to the coffee table before kneeling on the floor next to her, my cheek pressing against her belly and a few renegade tears wetting the fabric of her shirt.

"You'd be okay with that name?" I ask, but even before I do, I know in my bones it's the right one. But she has to be sure. She's given me so many words over the years, but this one...this one might be the greatest gift of all.

Scarlett smiles down at me, running her fingers through my hair. "More than okay. I love it."

I let my gaze linger on her face for a moment longer before I close my eyes and press a kiss to her belly.

"Hi, baby Lucas." Even trying on the name feels right, like slipping into a warm sweatshirt. Like a satisfying end to a book. Like coming home.

Scarlett's fingers twine into my hair. Our baby rolls back against my lips.

"I'm your dad," I say. "I can't wait to meet you."

Acknowledgments

WITH EACH NEW book, I am even more grateful for the entire team of people I have on my side. This book simply would not exist without the help of so many.

First and foremost, thank you to my husband for all the usual things—taking the kids, offering me quiet, cooking dinner so I can meet my deadlines—and for so much more. Thank you for seeing me even in my darkest moments and loving me anyway. Thank you for making me believe in sunshine, even when I'd rather be the grump. You're my favorite and my only, and I'm so glad we're on this journey together.

Thank you to the best of friends, Hannah. Your beautiful brain has produced so many gorgeous stories, and your fearless use of gorgeous prose inspired me to try my hand at some metaphors, as well. If I wrote something even half as beautiful as your books, I'd be happy.

Jillian... I still remember sitting in your Chicago apartment planning a wildly different book, and over breakfast on one of your visits as we planned yet another. Thank you from the bottom of my heart for never giving up on me.

A huge thank you to my early readers: Cait, Lexi, and Kayla. Your love of Scarlett and Ryan helped shape them and give me the courage to continue. Your comments gave me life...and made me laugh. Thanks also to Stefanie for your moral support. The beta group chat is my favorite place to be.

I can't forget to thank my street teams. From help with promotion to moral support (and enabling even my wildest ideas), I couldn't do any of this without you. I am so grateful you're here to cheer me on.

Mandi Andrejka of Inky Pen Editorial Services did the first editing pass on the indie version of this book, and it wouldn't have gotten this far without her. I'm so glad you reached out to me and we connected over several themes in this book. And your GIFs??? Perfection.

How do I even begin to thank Lorissa Padilla for being such a dear friend and for your amazing artwork to help with this book? Thank you for always taking what's in my head and making it more beautiful than I could even imagine. I am so grateful that you share your art with me, and that you always seem to know what I want even when I don't.

A massive thank you to my agent, Katie Monson at SBR Media. Thank you for helping my books find new readers all over the world, and for making me feel like my dreams are possible.

Of course, I want to thank Meredith and the team at Page & Vine. The fact that you picked this story to publish is so special, and it has already been a wonderful experience. Thank you for loving Scarlett and Ryan as much as I do and showing so much care with them.

Thank you to my family and friends. To Julia, Sandy, Elizabeth, Jill, and so many others who have supported me from the start.

To Dr. O—language is limiting, but it is also freeing. You taught me that. And it connects us. When you sent me that list of books about grief, you actually gave me a lifeboat tethered to the shore. Thank you.

To my mom, dad, brother, and sister-in-law who have been endlessly supportive for years. It means the world that I said, "I'm writing a book," and you all essentially said, "Finally." Thank you for believing in me even when I wasn't sure I believed in myself. And, of course, thanks for listening to all my stories, both then and now. I literally couldn't do this without you.

And last but not least, thanks to you, dear reader. May you always see and honor your own strength.

About the Author

Allie Samberts is a romance writer, book lover, and high school English teacher. She was voted funniest teacher of the year for 2023 and 2025 by her students, which is probably her highest honor to date. She has many hobbies but reading and writing are her favorites. She lives in the Chicago suburbs with her husband, two kids, and dog. You can find her social media, sign up for her newsletter, and get other updates at www.alliesamberts.com.

Also by Allie Samberts

Strong Enough Series:
Not a Strong Enough Word
Not on the Same Page (August 2026)
Not the Way It Ends (November 2026)

Leade Park Series:
The Write Place
The Write Time
The Write Choice

Standalones:
Common Grounds
Love Out Loud

Novellas:
Pumpkin to Talk About
Christmas by Design
Love in the Time of Conversation Hearts (with Hannah Bird)

They agree on no strings.
But their hearts keep
landing on the same page.

Not on the Same Page

ALLIE
SAMBERTS

NOT ON THE SAME PAGE

Coming August 2026

They agreed on no strings. But their hearts keep landing on the same page.

A year ago, literary agent Trina McBryde and editor Casey Endersen ended their no-strings arrangement. It was perfect for two people who didn't want a relationship. But what started as a way to blow off steam and have a little fun almost put their careers at stake, along with their feelings for each other.

When an important publishing conference brings them together again, the desire they tried to deny is back, and stronger than ever. But the real challenge comes afterward—Casey needs Trina to sign a promising new writer, which means that after a year of avoiding each other, they'll be forced to work together again. Late-night calls, whispered strategy sessions, and stolen glances make every professional interaction dangerously personal.

Every secret meeting carries the risk of exposure. If anyone finds out, they could lose more than just their jobs—they could lose their reputations.

But Casey has already fallen...again. And Trina is running out of ways to resist.

As professional boundaries blur, they'll have to decide if being on the same page means following the rules—or finally writing their own.

www.alliesamberts.com